With Love, Juniper

Inked in Gray Press

InkedinGray.com

ISBN

Paperback: 978-1-952969-21-8

E-book: 978-1-952969-23-2

Cover Design by Amanda Cessor

With Love, Juniper

Amanda Cessor

To every person who has ever been told that they were too much.
I hope you never make yourself small.
I hope you find the people worthy of your light

CONTENTS

Before You Read

With Love, Juniper has trigger warnings. In full transparency, we will list them here if you need them. 🩶

Trigger Warnings: Mentions of past murder and war, blood and violence, mentions of injured veterans and PTSD, mentions of ritual murder, allusions to cults, depictions of social anxiety and panic attacks (mild and severe), alcohol consumption and gambling, physical altercation (one instance), some depictions of deep self-loathing, vomiting (non-graphic), emotionally manipulative, mildly sexist antagonist, witchcraft-centered setting.

Prologue: Respite

Theo Vervain never dreamed.

When the young man closed his eyes for sleep, he never saw any scenarios play out behind his eyelids; never found himself flying, or falling, or otherwise. He was simply asleep until he was not.

But that changed when he rode the train into Linseed Village.

He had booked passage to the countryside at his mother's behest; something she had begged him to do after spending a sleepless week in his father's study. He was combing through old files in the hopes of finding some information to aid his father's investigation into a string of ritual murders in Kingsborough.

It was the first, and hopefully only, time he had ever snapped at his mother, who kept encouraging him to put the files down and get some rest. He had been in such a state of focus that her gentle urgings registered more like the incessant buzzing of an insect. Yet, seeing his mother's eyes — his own eyes — crumple in hurt and worry was enough to make him regret it a hundred times over.

He was on the train two days later.

Normally, Theo hated train rides. He hated the forced idleness — the inane chatter of other passengers that seemed to never cover anything of importance. Even more, he hated that he couldn't get any rest; his mind too active with thoughts of what would be done at his destination or whatever busy work he could get done while the scenery passed by outside.

But the exhaustion from his obsessive hunting for information lingered, and not long after the train pulled out of Kingsborough station, Theo found himself drifting off, his cheek propped up on a closed fist as the train car rocked back and forth. And when he slept, he dreamed. Even though Theo Vervain never dreamed.

He dreamed of his pale hand brushing through dark, silken hair. He dreamed of parted lips flushed rosy pink. He dreamed of the smell of lush soil and warm licorice tea. Even in his dreams, his heart beat at a strange tempo.

He was equal parts captivated and frustrated. Captivated by the simple beauty of the woman before him and yet frustrated that he couldn't quite grasp the full picture of her. It was as if he was looking at a painting where her face had not yet been fully rendered, as if he was smelling the bouquet of perfume many hours after it was dabbed on her collar bone.

It was enough to set his teeth on edge, even while he slept. A muscle tensed faintly on the side of his jaw. He squinched his eyelids tighter as his chest rose and fell a little faster.

"Sir?" someone asked him.

He didn't rouse.

"Sir, wake up. It's just a bad dream," they said, jostling his shoulder.

He startled awake, indigo eyes blinking in the slanted sunlight of late afternoon. He inhaled deeply and rubbed a hand down his face, somehow feeling more exhausted than he did before the nap. This was why he thought naps were such a waste of time.

Before him stood a young woman of somewhat average beauty in a train-staff uniform. She had mousy brown hair and eyes to match them. Her skin was tanned, likely from all the time she spent walking through well-lit train cars for her profession. She carried an usherette tray filled with tidy, colorful rows of chocolate bars, cookies, roasted hazelnuts, and tins of cigarettes with various herbal infusions.

He looked blearily up at her and she flushed. He wondered at the expression on his face because she looked like a child caught stealing.

"F-forgive me sir. I shouldn't have woken you up. It's just that the quality of your sleep seemed rather haunted," she stammered. "E-er. Would you like any refreshments?"

Haunted indeed. For a moment he found his eyes trained on the flush of her cheeks, straining to remember the particular hue of pink that he'd seen while he slept.

Theo reached into his interior pocket and plucked out a few stag bills. "Think nothing of it," he said as he handed them over to the young woman. "A tin of cigarettes will do, and a book of matches if you have them. Keep the change."

"Of course. Would you prefer clove, juniper, or lavender cigarettes?" she asked, seeming relieved to not be on the receiving end of a tongue lashing.

"Juniper, please," he said.

The exchange was made, and Theo lit up one of the cigarettes as the young woman bustled away. He opened a window just as the train started to pull into one of the many fields of flax which gave Linseed Village its name. He struck a match, lighting a cigarette and taking a drag, willing the tobacco to give him a bit of energy. His mother would hate to see him smoking, but one cigarette wouldn't hurt.

A few benches behind him, he heard a cheerful voice speaking to the very same woman.

"Is that Hailey Connifer I see?" it said.

"Oleander?" she said just as gleefully. "Don't tell me it's been two years already. It must have been."

"I'm surprised to see you working on the train home. Last I remember you were just a girl."

"I was fourteen when you left," she said quietly, sounding almost put out. "I turned sixteen in the summer, so I decided to get a job to help Papa out with the cost of things."

Theo looked over his shoulder to watch the exchange. Past the young woman, whose name was apparently Hailey, he saw a man with dark hair and pale blue eyes. He wore an arm band with the golden seal of Kingsborough Conservatory on his upper arm, revealing him as a newly minted sorcerer fresh out of his studies.

He looked oddly familiar, to the point that Theo wondered if he was one of the new students he had helped welcome into the Combative Arts Department, of which he was an alumnus. Theo squinted a bit trying to see what symbol sat in the upper right side of the seal, and found a sprout stitched in iridescent green thread.

Herbalism? He'd completed his diploma in *herbs*? What a useless skill.

There must have been some other reason he seemed familiar then . . . if only he could put his finger on it. He continued to eavesdrop to see if it would become clear.

"That's kind of you," Oleander said, smiling up at Hailey. "How have things been the last couple of years?"

"Oh, you know, the village folks always pull together to get us through; or we'll rent to one of the travelers to make ends meet. We're hoping to get a late harvest in this year if we can, but it's not looking good— ah, but you must be looking forward to being with the Harlows again! Juniper has been trying to help us with some bespelled seeds that will grow through the winter."

The Harlows? Theo thought on it, and according to his recollection — yes, that's right. After the Battle of Oblivion, one Rowan Harlow wound up retiring in the countryside with his wife, a nurse he'd met on his medical bed during his recovery. If he remembered right, Rowan Harlow had been a friend of his own father. Perhaps he should visit and pay his respects to a friend of his father; make a good show of being a well-mannered young man.

"I can't wait to see how she does it," Oleander replied. "I miss her most of all. I can't wait to see her tomorrow."

Theo observed a slight dimming on Hailey's face. Unrequited love, he hypothesized. A girl who pined after someone far beyond her social standing, no doubt. He'd encountered it himself a number of times. Oleander appeared oblivious, though.

Hailey cleared her throat. "Well, I have to keep moving, but hopefully I'll get to see you at the upcoming Solstice. It was good to see you, Oleander," she said as she began to scurry off.

"Oh wait, Hailey!" he called after her.

She turned to look at him, her eyes glittering with hope.

"I just wanted to buy a couple of those cookies and three of the chocolates before you head off. We've got a ways to go before we get to the station tomorrow morning," he said.

Hailey huffed a laugh and came back. "Always such a sweet tooth on you, Ollie," she said. "One stag for that, please."

The young man pulled a pocketbook out of his coat and handed over a ten-stag bill. "Hang onto the change, alright?"

"I couldn't," she said quickly. "Oleander that's too much."

"I insist," he said. "We'll call it even for that time I smashed through your father's fence with my besom, alright?"

"That was — you were twelve, and Mr. Harlow paid to have it fixed," she mumbled.

"Still, I insist," Oleander said.

Theo watched Hailey hesitate for a moment before placing the money in the slot on her usherette box and nodding. "Thank you," she said before finally handing over the sweets.

Damn it all, who was this man? Why couldn't the girl use a bit of propriety and refer to him by his family name? And moreover, why did it bother him so much that he didn't know?

Something hot seared the space between Theo's two fingertips, and he looked down to see the cigarette had almost entirely burned down as he'd watched the exchange between the old friends. He hissed out a quiet vulgarity before flicking the spent stick out of the open window. He paused a moment to say a quiet incantation over his burns, nothing terribly advanced; just enough to numb the pain while he healed naturally. Once finished, he lit up another cigarette, taking a moment this time to enjoy the freshness of the juniper lacing the tobacco.

Whoever the stranger was, Theo was sure he would learn soon enough. After all, he would be in Linseed Village through Solstice and there was only so much to do in the tiny town. So, he focused on the gentle swaying of the flax out in the fields as he tried to think of something other than the strange familiarity of Oleander or the blurry beauty of the woman in his dreams.

Tried.

And failed.

Homecoming

Juniper flitted about the sitting room in the cottage that her family called home. There was so much she wanted to have ready for Oleander's return, and she wasn't one to laze about when there was so much to do.

Outside, the autumnal day was cool and gray, but not in a way that made you feel glum or morose. The boughs of the oak trees outside of the sitting room window were still heavy and vibrant with the gold, scarlet, and tangerine hues of the burgeoning fall. They stood looking like bonfires reaching into the sky, as if to keep the pillowy violet clouds warm, or perchance, even to scare them away for a few more moments of vibrant blues stretching across the idyllic horizon that acted as backdrop to Linseed Village.

It was the kind of day that stoked the warmth of excitement in your heart for the coming holidays; for spending time with family — for reunions. It was perfect weather for the occasion, the return of her dearest friend and confidant.

Oleander was coming home after his time in Conservatory.

A time that was demanding for any young witch and an important rite of passage. He successfully completed the heavy workload, passed all his classes with excellent marks, and was well on his way to being recognized as the talented sorcerer Juniper always knew him capable of being. She hoped that Oleander could fill some of the void left in the wake of her own inability to get her Sorcerer's Diploma.

Her parents, of course, never said anything to disparage her inability to attend Conservatory, but she couldn't help but feel a bit guilty for failing to carry on her parents' legacy; for being unable to do much of anything really.

She would always be just a simple cottage witch with a penchant for herbalism. And she was doing her best to make peace with that.

Juniper smiled to herself as she adjusted a plate of delicately iced cakes on the small table they used for tea. It was adorned today in a cloth of white eyelet lace with a series of cream, mauve, and violet doilies which Juniper sometimes liked to fashion in her boundless free time. A kettle of black tea was kept warm by a spell not far away; the herbaceous, nutty aroma wafted toward her. It was one of Oleander's favorite blends and one of her own design: Black tea, bergamot, peppermint, and star anise, all carefully steeped in perfectly heated water.

She wondered idly if Oleander had done any work creating his own blends of teas. He'd studied Botany and Herbalism, after all; insistent on following in Juniper's footsteps, even though he would be ridiculed for doing so.

Not all witchcraft was equal these days. There was a time when every discipline had its people of influence, when those outside of that discipline respected it. But that was long ago, before the war. Many expected young men like Oleander to study Defensive Arts or Combative Arts, or perhaps more theoretical paths if they didn't have the power and physicality to wield such things. The expectation was that every young, capable witch should learn to protect their women and their families. Everyone was expected to be prepared should war ever darken their doorstep again.

Even though it was unlikely there would be another war, careers available in the combative arts were coveted and highly sought after. Her own father still worked for the Ministry of Defense, traveling between their small village and Kingsborough to meet with the powers that be, albeit only once in a long while.

Typical of Oleander, he saw no reason to pursue a discipline he simply had no interest in. *"I've seen what you can do with a fist full of herbs, Juniper! I don't need to study combative magic for two years to protect you. I want to study this so I can work with you."* Juniper's smile held, remembering the words he'd said the day he chose his course of study. His blue eyes had been so bright, so full of life and certainty — unshakeable as always. She wished she had his utter lack of regard for the opinions of others. He was unapologetic in his pursuit of that which he loved.

Her brows settled softly as she stilled in quiet recollection. She hoped he wouldn't regret his choice later in life, and that his heart truly loved to tend plant beds as much as her own did. She checked the clock on the wall; Oleander would be home in perhaps fifteen minutes if his train wasn't delayed. It was just enough time to get the last of everything ready.

If Oleander's tastes had remained the same as when he left, he had a voracious sweet tooth. Juniper hoped to spoil him upon his arrival. She already set the table with a small plate of cakes purchased from his favorite bakery, a box of chocolates, and plenty of sugar cubes and cream for his tea, but there was more to set out.

She stepped into the kitchen, a well-loved and often-visited part of the house that showed plenty of signs of use. Juniper hardly noticed the etchings in the worn whitewashing of the doorframe where her father had marked her growing height and then Oleander's. She hardly remembered what caused the scorching on the dark-stained cupboards over the enameled green stove, or which winter it was that Oleander had accidentally left the window open before a blizzard — letting near two feet of snow gather on top of the counters. The swelling and bucking of the countertops from that snow had bothered her mother up until Juniper and Oleander made a day of hiding the damage with some grout and a patchwork of broken plates and teacups from all the years Juniper sacrificed them to her clumsy gait.

It was that same colorful patchwork counter where a three-tiered stand now sat; one that her mother typically used for the tea parties she hosted once in a while. On it already sat some jam sandwiches on soft white bread, cut into stars and moons. Beside the sandwiches, there were several small ramekins filled with various candies that he loved: chocolate-covered almonds, candy floss, and lavender lemon drops. Juniper reached up to a swag of dried lavender hanging from a piece of tired-looking ribbon in front of the bay window and plucked a few sprigs from it before placing them strategically around the candy dishes.

The smell of baking cookies wafted through the house, nearly done in the oven. They had to be warm for his arrival, naturally — nothing short of that would do.

A bespelled brass bell snuck up behind Juniper and aggressively chimed, making Juniper's heart lodge in her throat. She whirled on the thing and scowled lightly. "I really need to make a new one of you," she said in soft scolding to the little bell. "Every time you do that, you spook me out of my skin! One of these days I'll wind up having a heart attack and my family will come into the kitchen or the parlor to find me dead on the floor!"

The magicked instrument merely loped through the air back to where it always sat in the kitchen, seemingly unapologetic for the disturbance. She simply rolled her eyes as she took up her oven mitts and made her way to the stove.

She opened the olive-green stove to draw the baking sheet full of cookies out, sat the tray down atop the oven, and with a flick of her delicate fingers, turned off the heat. The smell of butter and caramelized sugar filled the room, and she breathed a dreamy sigh before setting them on top of the stove to cool.

Finally, she fetched a glossy fruit and custard tart out of the icebox, the most impressive thing among the entire spread on the table, she set the small tart on the very top of the tiered stand. Certainly, no expense was spared in ordering the tart — that was the Harlow way. They were no greedy misers; they had gained affluence through their lives and saw no issue in using it to treat those they cared for in a manner that comforted them and brought them happiness.

Juniper placed the fresh cookies on the three-tiered display and negotiated lifting it. She ground her teeth as she carefully carried it to the sitting room where the other desserts were displayed.

Ollie was family now, though he still carried his family's surname, Ambrose. He'd come to live with them ten years prior, after being orphaned in Kingsborough. His father had narrowly saved Juniper's father's life during the war. It only made sense, her father had explained, that he care for the son of the man who allowed him to have his own family.

Juniper finished some last-minute preparations as the clock continued ticking in the foyer not far away. Each clack of the moving minute hand filled her with more glee and excitement to see her dearest friend. Finally, a knock came.

Juniper's heart soared as she hurried to the door, and her face and ears warmed with her excited flush. She threw the door open to greet her dearest and oldest friend.

"Ollie, I—"

The words caught and extinguished in Juniper's throat, her heart lodging painfully there instead.

Dread set deeply into her bones.

It was always this way. An invisible rope snaked around her ribcage and constricted tighter than any stays or corsets she'd ever worn. Each inhale was stilted and painful. The blood left her face and nausea curled in her stomach.

This man in front of her was not *Oleander.* It couldn't be. When Oleander left, he had been no taller than Juniper's shoulder — though he would have debated the issue rather hotly when this was pointed out. At age sixteen, the pudginess in his face still betrayed his age. Back then, he had the lanky awkward build of what he was and what he still *should* be: a normal teenage boy.

But the boy standing here now, on their front steps, well — he was not a boy. He was a man. A grown man! He'd promised her that he'd return as a man. But two years certainly couldn't have made such an impact on his build.

Warmly hooded blue-gray eyes crinkled in a smile down at her from where he suddenly stood, nearly an entire head taller. Dark, shapely brows rested low and relaxed above them. Beneath his eyes were the faint wrinkles of many sleep-deprived nights and so many smiles. Full lips curved and made his high cheekbones round out pleasantly, the only lingering softness from his once youth-tender face, it seemed. Below his mouth, his jawline swept beautifully to where his ebony hair was perfectly coiffed and combed behind his ear. Juniper's eyes fell to his torso, ears growing hot with her growing flush that now made a betraying return to her face. She'd hoped to find relief there — escape from the burning smolder of his gaze. She didn't.

Of course, her mother had mentioned needing to send off some new clothes to Oleander over the past couple of years. But she had never imagined this. That lanky build she'd expected had filled out. Where he used to swim in his dress shirts and coats, now every line of his jacket and vest perfectly traced the attractive broadness of his shoulders and his chest. The elegant taper of his waist stopped at high trousers, silver buttons shining. A perfect straight-legged pleat went straight to the floor where he wore stylish, polished leather shoes.

No, this was not Oleander — not her Ollie. Not the boy she sent off to school.

The stranger on her doorstep took his stylish pointed hat off his head and held it politely in front of his chest. The perfect gentleman. The movement made Juniper lift her dark gray eyes to his bright blue-gray ones and they crinkled further.

"Juniper," he breathed with sweet joy and affection, his voice a stranger's voice. It was so deep. The timbre of it rattled through her tightened chest. "I have missed you so very much," the stranger said.

Juniper swallowed, willing her heart to return to its home back in her ribcage. Her ears were ringing as she forced herself to speak. "O-Oleander. Extended periods of transmogrification can be incredibly dangerous. I know you have a penchant for pranks but—"

The man's brow knitted with consternation, head tilting in the way Ollie's always did when he was startled or confused. Then, his brows rose higher, deciphering Juniper's stammered words. The look of confusion gave way to a brilliant laugh, perfect teeth shining in the calm autumn morning.

Juniper's heart squeezed as the laugh quieted.

"Am I so changed," he asked as he lifted his hand to his mouth, "that you think this form is something other than my natural one?" He gestured to himself in demonstration.

The light twinkled in his eyes as he said the words that hammered the last nails into Juniper's nightmarish coffin.

"I assure you; I am still very much the same Ollie that left home two years ago."

He began to take the few steps left between himself and the threshold and Juniper's fingernails dug painfully into the palms of her hands. Her knuckles strained white with how tightly she balled them next to her, skin clammy and cloying with nervous sweat on her palms.

"I've come to collect my hug hello," he said as he took another step.

Juniper eyed the distance between them, only one step remaining before he would be there. In the house. With her. Her chest squeezed again; the invisible rope tightening even more. She couldn't get any air in her lungs.

Oleander seemed finally to register her emotional state. He slowed in his pursuit of her.

"Juni? Are you alright? You look like you've seen a ghost," he asked as he came to a stop just at the threshold.

Juniper registered the pause in momentum, the question hanging in the stale air between them.

Oleander inhaled to speak again, but before he could manage a word, Juniper had slammed the door shut in his face.

Unexpected Reunion

O leander started when the door abruptly closed, leaving him stranded out on the porch of the small country cottage he called home. Whatever it was that he was about to say whooshed out of him with a baffled exhale. Juniper had looked upset, even fearful, upon seeing him. He knew that she struggled with her nerves. Surprises of almost any kind had always put her off. Either way, he'd never imagined she would be so startled by *him*.

As he heard her feet retreat farther into the house, a pang of worry stabbed at his chest. Oleander knew Juniper better than he knew anyone else in the world. Her preferred tea strength and favorite colors were both committed to memory. He was aware that she enjoyed mushroom hunting and collecting but despised actually eating the fruits of her efforts.

He also knew the darker side to her — her quirks.

He was aware that even a modest dinner party with only six people could send her into a fit of hysteria, that she couldn't get any words out when talking to boys her age in the local lounge, and how she skulked away during the village's communal ceremonies so that she wouldn't have to join in the dancing with anyone other than her father and himself.

Still, he would never have guessed by any stretch of the imagination that she would have reacted to his appearance with such intensity. Guilt tugged the corners of his lips into a frown when he realized that he probably should have seen this coming. He should have warned her that he was different: sent his school portrait, mentioned his growth spurt in letters. *Something.*

But when you're the one occupying the changing body over the course of years, you don't really pay attention to those changes.

Oleander heaved a soft breath and reached for the doorknob, thumb pressing down on the brass lever to open the door.

"Juniper?" he called gently into the home.

The surge of warm air from the fire burning in the hearth intensified the scents of his favorite tea, along with the aromas of chocolate and warm butter. He stepped in, his bags forgotten on the porch as he shut the door quietly behind him.

"Juni, I'm sorry for startling you. I should have sent word before I came about how I've changed," he called into the house as he made his way to the sitting room.

The sight of the spread on the table immediately lifted his spirits. His eyes glittered at the glossy fruit atop the tart on the tiered display of sweets. He reached for a cookie and delighted in the warmth coming from it. These were fresh. Fresh cookies made by his beloved, just for his arrival.

He happily bit into it as he wandered deeper into the house. He hummed, the sound throaty and warm. He recognized the taste, lemon-rosemary madeleines, among one of his favorite treats she made. The rosemary and lemon that flavored the confection undoubtedly came from Juniper's own garden, brought to life by her own hands.

As he walked, he heard a door shut on the second floor of the house. From where he stood in the corridor, he could hear boot-clad feet pacing back and forth above him. Juniper had run away to her bedroom. He made his way up the stairs, the fourth stair creaking the way it always did — something Mr. Harlow always vowed to fix, but if Oleander was honest, the sound was now a welcome comfort after being away for so long.

He ate the final bite of his treat as he approached a violet door painted with blue-green vines and light pink peonies — Juniper's room. He raised his hand and gently rapped on the solid wood.

"Juniper? Are you alright?"

His voice was soft, as if trying to approach a startled deer in the forest, speaking only so that he knew he would be heard, and not any louder.

"I-I'm fine," a soft voice trembled from the opposite side of the door.

"Will you come out? So that I can say hello to you properly?"

"I . . . well I . . . it's embarrassing, uhm, but I have been feeling ill all morning. I thought I was on the mend, but I fear I may be getting another bout of it. It's probably better that you don't see me like this," the voice on the other side of the door said, wavering slightly.

Oleander's brow knit. Worry tangled in his gut as he rubbed the back of his neck, a nervous habit he'd had since childhood.

All the same, he knew now was not the time to push Juniper. Now was not the time to ask her to be more than herself, more than her fear. He exhaled softly so that she wouldn't hear and cleared his throat, willing his voice to sound a bit more chipper than he actually felt.

"Take your time, Juni. Get some rest," he said.

He waited for a moment to see if Juniper would respond. When she didn't, he turned away from the violet-hued door and made his way back down the stairs.

Oleander sighed as he made it back to the spread on the small breakfast table in the sitting room. He once again surveyed the treats placed out for them — for him — to enjoy. So many sweets that were his favorite, all carefully curated by Juniper.

Oleander sat down at the table and poured himself a cup of tea, the familiar fragrance bringing a warm curve to his lips and a crinkle to his eye. He added no less than four sugar cubes and a splash of cream, setting a spoon to automatically stir with a twirl of his finger. He glanced at the stairs just outside of the door, his thoughts wandering to Juniper who was still silent in her room.

Juniper had always been . . . nervous. As long as he had known her, she had been that way. Even as a child, Juniper always froze in most social situations. Before her adolescence, when Oleander had first come to live with the Harlows, she used to hide behind her mother's skirts. Now, her favored hiding spots were her greenhouse, her bedroom, and the forests — she hid behind her passions and her work.

The other side of that, however, was her softness. Juniper was a heartbreakingly gentle woman. Her strength lay tangled up in her weakness. Yes, perhaps she could be a bit fragile. But it was her fragility that allowed her to be so kind and sweet.

If Juniper was a recluse, Oleander was the opposite. The things that frightened Juniper were as easy as breathing for him. Oleander had a sort of innate charisma. He could easily steer a conversation, keep it warm and engaging. He was observant, thoughtful, and had a sharp wit. It was no accident that he was this way, though. He had cultivated and honed himself to wield this power.

Oleander sipped his tea, and a low hum rumbled through his chest as warmth spread through him. He closed his eyes, settling into the sounds of home. The ticking of the old clock made by Mr. Harlow's father. The slow and steady drip of the faucet in the kitchen. The wind blowing through the collection of wind chimes that hung from the old tree in the gardens.

He was so happy, so very content, to finally be home again.

It had been a long two years. Oleander tried to smother the worry making his ribcage taut. He had hoped, perhaps foolishly, that his absence would have awoken some sort of romantic interest in Juniper. He'd thought that his absence would have made her heart yearn for him in the same way that his did for her. He had hoped his growth spurt would have impressed her. Helped her see him as a man — a man that would adore her and provide for her. Of all the ways he saw this reunion going, sitting alone with a mountain of sweets and no company was not one of them.

His finger tapped the table. *Tap. Tap. Tap.* Impatience and frustration swelled beneath his worry. Maybe . . . maybe she truly was ill. Maybe the timing had been so poor that he happened to arrive home just as she was swooning with dizziness and nausea. If that was the case, well, he was being very selfish indeed.

He breathed a long, slow exhale and rose from the table, grabbing a few chocolates in his hand for the road. It wasn't just Juniper who had missed him, after all. And she was also not all who he had missed. Mr. Harlow, Mrs. Harlow — they were his guardians, and he wished for them to see how he had grown.

It wasn't uncommon for the man and lady of the house to be absent while Juniper remained. If things were truly as unchanged as they seemed to be, Oleander knew which haunts the couple frequented, both while together and while doing separate business. He stepped out of the sitting room and looked once again around the house. He listened for movement from upstairs, for any retching or sickly moaning. When he heard only the metronome of the familiar clock on the wall, he stepped back out of the front door to the porch outside.

Oleander took some time to get his trunk and a few

wrapped gifts into the foyer. Then, after checking himself in a mirror by the doorway and straightening his lapels, he started to make his way down the front walkway of the house.

The Harlows were a humble family, despite their affluence. While the family had more than enough to afford a proper estate, they chose instead to live in a two-story cottage on the outskirts of the village. What they lacked in house size, however, they made up for in land. The Harlow deed stretched a thousand sprawling acres beyond the modest home. Those acres consisted of developed farmland, small ponds and marshes framed with swaying cattails and sweetgrass, and untamed woods filled with any manner of brambles among a few other structures placed by the family.

When Juniper debuted as a young woman, her parents presented her with her very own two-storied greenhouse. All ornate bronze framing and iridescent glass, making the soil and planting beds inside glitter with rainbows when the sun shone through. The only reason Juniper had been surprised was thanks to a glamour her mother had placed on the structure until it was time to unveil.

His feet crunched on the gravel walkway and he found his mind preoccupied by remembering that day: How it had been an open field one moment, and a beautiful glittering greenhouse the next; how Juniper had cried and cried and thanked her parents so profusely; how that structure soon became where she, and by association, he himself, spent most of their time, working late into the night bringing life into that little place.

The cottage itself was charming. The Harlows first bought it as newlyweds. At that time, it was a simple single story with only two or three rooms. The home had grown with them and their family since. What was once the Harlows' bedchambers became the library and study, where Mr. Harlow did most of his work. What was once Juniper's nursery had become the sitting room. The bedrooms now took up the second floor, with

Oleander's across from Juniper's, and Mr. and Mrs. Harlow sharing a room which faced the guest room, which was most often used as a storage room for any assortment of Mrs. Harlow's most recent diversions — before he had left, it had been made a shrine to her deceased interest in oil painting — he could only guess what was in there now.

The cottage had a broad white deck that wrapped around the entire house, seamed in by white railing. On the deck sat a few tables of varying sizes. Some for tea, for breakfasting, for casual dinner parties, and so on. The wood paneling on the walls was painted a desaturated pale violet, like lavender flowers. The windows were each framed by dark gray shutters which remained open except in the case of a particularly sweltering summer or should a worrying storm roll through. There was a curving, sloped roof with shingles of the same deep gray atop the walls and a single turret with a similarly rounded roof. The observatory, as the family called it, was a tiny loft with a telescope and maps of various stars and constellations. The place where Mrs. Harlow spent a great deal of time communing with the heavens.

Oleander looked back at the home as he made it to the mailbox at the end of the long walkway. He stared for a time, as if the house would betray the state of the woman he loved still hiding somewhere in there. But, of course, it did no such thing, and he could hardly think of a spell or incantation that might will it to. The fact of the matter was he would have to remain patient, as he always had been when it came to the matter of Juniper. He sighed and turned to make his way into the heart of the village.

Lady Troubles

Linseed Village, being perhaps a mile and a half away, was a sleepy little town where everyone knew everyone — and on the very rare occasion that someone did not know everyone, someone knew someone who knew everyone. They knew their names, their families, their lovers; they gossiped about their blunders and prejudices, and envied their successes and their commendations. It was easy to feel suffocated by a village like that. Even Oleander sometimes felt the pressure of his every move being scrutinized, so it was no real surprise that someone as nervous as Juniper would pick up the habits of a recluse.

Dirt roads leading from the cottage gave way to a central cobbled street marking the beginning of the tiny place. This single avenue held many of the businesses in the sleepy village. Each was both a home and a storefront. Oftentimes, the shop was in the front and the house was through a door behind the counter. A few businesses kept the shop on the first floor with their home on the floor above.

The shops had remained the same since Oleander arrived to live with the Harlows. He strode now on the avenue past the same stores: first the tailoress, then the bookshop, then the general store. He turned his head to the right to see the bakery cafe, the apothecary, and the hat shop. He passed a few other businesses: the solicitors, a dentist, and a tiny chapel. Finally, he reached the first stop on his outing, The Cat's Cradle.

It was a stylish little building. The plaster walls were painted a deep wine red with black trim and black and white striped awnings. Below the ornate steel-framed windows were brick garden beds laden with bushels of a variety of mint plants, attractively trimmed rosemary bushes, and different strains of sage. They were bespelled to fill the small patio dining area with their pleasant aromas. Oleander inhaled deeply, his lungs seeming to open to accommodate the nostalgic comfort of their scents.

The small lounge appeared mostly empty as Oleander entered. During the day, it was a gathering place for all sorts. The women of the village seemed to like the light lunches that were served, usually featuring dishes comprised of fish from the lake that had been delicately steamed and dressed in bright herbs and fresh lemon from the gardens kept in the front. During the hot summers, they would serve shaved ice with bright, sweet syrups and sweetened milk drizzled over them. But at the tail end of fall, it was not a huge surprise to see the place mostly empty. The lake was too cold to fish in, and during this season, The Cat's Cradle was mostly where young gentlemen would gather in the evenings for cards and socializing, and perhaps a stiff drink.

Oleander's pale eyes scanned the establishment until they landed behind the large mahogany bar where a man stood. He was a slender, lithely built man. He wore a simple white dress shirt with black sleeve garters. Likely a stylistic choice but also a practical one, keeping his sleeve cuffs from getting damp or dirty with the various tasks required for keeping a bar. He wore a finely tailored silk vest bearing fine embroidery of flying white cranes with wings tipped in gold thread. The silk was the same color as the building was painted outside, a deep wine red. His pale, silvery hair was cropped short on the sides, with the top kept long and slicked with careful precision to the side and toward the back where it gathered to a neat point.

Oleander took another step and the man behind the bar stiffened. He turned his head slowly until his face could be seen in profile. A golden eye with a slitted pupil slid over to Oleander. The eye of a sleepy, unbothered cat. The man then turned to face him.

"Sneaking up on me again, Ambrose?" the barkeep purred with a cool voice.

"Dante, it has been entirely too long!" Oleander beamed.

Dante, the owner of the fine establishment smiled calmly. The expression only barely reached his eyes; an expression Oleander knew as elation where Dante was concerned. He was a man of few words, and perhaps even fewer emotions. Oleander returned the expression, though warmer. Two years it had been, and yet the strange man hadn't aged a day. Just as he hadn't aged since he was Little Ollie.

"Come sit, Ambrose," Dante said. "I'll make you a drink to celebrate your much-anticipated return."

As Oleander approached the bar, Dante finished his work of drying out a short glass carved of crystal and set it up on a shelf, neatly lined up with a dozen other identical ones. Oleander took a seat on one of the barstools, propped his elbows up on the bar, and folded his arms. Dante mirrored him on the opposite side of the bar, bending at the waist, one ankle crossing behind the other.

"I'm surprised to see you here so early," he continued, golden eyes calm and heavily hooded. "I thought you would be spending most of today with Miss Harlow. You both seemed to miss each other terribly."

"Ah, she's . . . unwell, apparently."

Dante's pale brow twitched almost imperceptibly. He moved then, fetching a tall glass out from beneath the counter as he started to fashion a drink for Oleander. He started by chipping a block of ice into a glassy sphere. The man made it look easy. Oleander made a note to ask him how long he'd been doing this line of work the next time he had a chance to chat with him.

"Is that right?" he said as he worked.

The question, stated by anyone else, may have seemed like a skeptical jab. However, Oleander knew the stoic man well enough to know that he was genuinely concerned after Juniper's welfare.

"I could see to making her a tonic," the man offered quietly, "Ginger, chamomile, peppermint . . ."

"I'm sure she would appreciate the gesture, Dante," Oleander replied. "However, if I'm to be quite honest, I'm not entirely sure that she is actually ill."

Dante eyed Oleander with those cat-eyes and sighed. "I see," he stated flatly. "Her nerves again?"

Dante was a dear friend of the Harlows and one of the few people who understood Juniper the way that he did. Most folks in town only seemed interested in speculating about her health, her looks, or her level of arrogance to explain her lack of involvement in society.

"Potentially?" Oleander answered. He wasn't entirely sure, and he cursed himself for betraying his emotions so plainly.

The cat-eyed individual standing across from him was quite the rarity. Dante had spent his first eight lives as a Familiar to a powerful sorcerer. The relationship between Familiar and witch was one of service; a bond at the spiritual level not only to the witch themselves but to the very blood running through their veins. It was a bond that was forged through literal blood, sweat, and tears and required sacrifice both from the witch who performed the rite, and the spirit they claimed.

Dante had served not only the witch but the witch's father and his father's father and so on and so forth (though, once for a father's mother). The magic of the bond allowed Dante to live for centuries in the body of an ordinary house cat. He had served the family happily and with pride. He loved them like they were his own family; in many ways, they were his only family.

After many years of faithful service to his master, Dante was gifted a human form for his ninth and final life, a gift about as rare as freeing a genie with a final wish. Oleander read up on it at Conservatory. He could only find four examples of this happening in recorded history, Dante being one.

Over the years, summoning a spirit to act as one's Familiar fell out of favor with most civilized witches. Something about ripping a spirit out of the aether to do one's bidding just didn't feel like something good people did, regardless of how venerated and powerful Familiars could be. Dante was a rare specimen in more than one sense of the word.

"Yes, yes." Oleander frowned at his drink. "You know . . . you could have made me something a little . . . stiffer than lemonade, my friend."

"It's still the morning yet, Ambrose. I'm not sure being inebriated will aid with your lady troubles," Dante quipped with a smirk. "Besides, you had no interest in liquor before your departure."

"I *am* a man now. I developed a taste for it at Conservatory," Oleander said. "And I'm not having . . . lady troubles," he grumbled.

"Quite a surprise with your voracious sweet tooth. Regardless, the time of day remains the same. I'll treat you to a short glass of something tonight if you come for cards."

"Fair enough." Oleander mused as he took another sip. He

paused for a long moment afterward, eyeing his old friend. "Well . . . what do you make of it?"

"The situation with Miss Harlow?" Dante asked, eyes steady on Oleander's.

Oleander nodded.

Dante considered for a moment, propping his chin in his hand. "I have known Miss Harlow since the girl was a babe in her mother's arms. Even then, she was fearful of new environments, new people. She is much like my kind in that way," Dante muttered as he looked at nothing in particular. "With that in mind, I would say that she likely expected the same boy who left her home two years ago to be the one that arrived at her doorstep today. The shock of her subverted expectations may have very well caused her to feel ill."

Oleander looked down at his half-empty glass as he considered that. His brow tensed and dipped, narrowing his eyes as he frowned. He hated the idea that she could be feeling ill solely because he didn't fulfill her expectations. His hand took to idly turning the cool, dewy glass in his hands, fidgeting and restless.

"She's fearful of me . . ." He realized.

"She may be, for now. While she adjusts." Dante shrugged. "I see your time at Conservatory didn't do much for your patience."

The words hit their target, Oleander tensing before defensively biting out, "It's just that I had my own plans and expectations too, Dante."

"Well, that was your first mistake," Dante told him. "Having expectations when you are owed nothing."

The two stared at each other for a few long moments, somewhere in the room an insect buzzed. Oleander's temper roiled a bit at Dante's bluntness, at his seeming lack of care for his plight. Despite it, after a moment, Oleander forced himself to deflate. He was on edge, and he knew it. He had no place being rude to his friend, especially reuniting after having been apart for two years.

"Dante, I forgot how dry and direct you can be," he sighed.

Dante gave a smirk that didn't reach his eyes. "You're just far too used to your cohorts handling your delicate feelings."

"Yes, that most certainly must be it," Oleander said with a weak smile. "My spirit has grown flabby with the coddling."

Dante huffed and rounded the dark-stained bar. He reached Oleander's side and sat on the barstool next to his. "She did miss you, you know," Dante finally relented. "She shared as much with me at the few rites she was able to force herself to attend. She missed the comfort of having you there, the protection."

The information was bittersweet to Oleander. She missed him, yes, but only for the way he shielded her from the expectations and requirements of others? Of course, he was happy to do it but was that still the only way she saw him?

As if reading between the lines in the pause, Dante offered, "You've only just returned, Ambrose. There is plenty of time to court her properly. Be patient."

Oleander blinked over at his friend as the words echoed through his head like a revelation. Court her properly. Yes, he could finally court her!

He was a proper man, now. He no longer had to dance around the issue, make empty promises with no backing. Oleander could finally *court* Juniper. Treat her in all the ways he had dreamed to. Take her on outings, purchase flowers for her, invite her to dance at the festivals. And not just as a pitiful child, but as a *man*. His heart sang and raced in his chest with the realization. It raced with hope.

Oleander rose from his seat, taking a few spare moments to polish off the beverage his friend fashioned for him. He clapped Dante on the shoulder amicably. "I think I will come for cards tonight. For right now, I need to find Mrs. Harlow. I think she'll be quite cross if I don't seek her out while I have all this free time."

"She stopped by briefly earlier. I believe she's over at the clinic," Dante replied.

"Helping the nurses, no doubt. I thank you, my friend."

Dante gave a lazy cat's smile. "See you tonight."

"Indeed," Oleander replied, his long legs swiftly taking him out of the lounge and further down the avenue.

There was a sort of lightness present in his steps that wasn't there a moment before. Oleander chuckled to himself, smiling and shaking his head. Moon knew he could be dense, but this was a new low, even for him. How could he overlook the fact that he could finally compete with the other boys in the village properly now? So many times he had seen the young men in town vie for Juniper's attention, so many times he had protected her from it, but now he could do more than protect. He could properly participate.

As he considered it, he arrived at the clinic. It was a squat building, tan in color with dark brown roof shingles and a simple, natural wooden sign with a caduceus carved into it hung near the door. The pale-yellow paint that helped it stand out against the wood was mostly chipped off from age. The clinic had been run by the same people for generations; the sign was likely almost a family artifact for them. He wondered if they would bother to restore it, or if they liked the worn quality of it to represent how long they served the village.

Oleander made his way up a simple dirt ramp lined with bricks, and craggy little wisps of weeds and grass clinging to life, despite the autumnal chill starting to take over the remnants of summer. He opened the door and strode into the small lobby.

Seated at a small reception desk in the small room was Dr. Reed's daughter, a narrow-faced girl around his own age named Emelia. She was shorter than he remembered, but then again, so was Juniper. It was going to take some getting used to, these differences in height after growing so much so quickly while away.

Emelia's eyes grew wide as he approached the desk. It was an expression he couldn't really identify. He lifted a hand to gently rub his nape, remembering past interactions with the girl being . . . unpleasant at best.

"Hello, Miss Reed, I'm sorry to bother you. I've heard that Mrs. Harlow was here to help around the clinic and—"

"A-Ambrose! Is that you?"

Oleander blinked with surprise at the exclamation, mouth dropping open for a moment.

"Uh, yes, indeed it is me. I suppose I really must look different if no one is recognizing me," he muttered under his breath.

Emelia gawked openly at him for a moment.

She inhaled to speak, but before she could the door to the main room swung open. The sound of it was enough to startle both parties as they looked over. Emelia pouted and Oleander grinned.

In the doorway stood a woman of average height with black hair, the same shade as Juniper's. Dark eyes framed with tiny wrinkles from years of smiling crinkled, taking him in from toe to tip.

Juniper was the spitting image of her mother. If he was honest, Oleander was always taken aback by how much the two resembled each other: same expressions, same height, same gently curving frame. Both had dark hair, though Juniper's was a bit darker thanks to her father.

"Oh, *look at you*," Mrs. Harlow cooed. "You've grown into such a handsome young man, Oleander. Look at you!"

"Hello, Mrs. Harlow," Oleander gusted with a soft laugh.

Mrs. Harlow approached and pulled the boy into a fierce embrace, squeezing him in the way only a mother with a heart full of love could. Oleander's arms easily wrapped above her shoulders as he squeezed her once. He gave a chaste kiss to her crown, surprised by how small the matriarch felt compared to when he left home.

Mrs. Harlow held him at arm's length and looked at him again from head to toe, taking in the newness of him.

"Why aren't you home? I thought you'd be having tea with Juniper about now," she asked.

"I thought I would be too, I confess. But apparently, she isn't feeling well today. There was certainly a spread set out for me, but it didn't seem right to enjoy it by myself," he informed her with a slight grimace.

"Oh, what unfortunate timing," she responded. "Well, I'm nearly done here and then we can go get you a few things at the general store and head home."

"I'll help you!"

Mrs. Harlow beamed and patted him lightly on the cheek. "Come on then, let's see what you learned while away at Conservatory."

Greenhouse

*J*uniper was still seated on her bed when she heard the front door open and close with Oleander's departure.

Her heart hadn't stopped racing since she saw him standing at the threshold. Her ears were ringing the entire time as she spoke to him through the door, as she heard him wander about the house, no doubt enjoying the treats she set out for him.

She felt . . . terrible.

She was the worst kind of friend, the worst kind of coward. How could she not face him after two years of distance? Not welcome him back into their home? *His home?*

The chill of self-loathing moved through her veins like ice, tightening and twisting her gut like a wrung-out dishrag. She shrunk into her bed and curled around one of her feather-down pillows. She inhaled deeply and the lingering traces of lavender and chamomile from a home-distilled spray took some edge off her distress. Still, she couldn't stop seeing the image of Oleander's falling face, hearing the disappointed, worried din to his words outside of her door.

"This shouldn't be happening," she said into the pillow. "What do I do? How do I fix this?"

Juniper lay there for a time, handling her emotions in the only ways she knew how — by herself and with a healthy dose of self-loathing. These moments were often unseen and often the most awful part of her nerves. Yes, there was the stress of facing social interaction, the requirement to perform and meet expectations (sometimes the stress came from not knowing the expectations she was meant to meet), but it was the moments afterward that truly rendered her paralyzed: the guilt, the embarrassment, the shame, all crashing into her like a wave. Juniper felt trapped, unable to see the small moment for what it was — small.

So many years of living this way had practically made her into a recluse. Not only nervous about interactions themselves but for the potential they had to destroy her — to bring her to her knees like this.

Her eyes burned as she lay there, curled up. They welled with large tears, and she did the only thing she knew to do to release the tightly wound tension in her body.

She cried.

Sometimes it was the only thing she could do to relieve the coiled muscles in her shoulders, in her belly; the only way that she could handle the emotions that came with being so inept, so much of a disappointment and a failure. Her only way out was through. So, she gave herself leave to have a good little cry in the privacy of her room. She allowed the fragility to seep out of her through her tears.

After an hour or so she eased out of that state; she was still raw, still aching, but the edge of her distress was worn down, dulled. She wiped her face before she rose again and went to her vanity. She saw to some of the swelling brought on by her tears, daubing a cooling tincture from a bottle in the drawer under her eyes. She gathered her hair over one shoulder, and brushed through the tangles, trying not to ache at the memory of receiving the brush as a gift from Oleander for one of her birthdays.

She grabbed her hat from the vanity, a straw one she recently purchased from the hat shop in town. It was made in the traditional style, the cap coming to a stylish, slightly curved point. The brim of the hat was just wide enough and decorated with ornately painted roses and peonies in the same dusty pink as the dress she wore. A thick, white ribbon tumbled from the inside of the hat, which she tied into a well-shaped bow beneath her chin. It was paramount that she lifted her mood before her family came home. She couldn't go worrying them all over this stunt. Above all else, she didn't want to further ruin Oleander's homecoming by making him feel unwelcome, or like he was a nuisance. She exhaled, pinching her cheeks to draw some color into them, and exited her bedroom.

She opened her door and peered out, head craning to check the hallway.

"Hello?" she called. "Oleander?" she said a little louder. Taking a moment to be sure that he had, in fact, left the small cottage and that she wouldn't have to go through the same nightmare all over again, with an audience this time, she quickly moved down the hall.

She took the same stairs down to ground level, but upon reaching the bottom, she turned away from the front door. Juniper walked through the kitchen, still smelling of cookies, into another corridor that gave way to a family library on one side and her father's study on the other. At the very end of the hallway stood a door that opened out to the back garden.

The witch opened the door, stepping out into the autumn chill and damp. She walked on the soft dirt path which flowed through the various plants throughout the garden, all tended and grown by her own hand. She walked past beautiful, full bushels of chrysanthemums, swaying pansies, tall fountain grass, and vibrant asters, all arranged in tasteful disarray. The blooms looked as if they just gravitated to their home — to Juniper herself.

Not far off stood her beloved greenhouse, a gift for her debut when she was sixteen. In the six years since then, the bronze structure had oxidized. The once orangish-yellow metal now appeared mottled brown and turquoise. Juniper loved it though; it made the building itself feel alive, made it feel like it was growing and changing with her.

As she neared the structure, something in her stomach and chest loosened further. This greenhouse was her sanctuary. She loved all of nature — any forest, any meadow — but this greenhouse was the only thing in her life that was entirely hers. She stepped in and found the warmth trapped inside even on this cloudy day was a boon of its own. The smell of damp soil and water filled her nose and the tension inside of her was further unwound. It was so still and quiet, and yet somehow alive.

When she was first gifted the greenhouse, it was entirely empty. Just a simple glass and bronze structure with a loft made of the same bronze covering a modest portion of the upper space. Her parents wanted to give her something that was her own.

She ordered soil brought in and started to harvest seeds from her journeys into the forests and the personal gardens there that she already tended. She had a small writing desk placed in the loft along with a chaise for sunny afternoon naps, and of course, bookshelves where she kept references on plant identification and seed starting. It wasn't long at all before she started to fill the space with life of her own creation.

Juniper went up the stairs, laced boots clanging on the metal, and made her way to the bookshelves. There, she checked on her sprouts and her experiments.

"Good morning, everyone," she cooed. "I hope we're all faring well." She reached out to pick up a cracked teacup the color of the sky with a happy little stalk growing out of it. She touched the leaves so delicately, like they were the wings of a moth. "Well, you're responding well to your new soil. It's time to find you a new container, don't you think?" The plant remained silent, but the smaller tendrils of its greenery gently, and very slowly, curved around the finger offered to it. She let a soft breath escape her as she gently petted the curling leaf with her thumb.

"I shall take that as a yes," she whispered.

Juniper knew plants better than she knew anything else. Better than she knew other people. She had always had an inexplicable draw to them, even as a child. Growing up, she had a knack for finding rare plants: four-leaf clovers, puffball mushrooms, magical ingredients. When she was a little girl, she used to tell her mother that they sang to her and that's how she found them.

Juniper didn't hear them sing anymore, nor ever remembering a time when she did. She just assumed that it was the only way she could communicate what she felt as a child with her limited vocabulary. She ruminated on the memory as she made her way back down the stairs, the plant's tendrils still curling around her extended finger. She made her way to the shaded area beneath the loft, a spot she reserved for plants that preferred partial sunlight and for storage of tools, seeds, and various sizes of planting containers.

"Hmm," she said half to herself and half to the sprout. "Let's see, perhaps a ceramic container to help maintain that moisture in your soil, no?"

The plant, of course, did not respond. Her gut tightened, though — an intuitive cue.

"No?" she repeated, "Hmm, perhaps you'd like something prettier."

The tightness in her stomach ebbed a bit. Juniper laughed softly. "I see," she replied. "Let go then," she coaxed.

After the plant released her outstretched finger, she reached out for another porcelain piece, this one an old casserole dish that her mother no longer wanted to keep. Juniper's belly warmed now, a silent cry of joy from the sprout in her other hand. Juniper hummed to herself and to all the life thrumming in the little greenhouse as she made her way to a round wrought iron table with two chairs and set the plant down on the iron table along with the casserole dish. She then returned to the shaded area to grab a small burlap sack of damp soil as well as a large jar filled with dry leaves and wood chips. She returned and sat at the table, setting to work.

"Now," she said to the plant as she started to carefully measure out the proper ratios of soil to the dry leaves, "we have a custom in this greenhouse, perhaps you've heard of it." The plant remained silent as Juniper began to mix the soil together with her bare hands, delicate fingers coaxing the two textures together. Her heart softened at the feeling of the soil beneath her manicured fingernails. This was home for her.

"When a sprout is transferred from its seeding container to its first growing container, we choose a name for it," she said as she drew her fingers out of the dirt and clapped some of the dust off her hands. It fell onto her skirts, her boots, and onto the floor; a stain of grime remained tinging the pale tips of her fingers.

An errant wind blew through the greenhouse, rustling the seedling and making it look as if it danced. She knew that it was unlikely that these little moments meant much, she knew she had the bad habit of anthropomorphizing her little friends. But it brought her so much joy and peace to feel like they were as happy to see her as she was to see them. How terrible it would be for them to run off and retreat into their pots! *Oh . . .*

She lifted the teacup and carefully — so, so *carefully* — tipped it over into her open hand. She allowed the sprout to come out of its old planter and nestle in her gentle fingers. She carefully turned it upright again and began gently massaging the old soil out of its thriving roots.

"So, let's think . . ." she trailed off to the plant quietly, eyes so attentive as she gently cleared the soil out. "You should be a . . . hmm . . . you're a cross between a lavender and a chamomile seed," she said as she considered, "which should be good for relief of nerves, sleep aid, and promoting pleasant dreams."

She reached into the new container and gently opened a pocket in the dirt. Once done she placed the roots into the soil, watching as the roots snaked and tangled into their new soil bed. Juniper beamed. "Very good!" she said with effusive praise. "You're a resilient little one. Let's hope you actually produce some flowers."

Juniper had been working on this particular project for some time, almost a year now, after a run-in on an especially unpleasant night in town for her nerves. Dante had been the one to find her, taking her to the lounge and helping her settle. This plant had been intended to be a gift of thanks. She had long since given up on using it for that purpose, opting to bring him wild sarsaparilla that she had foraged instead, to use in his drinks of course. But after starting the project she certainly wasn't going to quit.

"Hmm," she said as she gently patted soil over the roots, "a strong, tiny, resilient sprout, that calms and brings sweet dreams. How about Lula? Like a lullaby!"

Another wind whipped through the small space. Lula danced with it and Juniper laughed and brought the plant over to a makeshift wooden shelf where she kept a variety of others in different stages of growth.

"Welcome to the family, Lula," she said warmly as she set it down delicately, as if handling a babe.

A voice rose then, but not a voice from the little plant. A voice from behind her. Warm and deep and gentle.

"Welcome, Lula," it said.

Juniper started, nearly jumping out of her skin, blood draining from her face. She turned to face the source of the voice in segments. First, her head turned and then her shoulders, finally she fully faced it. There, leaning in the doorway with both arms and legs crossed in easy grace, stood Oleander.

The wind . . . it had come when he opened the door. She must have been so focused on her conversation that she didn't hear him step in. She stared at him. He didn't speak, he didn't move, he just looked at her with a relaxed gaze and a gentle curve to his lips. His face was so familiar but so different. The smile was the same one that he once gave her as a boy. However, in this new slimmer, sharper face, his pale blue eyes smoldered like ash-covered embers.

Juniper set a hand down on the surface behind her, a steadying touch.

Oleander didn't move, still standing there, calm and constant. "Are you feeling better, Juniper?" he asked quietly.

"I — better?" she asked, not entirely sure what he referenced, still reeling from the shock of finding herself no longer alone in her greenhouse.

His brow knitted, and he finally pushed off the door frame, standing properly. "Your stomach, Juni," he clarified.

Juniper wanted to slam her face into her hand. That's right, that was the excuse she used when she fled from him the last time. And she'd just let slip evidence that she never felt bad at all. "Oh, uhm — yes. I am," she stammered. "Mmm — but I'm afraid that your arrival is poorly timed, I was just about to leave."

"I seem to have a lot of bad timing, today," Oleander told her, brows rising with what she knew to be skepticism. "Where will you go, Juni?" he asked patiently.

Where? Where? *Where?* Her fingers nervously tapped on the rough wood that they rested on as she looked about her greenhouse. Where could she go to escape him? She couldn't face his scrutiny and disappointment in her.

"Juni," he stated softly, pulling her focus back into the room.

Her chest felt so tight, so unbearably restrictive around her hammering heart.

"Th-the clinic, to find Mother."

"Mrs. Harlow returned home with me, if you'd like to see her," Oleander countered.

Damn it all. Why was she always so *stupid?*

"Juni, what's wrong?"

His voice was so kind, so patient. It made her hate herself more.

Her other hand reached up to grasp at the fabric over her chest. It was so hot — too hot — in the greenhouse. She felt faint, she felt nauseous.

"I have to go," she said, moving before Oleander even had a moment to process the quiet words.

"Juniper!" he exclaimed.

She didn't stop when he did, heading straight for one of the larger windows near her.

"Juniper, what are you—"

She fumbled with the window, barely the dimensions to fit her body and voluminous skirts through.

"Juniper don't use the window . . . please . . ." he stated as he started to walk toward her.

Juniper gasped, pressing herself against the glass, feeling like a caged animal. Her heart sank into her boots as she watched his expression crumple with realization; watched him see her shame as clear as words on a page.

She needed to be out of here. She needed to run away from it. She panted as she slapped her shoulder into the window once, twice. Distantly she noticed how the iridescent glass started to warp and bend. She worried for a moment that she would have to smash the pane out to flee. But just before she was getting ready to lift her foot to kick through, the window's rust-covered hinge gave way, sending her tumbling in a graceless heap into the dirt and moss below.

She didn't wait for Oleander to move any closer.

She ran.

Good News!

Oleander stood there for a long time, just trying to process whatever had just happened. His brain kept turning over the details in his head repeatedly. The look of dread on Juniper's face as she stutter-stepped anxiously toward the window kept playing over and over in his mind. As though going within striking distance of him to unlock the door was a sentence worse than death.

He stood there long after Juniper vanished into the forests at the other end of the estate, long after his head emptied of most of his coherent thoughts. In the awful stillness of the greenhouse, his heart ached and thudded horribly in his chest.

Juniper was frightened of him. Why? Whatever had he done to scare her, to make her feel unsafe with him? His mind combed over the letters they exchanged over the last two years, searching for anything that he said that was rude or uncouth or easy to misconstrue as insult or critique. Was she finally tired of his constant insistence that he would make her his wife one day? Did she dislike that he'd studied Herbalism despite her warnings not to?

When he found no evidence there, he reviewed his arrival. There was nothing of note there, either. Of all the variables there were to think about, he was the only constant, as far as he could tell. He was precisely the same person he was two years ago, save for a few more magic tricks and a six-inch growth spurt.

Did she find someone she loved while he was away? Was she afraid to tell him, to hurt him, so she just kept avoiding him? Mrs. Harlow would undoubtedly be aware if her daughter was the subject of a courtship.

It was then, remembering lunch with Mrs. Harlow, that he recalled a moment that he'd glossed over. Something Mrs. Harlow told him which he had easily and thoughtlessly dismissed. "I worry about Juniper," Mrs. Harlow had stated while she idly stirred her tea. "I fear she's getting worse. Becoming truly reclusive." What had happened to her while he was away?

He had told Mrs. Harlow that he didn't think there was anything about Juniper to fix. That she was perfect just as she was. He still believed that. And perhaps it was hubris, but something must have occurred while he was away and unable to protect her. Something horrible.

Oleander glanced outside. It was getting late in the day, the air chilling. Juniper had no coat, having not needed one in the warmth of the greenhouse. But she would catch her death if she was out there too late after sundown. Oleander hissed to himself and hurried back into the cottage, long legs taking him there much faster than they used to. He grabbed one of Juniper's cloaks from the hooks arrayed just by the back door and ran back out before Mrs. Harlow could ask after him.

Broom, he thought. He should fly to find her. No . . . Juniper was afraid of heights. Still, what if he did find her and she was too exhausted to walk back to the cottage? What if she had injured herself after her spill? If she was fearful of him, she surely wouldn't allow him to carry her.

No, it would have to be the bike. Not the best for the terrain, but as long as it was close enough, he could bring it down to her and walk the bike with her astride it. He would bring the bike. She would have to hold onto him, but hopefully, he could manage to convince her that it would be okay.

Then again, maybe it would be a better choice to go get Mrs. Harlow to help. No, that wouldn't do. Mrs. Harlow was already convinced that Juniper was becoming a true hermit. To Oleander, it felt like some strange kind of betrayal to confirm that theory. It wasn't correct. Juniper just required a little bit of patience and understanding. *She wasn't broken.*

A muscle tensed and relaxed in Oleander's jaw as he strode to the shed in the garden. He opened it, scanning the various tools and supplies. After a few moments, he finally spotted the bicycle behind a bit of bric-a-brac. He hastily moved it all out of the way and grasped the bike by its handles. He started to roll the bike and was met with a disheartening *flup, flup, flup.*

He glanced down to the source of the sound and found a flat tire, the rubber worn completely through in places. He didn't know if it was rats, squirrels, or just time that had worn through the rubber of the wheel. Regardless, he muttered an ungentlemanly curse beneath his breath, gritting his teeth and dropped the bicycle.

Okay, no bike.

Oleander paced, his own panic rising and roiling. What could he do? He didn't wish to further distress Juniper. What if she just kept on running? He needed to be smart about this. Yes, it hurt to think that Juniper could be frightened of him. Yes, it was painful to think that she may not be close to him in the way that she was before. But this moment was not about him. *What did Juniper need?* What would do the most help and cause the least harm?

He ran through options in his head. Who, besides himself, did Juniper feel safe with? He paced and pondered for a few more precious moments. He ran through the roster of girls and women in town, wringing his brain dry for any semblance of a young lady that Juniper would consider a friend or a mentor. He was so focused on finding someone of the same gender that he nearly forgot an obvious possibility; one he had even had a discussion with that very day. His pacing slowed to a stop and after a moment he was running back to the house for his broom.

Dante.

Dante was someone safe and wouldn't judge or gossip.

He threw open the door, grabbing a stylish besom with a raw birch handle. He wasted no time hurrying back out, ignoring Mrs. Harlow as she called out to him in concerned question. He mounted and took to the skies. There wasn't time to waste traveling to The Cat's Cradle on foot.

It was only moments before Oleander landed smoothly outside of the bar. He strode in with purpose. Dante was already rounding the bar; no doubt having seen Oleander's expression. Eight lives of observation helped the man know how to read a room.

"What's the matter?" Dante asked, pupils constricted into fine, thin lines.

"Juniper ran off. She was in a panic. She knows the forests but—"

"But a panic can make anyone stumble," Dante finished. He turned his head to a young man standing behind the bar with ginger hair and warm brown eyes. Oleander glanced too, recognizing him as Tucker Frond, a young man a bit older than Juniper who lived in the village. "Frond, watch the place until I get back. You know what to do," Dante instructed.

Tucker bobbed his head birdishly, eyes wide with confusion and worry. "Is Miss Harlow—"

He didn't have a chance to finish his question before Dante's form changed. The man spirited into a plume of gray smoke which bellowed and curled in the cool fall air. It whipped away in mere moments, leaving behind a silver-coated cat with large, golden eyes.

Oleander didn't flinch as the creature easily bound from the floor, landing smoothly atop his shoulder. He merely nodded his thanks to Tucker before turning to run outside once again.

Oleander mounted his broom and pushed off the ground, soaring quickly into the skies. Dante didn't wobble from his shoulders, simply peered down to the ground far below as they zipped over the dense forests of oak and willow trees. After a few moments of them both looking across the stretching acres, Oleander heard Dante's voice in his head.

"How long ago did she run off?"

Oleander swerved in the skies, losing some altitude from the shock of unexpected telepathic communication. While Oleander didn't balk at the shift of man into cat, it was purely because he had seen so much transmogrification during his time in school. Hearing a voice other than one's own in your head was a different story entirely.

Dante didn't react, he simply waited for Oleander to stabilize and answer his question.

"I-I'm not entirely sure. I was a bit dumbfounded when she first bolted and didn't immediately react. Perhaps twenty minutes, or a bit more than half an hour?"

In his peripheral vision Oleander saw the feline bob its head in a nod.

"How far does that mind-to-mind communication work?" Oleander asked his friend.

"Around five miles, if my energy level is good; which luckily, it is today. I take it you came to get me to avoid chasing her around like a

runaway dog? After all, a dog runs away by accident; a cat runs away with intent."

Oleander's mouth tightened and his brow drooped. "Yes, that's right," he said glumly. Oleander's heart squeezed and ached again. He felt like a villain chasing after a damsel. How many times had he mentally cast the boys in the village in the same role after Juniper avoided them? Too many times to count. It made it hurt all the more that he was now one among them.

"Don't be sour. This is good news, isn't it?"

"How could this possibly, in any light or any circumstance, be *good* news?" Oleander spat. He wondered how mad he looked having a one-sided conversation with a cat.

"Come now, Ambrose. Use your brain," the feline teased. *"What are the circumstances in which Juniper has fled like this before?"*

"She's always fled any young man in the village! What are you playing at?"

"Any young man?" Dante asked leadingly. *"Any at all?"*

Oleander quieted as he flipped through old memories like pages in a book. Many of them felt very old indeed after two years away from home. There were very few events in the village which even required Juniper to interact with the young men in town. There was Midsommer, during which one of the dances required that the eligible bachelors dance with the debuted young ladies, mimicking the union between the Moon Goddess and the Great Stag. Juniper always avoided that one, filling her dance card with Dante, Oleander, and her own father instead. There were also the odd group dances at this rite and that rite and of course just parties at estates in the village. Juniper never went to those, though.

Oleander's brows knitted as he remembered the very first time Juniper went to one of the festivals after her debut as an eligible young lady. Midsommer, some six years ago:

. . .

He stood next to her, as always at these events. He fancied himself a sort of knight of hers; a silent protector with an eye on the crowd, peering around for possible threats to Juniper's fragile sense of safety. All seemed to be going just fine, at least until the music was struck and the crowd dispersed to dance.

Oleander's attention homed in on her as he felt her stiffen next to him. Not unusual at events like this, but when he looked up at her he found himself surprised. He saw her eyes wide and terrified. Oleander, younger then, heard her praying repeatedly to the Moon for some sort of mercy.

"No, no, no, no! Anyone but him!" she gasped beside him.

Oleander followed her gaze to a boy, two years older than her. He knew him only as an acquaintance since most of the boys in town didn't bother with him at that age, being only twelve. The boy was tall, with green eyes and auburn hair. The eldest of the Frond boys; Tucker's older brother.

"Do you not like Ethan, Juniper? I can tell him to shove off, just say the word." He squared his shoulders in quiet preparation, making himself as tall and formidable as possible.

"That's not it at all, I like him entirely too much! I can't dance with him, Ollie. I'll make an absolute idiot of myself. I won't even know how to speak to him," she hissed, staring down at him. "I—"

Before she could speak more, Ethan reached them. His green eyes focused quietly on Juniper, his high cheekbones, faintly pink as he gave a small bow, and cleared his throat.

"Miss Harlow, would you do me the honor of allowing me to claim your first dance of the evening?" he asked.

Oleander looked up at her again and she was frozen stiff. Frozen in a way he had never seen her freeze before except for maybe the few times she had dealt with her fear of heights. She stammered unintelligibly for a few, painful moments before Oleander stepped in, ever her protector.

"Sorry, Frond, her card is full. Just Mr. Harlow and me tonight," Oleander told him.

Ethan looked to him, brow tensing for a moment before he looked back to Juniper. There was a long moment of silence then. Juniper said nothing at all: A doe frozen in a meadow.

"Very well," Ethan relented. "Enjoy the festivities."

Oleander's broom slowed to a stop in the air and started to descend steadily. His blue eyes stared ahead but saw nothing as the old memory became nothing but noise in his mind. It was as if his brain had come to the conclusion Dante had hinted at, but not his heart. His heart was still ambling to catch up.

Oleander heard the dark, amused chuckle of his friend in his mind, bringing him back to reality.

"Well?"

"She only responds this way to—" He swallowed tightly, his throat having run as dry as sand and stated dumbly, "to young men that she's . . . attracted to . . ."

"So she does," Dante affirmed. *"Excellent deductive reasoning, Ambrose."*

Oleander was still too dumbfounded to be offended by Dante's condescension. He descended into an area of the forest that would have had the straightest path to the Harlow estate, the most likely way Juniper would have fled instinctively if she was running in terror. His feet landed softly on the damp forest floor, fallen oak leaves crunching beneath his soles.

Dante lifted his feline nose, whiskers quivering slightly as he sniffed the air, still expertly perched on Oleander's shoulder. A moment more and he stopped sniffing, then sharply turned his head to the east, away from the village and off the beaten path.

Oleander looked the same way. It wouldn't be a shock for Juniper to leave the main road. She was afraid of most things, but the wilds of the forest had always seemed to be a sort of home away from home.

"I have her scent. Wait here, I'll return with her."

Dante leapt from his shoulder and loped through the trees, disappearing from Oleander's line of sight in a matter of moments. Oleander was left with only the sounds of the forest and the rising volume of his own roaring thoughts.

Given no other recourse, he sat on the exposed roots of a massive oak tree and exhaled slowly, the air passing through his tight lips. He inhaled sharply as soon as his lungs emptied, the breath shaking as his chest inflated once again. A spare glance down at his hands found them . . . shaking? By the Moon, why was he so nervous all of a sudden? Wasn't this what he had wanted all these years? Maybe it was that it still didn't feel quite real; the truth of it not yet settling in his bones.

Yet, it all made much more sense as he went back over the day in his head. With this new context available, he could now see what was plain as day from the very start. Juniper's shock, her hiding — it all corroborated the conclusion Dante had helped him to. This day felt more like an entire week with how chaotic and haphazardly events had unfolded. Every hope, every daydream, every expectation had been subverted. Every plan went awry, and yet . . .

Oleander drew a broad hand down his face, stopping it over his mouth as it curved into an involuntary smile. A reality settled in him, deep in his bones, making his heart hammer away against his ribcage and pound in his ears. His cheeks hurt as he dropped his head into the same hand and laughed to himself.

Juniper thought he was attractive.

Five Things

Juniper hated herself.

She sat, huddled to herself, in the chill air. She was sealed off from the world behind the thick blue-gray curtains of a weeping willow. The same blue-gray as Oleander's eyes. She willed herself to sink into the bark of the tree, willed herself to be enveloped by its branches and roots and the soil beneath her. The willow seemed to answer her wishes or at the very least, attempt to. Lazy, weak roots snaked their way out of the soil and around the tips of her shoes. The branches seemed to undulate and sway, hiding her away.

She wept there for a long time, arms wrapped around herself like it would somehow keep her from falling apart at her fraying seams. Her thoughts were a maelstrom of distress and self-loathing. It was like an endless black pool with a stirring current that pulled her deep under. She drowned in it. She couldn't find the surface or break free of it.

It was in this sorry state that Dante finally found her.

His paws were silent as he came into the shade of the willow and saw her. So small, so sad. Brown woody roots tangled from the soil up her boots and her stocking-clad calf. He sat a distance away, feeling out the energy encapsulated in the little shelter she found for herself there. He had seen her in a few wretched states since Oleander's departure, but none so awful as this.

After a few more moments he quietly approached her. The tickle of a whisker made her fingers twitch, then a small wet nose nudged her white-knuckled hand. Her breath hitched as she opened that hand, and then opened her tear-swollen eyes. Dante arched his head into her cupped palm, smoothing himself past her fingers. The silken texture of his coat jarred her enough that she was able to break through the surface of that deep pool of despair.

"D-Dante," she rasped with quaking, hitching breaths. "How did you—"

She stiffened sharply and sat up, looking around with panicked eyes.

In only a moment, Dante was there in his human form, squeezing her tiny, freezing hand in both of his large, warm ones. The touch wasn't an intimate one, not the touch of a man courting a woman. In fact, he squeezed so hard that it almost hurt. The touch was one meant to jostle her out of her panic — bring her back to herself.

"He isn't here. He sent me in on my own," he assured her.

Dante reached into his vest and pulled out a black handkerchief from his inner pocket. He fussed quietly over her, drying her face. His brow dipped and his yellow eyes narrowed in gentle worry. He had never seen her so distraught.

"Does h-he hate m-me?" Juniper hicupped out.

"No," Dante answered immediately. "I don't think he'd ever be capable of such a feeling toward you, Miss Harlow." He lightened the situation. "Or *anyone* for that matter."

"But I've treated him horribly—" Juniper wept. "I saw the

hurt on his face when I ran. I can't face him. I'm such a coward, Dante. He should hate me, he should—"

"Shhh, shhh, shhh," Dante tutted, hand squeezing painfully again. "Tell me five things you see."

"W-what?"

"Five things you see in the clearing," Dante repeated patiently. "Anything will do."

Juniper's brow tensed slightly, and she began to look around the space. Her eyes fell first to Dante's hand as he dabbed wetness from her face again.

"Th-the handkerchief," she stated dumbly.

"Very good. Four more," he instructed as he folded the cloth and placed it in Juniper's other hand.

She lifted it to her own face, swiping moisture away and wiping at her own nose as she sniffled. "The tree."

"Mhm, and?"

Her eyes roved again around the small space under the canopy. There wasn't much there. She managed to find something on one of the boughs above her, a spider-silk web that had a few fallen leaves clinging to it but no spider in sight.

"The spider's web up there," she said sullenly.

Dante peered over his own shoulder, following the line of her gaze. "That's a pretty one, isn't it?"

The world returned around her, as if coming out of a horrible waking nightmare. Her chest properly expanded with her breaths, exhaustion replaced the horrible sadness and ache there.

"There's a pebble by your shoe," she said quietly.

"So, there is," Dante said, looking down at it for a moment before lifting his gaze to her and smiling kindly. "That leaves you with," he said, gesturing as if he were crossing off the other four on an invisible scoresheet, "well, would you look at that. Just one more."

"Dante, my old friend."

"There she is," he stated with caring mirth as he released his tight grip on her hand. "Take some deep breaths for me, Miss Harlow, and sit up from the tree. Try to sit up nice and straight."

Juniper felt a bit numb as she pushed herself off the tree, sitting on her own accord but still slouching. Moon above, she was so tired. And her throat and her head were both so sore. She wiped away a few errant tears and sniffed before inhaling full and deep into her lungs. Her self-loathing eased up, quieting to the normal murmur in the back of her mind. It no longer screamed at her or blocked out other thoughts.

"This is the worst episode in a while . . ." she whispered after a long time.

Dante had rested back on the palms of his hands, folding his slender legs and staring ahead at the swaying branches, allowing Juniper the time she needed to ground herself. When she spoke, he angled his head slightly and looked at her, his pupils widened ovals in his golden irises.

"Would you like to talk about it?" he asked, his voice gentle.

A genuine inquiry, she was sure. If she said no, she knew Dante would leave the matter alone and not ask about it again. She fiddled with her fingers in her lap, looking down at them for a long quiet moment. Dante only waited patiently. No pressure of expectation between them.

"What if I lose him forever?" she finally said.

"Ambrose?" Dante clarified.

Juniper only nodded in answer, as if saying his name would open the door to another episode of spiraling panic.

"I don't think that you could ever do anything to make him give up on you, Miss Harlow," Dante said, repeating the sentiment from earlier.

"I don't mean him. I know that . . . that Ollie would never be cruel to me. He'd never just up and leave me behind because he was tired of me. But what if . . . what if I lose him because of my own deficiencies?" Her voice was small and fragile. She rolled her pinky between the thumb and forefinger of the opposite hand. "When I see him, it's a purely biological reaction. I just freeze and I can't do anything."

Dante inhaled deeply and let the breath drain out of him slowly. "Do you remember when Ambrose first came to live with you, Miss Harlow?" Dante asked.

"Of course," she answered easily.

"He didn't speak for almost an entire year, remember? Didn't breathe a word to you, Mr. Harlow or Mrs. Harlow, or me," he stated. "Did you ever give up on him?"

"No, of course not. I knew he was trying his best, I just wanted to be there for him," Juniper stated.

Dante once again looked toward the swaying curtain of willow branches hemming them in. Their own private confessional. "Is it so hard to believe that you could be worthy of the same patience and care that you once showed him as a boy?" Dante asked her. "Don't you think that you could just allow Ambrose to understand you for all your deficiencies and quirks? Just until you can adjust, of course. It's only the same courtesy you once gave him, after all."

Juniper looked over to him, his eyes still not meeting hers.

"Ambrose isn't any of the Frond boys. Or the girls in the village who jab and gossip. He is your oldest friend," he said.

"And that's why I can't take advantage of him," Juniper quickly insisted.

"Needing kindness and support for a short time is not the same as manipulating someone into taking care of you hand and foot, Miss Harlow," Dante said, his gaze finally landing on hers. "Sometimes it's okay to let your friends shoulder the burden for a little while. Sometimes it's okay to just allow someone to be a little stronger than you — for you — until you can get back on your feet."

Juniper stared at him for another long moment. A faint line appeared between her brows before she looked back down at her hands, her fidgeting stopped, and they now sat still in her lap. "It sounds fair, but it still feels so wrong to do," she said in barely more than a whisper.

"It always does," he said as he lifted one of his hands to gesture in a half shrug. "It does help, however, to remember that it can be fulfilling for the other party. It can bring joy to be there for someone you care deeply about."

Juniper didn't say anything in response. She was too busy digesting the words — relating to them. She supposed that . . . yes, it was true. It did bring her happiness to care for Oleander, to spoil him, to support him, to root for him in all that he aimed to accomplish. And she remembered when he was a boy how badly she just wanted to be someone who made him feel safe, wanted to be someone that he spoke to, and confided in, and called a friend.

Was it possible that someone as charismatic and put-together as Oleander would want to provide something like that for her as well? That he would find fulfillment in aiding her through her own struggles with . . . whatever this was? Oleander had always seen her as so much more than she was. She had always appreciated his admiration of her. It was nice to have at least one person in her life that seemed to think she was worth-while, that what she was doing was worthwhile. But now . . . now that inflated opinion of her made her feel ill. She couldn't fulfill those expectations anymore. Any interaction she would have with him now would just be a disappointment to him. A failing on the most basic level.

"Tell me what you're thinking," Dante said softly, unob-trusively.

Juniper's dark eyes lifted to meet his golden ones, and she deflated with a sigh, looking down at her hands once again.

"I . . . don't think I've ever been the girl that Oleander admires. I think I've been living a lie and it's finally catching up to me," Juniper admitted.

Dante bent his legs and rested his elbows atop his knees, hands lazily hanging between them. He once again looked ahead to the swaying willow branches as he chewed on what she said for a few moments.

"Ambrose is certainly a man who sees the world through rose-tinted glasses," Dante said.

Juniper's face fell, feeling the wound of his acknowledgment of her fears as truth.

Dante looked at her. "That is not to say that you have been living a lie, Miss Harlow. Please don't take it that way," he quickly clarified. "It's just that, I think you're spending much of your life balancing on a tight rope."

"A tight rope?"

"It's not only the judgements against you that frighten you, but the idea that someone can think wonderful things about you as well. You see it as a role that needs to be filled; performed, if you will. Am I correct about that?"

Juniper nodded in answer.

"Perhaps Ambrose needs to curtail his idealized view of you…but perhaps you need to consider that you are not seeing yourself as clearly as you think you are," he said gently.

"But I hurt him, I saw it on his face," Juniper insisted.

"Perhaps, but more than anything, you scared him. Worried him." Dante looked at her and scanned her face once again, catching her eyes with his own. "He came into The Cradle with one of your coats in hand, and he just wanted to find you to make sure you didn't fall somewhere and hurt yourself. That you wouldn't catch your death out here." Dante's gaze was unwavering. "He didn't say a word about being cross or offended. He just wanted to see you back home safe, even if that meant he couldn't do it himself."

Juniper's mouth twisted to the side slightly. She had caused him a great deal of unneeded concern when she had run off and left him there, *after* jumping out of a window. In her mind she switched places with him, she envisioned a younger Oleander doing the same thing. She would have been beside herself. She never would have thought to be angry or disappointed; she just would have figured out how to help him. And that's what Oleander had done for her, in turn.

"Is . . . Ollie home?" Juniper finally asked quietly.

"I left him to come find you in the oak glens. I'm sure he remains near there, give or take a bit for his allotment of pacing," Dante responded with a teasing curl to his lips. "Can I escort you to him, Miss Harlow?"

Juniper only nodded.

Dante slowly rose back to his feet and offered out a hand to her.

She placed her hand in his and stood. She went to take a step and almost fell — only to look down to see the willow's roots still clinging to her boots.

"O-oh," she said quietly to the tendrils. "I'm okay now, you can let go."

As if a guard was called off by their charge, the vegetation snaked back into the ground.

Dante offered her an elbow.

"Shall we?" he asked.

Crone's Hare

Oleander was indeed pacing when Juniper and Dante made their way back to the main forest path. He began doing so not more than a few minutes after Dante left, when the quiet started to chew at his already-frayed nerves. Too much free space in his mind for his fears and they became incessantly loud — louder even than the creaking of the fourth stair in the cottage — he realized only now that he had forgotten to tell Mrs. Harlow to fix it this time around.

When Oleander heard steps scuffing from deeper in the forest, he turned to face them. He watched as Dante stepped over the hazardous roots of an oak tree before turning and extending a hand to help Juniper cross — then Juniper looked at him.

Her gaze felt different than before, even though the expressions on her face were the same: a little tense, a little worried, a little frightened. But now at least he knew *why* that was. It wasn't some mystery that he had to unravel through trial and error. He could be content with an obstacle he understood. He could address this whole messy situation strategically now.

Oleander remained exactly where he was as Dante and Juniper stopped about two yards away from him. He was silent, willing patience into his face as he allowed his lips to curve with relief. The sorcerer then willed his brow to soften and lift, letting his shoulders ease and drop. Both men conveyed, with facial expressions, that it was safe; they would let her set the pace.

Oleander watched Juniper's hand tighten a bit, curling into the loose fabric of Dante's sleeve. He watched her for a long moment, that same patient expression remaining on his face. Finally, Juniper's voice lifted from her throat, the sound as soft as a summer breeze and airily breathless with her own nerves.

"I feel terrible," she managed to say.

"You have nothing to feel terrible over," Oleander said, meaning it. He weaved his gentle care into every word, with the careful touch of a seasoned seamstress. Juniper's expression softened, then warmed. It broke Oleander's heart to see her smile like that. The first one she'd given him that day.

"I . . ." she trailed off and looked up to Dante. Oleander felt the little tickle of amusement as he realized she'd practiced what to say with their friend. "I don't think I can hug you yet," she said in nearly a whisper, staring down at her boots.

"That's quite alright," Oleander responded. "How about we just go back to the greenhouse, and I'll sit at the iron table while you work. I got nearly halfway through that book you sent me on the train home, the one about the soldier and his wife—"

"*Memory of Love!*" Juniper interjected.

"Yes! I've enjoyed it a lot. So, I'll read while you work, and if you're feeling up to it, we can discuss it when you're all done."

Dante smirked at his friend with cool approval.

"Would you like a ride back to The Cat's Cradle, old friend?" Oleander asked him.

Dante lifted a hand in polite refusal. "That won't be necessary, though I thank you for the offer, Ambrose," he said calmly. "It's been some time since I've taken my old form to get around. I'm looking forward to trying some old shortcuts." Despite what he said, he looked to Juniper then with a question in his eyes; he was weighing her willingness to be on her own with Oleander.

Juniper gave a little nod and relinquished the barkeep's arm.

"Perhaps I'll see you tonight then, Ambrose."

"I wouldn't miss the chance to rob you blind. I owe you for that game before I left for school," Oleander said warmly.

"I would like to see you try," Dante said back. He then turned to Juniper, giving a halfhearted bow, mostly out of politeness.

"Th-thank you," she stammered quickly, "for helping me."

"Always a pleasure to assist. Don't you think on it for a moment, Miss Harlow." (Without him having said that, she very well may have thought on it for the rest of the night, if not for multiple days, or even a week; spiraled and obsessed and self-loathed as she did earlier that day.)

Juniper stepped over to Oleander's side, giving Dante room to shift, watching him vanish into a plume of gray smoke which whisped away to reveal his tiny feline form. He looked at them for only a moment before he hurried away with loping steps, so much faster than he would have been as a man, and much more sure-footed. They both watched quietly as he vanished into the tree line and then Oleander looked down towards her.

"Ready?" he asked.

They began to walk on the path back to the house which was barely visible from where they stood. He let her fall into step with him at whatever distance she wished to remain. She seemed to settle at a bit past arm's-length away on his right side. Oleander hoisted his besom over his left shoulder and slid his other hand into his trouser pocket. Her cloak was thrown over his right shoulder — in case she wanted to grab it for herself.

The walk back was mostly silent, but for once, it didn't

bother him. Oleander had spent a lot of time with Juniper. He had spent a lot of time memorizing the things that seemed to fray and tear at her delicate nerves. Was it ideal that he was now one of those things? No, of course not. But he knew how to read her, when to push her, and when he needed to back off. He learned from years of observing people making those very same mistakes with her.

This morning, his lack of clarity during the entire debacle that was their reunion, threw him off. But now, having the context behind it and understanding precisely what Juniper had choked with, he knew what to look out for. And knowing that all this distance came from a budding attraction, well, it made it all the easier to deal with. He couldn't bring it up to her. Not now, and likely not even soon. Acknowledging the elephant in the room wouldn't serve Juniper in any way, and he didn't want her to feel that he was only showing her kindness and patience with the expectation of receiving her affections in return.

He wasn't expecting to be rewarded for allowing her the autonomy and space she needed to process whatever feelings she was experiencing. Those were Moon-given rights, as far as he was concerned. And there was always the possibility that she would never come around to him.

The thought of that made his stomach twist as they made their way through the forest, a chill starting to come through as the afternoon transitioned into evening. He hadn't let himself think about it until now, but there was always the potential that Juniper would always see him as the little mute boy he'd once been.

Juniper's arms folded and he saw her rub gently over her sleeves, an answer to an autumnal wind. He drew his hand out of his pocket and pulled the cloak off his shoulder, holding it out to her on an outstretched arm without a word. She accepted it, opening it and draping it tightly over her own shoulders against the chill.

Oleander was relieved, some knots of tension uncoiling, even for something so small as being able to make sure that she was warm on a cold day. Even if she never returned his feelings, he realized at that moment that he would be content to fulfill any duty that would make her happy and ensure that she was secure and unafraid of the world around her.

But he wasn't going to give up.

Not quite yet.

The pair returned to the greenhouse in due time, and Juniper continued her work as Oleander read at the table below her. No conversation was had, and Oleander dared only risk a few brief glances up at her as she worked.

After night fell, Mrs. Harlow came out to join them both as Juniper still toiled away. She brought with her a light dinner, a common courtesy she paid her daughter who often lost herself in her work. It was the perfect way to help Juniper adjust to this newer version of her oldest friend.

Oleander watched as mother and daughter stole alternating glances at each other, and he smiled encouragingly every time Mrs. Harlow gave him a pleading, worried glance.

Juniper, for her part, seemed more worried that her mother would pressure her to come down and join them.

Not long after dinner, the young man stood to excuse himself. "I'm sorry, ladies, but I'm afraid I promised Dante that I would beat him at cards tonight," he stated as he straightened his lapels. "I'd hate for him to tell all the gents in town that I'm a coward because I didn't deign to show. I'll be home late, I'm sure, so don't feel the need to wait up for me."

"Oh my, a little man you've become indeed!" the matriarch said with a bit of incredulity. "Going out to the gent's club 'til all hours of the night."

And for all the swagger and charm Oleander had shown that day, in that moment, he was merely a boy again. His brows shot up and his eyes widened. His mouth pressed as he flushed to his ears.

Hunched slightly, Mrs. Harlow reached to squeeze his cheeks but resisted the urge.

"Mrs. Harlow, you make me sound quite rakish when you say it like that," Oleander muttered with an unconscious glance upward to where Juniper sat inspecting seeds under a magnifying glass.

Mrs. Harlow gave a coquettish giggle in response. "With the way you've grown, who knows what sort of behavior you've picked up. I'm certain the girls in town will have trouble ignoring you now."

"The only girl in town that would ever catch my gaze is Juniper, Mrs. Harlow." The words came out firm and heavy compared to the levity in the room.

Juniper froze where she sat. Her mother only stared at him in surprise. The interaction froze there for a long time. Seconds dripped as slow as honey. All the same, Oleander didn't falter from what he said.

"It sounds so different now, from how it sounded just before you left," Mrs. Harlow finally said. There was a sound of almost . . . astonishment . . . in her voice. Not in a way of shock — no. She knew the torch that Oleander carried for her daughter. It seemed, in that moment, that Mrs. Harlow was realizing that Oleander was a man now, the same way Juniper had when she greeted him at the door of their shared childhood home.

"The feeling is exactly the same," he responded softly before he once again instinctively looked up at Juniper.

She felt his eyes on her, but she didn't dare look at him.

After a moment, he straightened his lapels again and cleared his throat a bit sheepishly. "Good night, ladies. Sleep well."

"And a good night to you, young buck!"

He glanced up once more; Juniper still didn't meet his gaze. He pressed a tight smile to Mrs. Harlow and took his leave from the greenhouse.

Oleander's footsteps became quieter and quieter as they receded from the glass and metal structure. Some invisible tension unspooled from Juniper in his absence. An exhale of what seemed like relief left her, drawing her mother's attention.

"Juni, dear . . ." she broached, "Why are you acting a stranger to our precious Ollie?"

The tension returned, invisible strings drawing her shoulders up like a poorly-made marionette. "I . . . don't know . . ." Juniper said quietly. She looked down past the railing of the platform at her mother. "I just can't seem to make my mouth work when he's about."

She returned her attention to her task, sorting seeds from a recent harvest by how many flaws they had. The one she was examining was neatly placed into a petri dish which held only two other seeds. Her mouth worked as she busied her hands examining another.

"It's not that I see him as a stranger," she finally muttered quietly. "It's that . . . he's so far beyond me now."

"Juni—"

"It's true," Juniper interrupted, looking down towards her mother once again. "He was always a good boy; he was always worthy of our pride. But now I'm a weight on him. A hindrance. And I know that everyone in town will see that, too. And once the people in town see it, so will Ollie. He deserves to see it. He deserves—"

Juniper shook her head, trailing off. She pinched the bridge of her nose and placed her magnifying glass onto the surface of her worn workbench. What was she saying?

"He deserves what, Juniper?" Mrs. Harlow asked.

Deserves what, indeed. What was Juniper even getting at? She had known for years, since the moment Oleander vowed to make her his bride, that he would find someone better. She had always seen him for the bright, vivacious boy that he was. She always knew that he would grow beyond her.

So why was it so . . . uncomfortable . . . to think about it?

"I just . . . wasn't anticipating him growing up so quickly. That's all."

Across town, Oleander arrived at The Cat's Cradle. On the sleepy village street, The Cradle was alive and kicking. Music drifted on a mild-mannered breeze out of the open steel windows. The herbs growing in the window boxes seemed to sway to the cheerful, yet relaxed melodies from violins and cellos inside. Along with the music came the chime of clinking glasses and the quiet rumble of laughter. From where Oleander stood, it was hard for him to tell if the instruments themselves were spelled by Dante, or if he'd gone through the trouble of hiring a proper band. Either way, it felt like a return to form for Oleander, even if he had only rarely frequented the establishment with Mr. Harlow once or twice before.

In the dying light of the day, the windows almost looked gilded with warm lamp light. They promised a different sort of richness, however. The richness of camaraderie and friendship. The promise of a threshold crossed into manhood proper. Oleander inhaled deeply as he entered the building and was greeted by the smell of cigar smoke and dark amber liquor.

Dante looked entirely at home behind the counter, the barest curve to his lips as he doled out short glasses of liquor and cocktails and tall glasses of foaming ale. The man's amber eyes fell on Oleander, and the two exchanged nods of greeting.

Oleander glanced around the establishment and saw mostly familiar faces but spied a few strangers as well; likely people who had come to the village by way of marrying a local, or perhaps were enjoying a vacation in the countryside away from the hustle and social pressures of the city. Oleander was just happy to be here now as a man instead of a boy.

As he approached the bar for the second time that day, he saw a few of the older gents look at him with surprise. Whether the surprise was in regard to his growth spurt or the surprise of seeing someone who was so recently viewed as a child sidle up to the bar, he wasn't sure. Oleander didn't shrink, though — he owned this moment as he owned every moment.

"What will it be, Ambrose?" Dante said casually, cementing Oleander's belonging there.

"Whiskey please, Dante. Neat." Oleander felt the itch of embarrassment under his collar. He rolled his shoulders and leaned onto his elbows over the bar. He belonged here as much as any other man in the room. He'd settle in soon enough.

Dante slid the glass to him, and Oleander placed a few shards on the countertop, which Dante pushed back toward him.

"The first one is my treat," he said. "I even poured you some of my best."

Oleander scoffed and placed the coins into his coat pocket. "You are a gentleman and a scholar," Oleander responded wryly as he took his first sip. It was good. Notes of almond and honey with a sweet finish. Oleander exhaled after his first sip and idly spun the glass in his hands.

"A busy night for you tonight, hm? I fear I won't get a moment with you for cards after all."

"I'll make time for that. You did promise to beat me, after all," Dante replied with wry amusement. "I'm not one to back down from a challenge, you know?"

Oleander looked toward the tables where cards were already being shuffled and doled out. Everyone was still in decent spirits, so most likely no one had lost too much money yet. He was reminded of the nights after exams where the boys would get together in one form or another to blow off steam or mourn their failures — fond memories, now. As he reminisced, a short older man tossed his hand of cards across the table and griped that the others were robbing him blind.

"We're playing for shards, old man! You just don't like to lose!" a younger freckled boy said with a friendly pat on the man's back.

"Well, so what if I don't! It's in a man's nature to want to conquer!"

"Oy, oy, oy," another young man said. "This is a game of cards, not a battlefield."

Oleander huffed and shook his head as he looked over to Dante, who had also been watching the exchange at the table. Dante sensed his movement and gave him a wry expression that barely touched his lips. He then looked over to the side where the ginger-haired Frond boy stood, sweeping the floor.

"Frond, mind the bar for a while. I need to humble this young man," he said.

Tucker grimaced, putting his broom aside to take Dante's spot behind the bar. He looked a little worried and Dante patted his shoulder.

"You'll be fine. Call for me if you encounter any obstacles," Dante encouraged.

Dante unbuttoned his shirt cuffs and rolled his sleeves up to his elbows as he rounded the counter and met up with Oleander. He gestured over to the tables where a couple of men were rising from their spots in a game.

"Seems we're just in time," Dante said looking sidelong at the young man.

"Rolling your sleeves up, eh? It must be serious for you to show so much skin," Oleander teased.

Dante lifted a hand and swatted the brim of Oleander's pointed hat, causing it to topple off his head.

Oleander caught it with a warm laugh and pushed at Dante's shoulder.

"Don't talk about me like I'm some virginal maiden," Dante said as he started walking with him to the tables.

"Don't act like one and I'd have no reason to do so."

"Oh, you will be eating a very large serving of humble pie very soon."

"What is it that they say about people who talk about winning too much?"

Dante clicked his tongue and this time swatted Oleander on the back of the head.

Oleander stumbled forward and laughed warmly.

"Just go get your ass in the chair," Dante said.

"Language, my lady!" Oleander exclaimed.

"I'm starting to think of just beating you, forget the cards."

This was the version of Dante that Oleander liked best. When Dante would let his guard and his poised demeanor falter a little bit. When he acted like a young man instead of the several-centuries old Familiar that he was. Oleander was still laughing as he dropped into one of the vacant chairs, hanging his hat from the back of it. Dante sat next to him, a bit of an angle to his fine brow, and Oleander beamed. Yes, Oleander knew the night would likely end with an empty purse, but at least it would be entertaining.

Across from them sat two other men, one was a stranger, one was familiar to them both. The familiar man was called Beckton Hawthorne. He was a tall man, taller than Oleander, with warm russet skin and dark mirthful eyes. He had broad shoulders and was well-muscled and athletic. He was the son of a traveling merchant who lived up on the hill but spent most of his own time hunting and pursuing other athletics. Oleander had even attended a couple of the hunts he'd organized.

He gave Oleander a pleasant grin when he and Dante sat

across from him. "Ambrose, it's been a long time. Have you just returned from Conservatory?"

"I have! This very day, in fact!" Oleander responded.

The second man sat in friendly proximity to Beckton. Where Beckton was brawn and muscle, this unfamiliar man was more like Dante in stature and mannerism. He was about the same height as Oleander, but everything about him seemed more elegant. Slender, long fingers collected up the deck of cards and started to shuffle with ease. He wore fine clothes, finer than Oleander's or anything he ever saw the Harlows wearing. A cobalt blue jacket with subtle embroidered brocade in a slightly darker shade. The coat had a high collar and a shining pearl button, a popular fashion in the city. An elegant column of a neck was dusted with the faintly curling ends of golden hair.

Oleander eyed the stranger with Beckton. "Who is your friend, Hawthorne?"

Under pale blond brows, angular eyes of deep blue met Oleander's pale blue ones. There was a slight narrowing of the stranger's features, an almost imperceptible tightening of the lips before the man stopped his shuffling to offer out that graceful hand.

"Theo Vervain," he stated easily, pale lips pulled back into a smile that didn't reach his eyes. "Oleander . . . Ambrose, wasn't it?"

"Yes, it's a pleasure," Oleander stated as he took the man's hand and gave it a good shake.

"Theo is visiting from Kingsborough for a bit of a break," Beckton said patting him on the back. "He's staying with us on the hill through Winter Solstice."

"That right?" Oleander said. "How do you find it?"

Theo began shuffling again before starting to deal out hands of cards.

"Well, it's certainly a change of pace," Theo said in a tone that was not entirely complimentary. "Seems you all live a little more simply out this way. No real need for any kind of ehm—" Theo gesticulated with his hand after setting down the remainder of the deck, twisting it as if searching for the word. "Variety, I suppose."

"Theo thinks we're all uncultured swine out here," Beckton said in good humor.

"Well, I wasn't going to put it that way, but if the shoe fits," Theo said with a shrug.

Oleander's mouth pressed a bit as he picked up his hand of cards. "Well, we're no cultural hub, but we have our own charms here," he said with a tight smile. "So, what are we playing?"

"Crone's Hare," Beckton said, picking up his own hand. "Bet is set at ten stags to start."

"On the Moon! Are you trying to get train fare back to the city or something?" Oleander said in jest to the new man.

"If the bet's too much, we could lower it for you, what shall we make it? A few shards?" Theo said coolly and with no lack of condescension. "However, I've always been of the opinion that a game isn't much fun without intriguing stakes."

Oleander fought the urge to scoff at the stranger's poorly placed intensity.

"Ten stags it is, then," Oleander said. The young man pulled his bill fold out of his pocket and drew out a ten-stag note, he placed it on the table tapping it with two fingers for emphasis. The other men followed quickly after him.

"So, Ambrose," Beckton started as he looked down at his cards. "How has your return been?"

"It's been a relief," Oleander replied easily. "It's nice to be back home with the Harlows again. I spent most of the day with Juniper in her greenhouse."

Theo's brow quirked as he looked down at his cards, but the rest of his features looked utterly disinterested as he arranged his cards in his hands.

"Juniper has hardly been seen lately," Beckton noted. "Some

folks in town have wondered if she went on some extended trip."

Oleander's mouth pressed. He didn't want to divulge any of Juniper's private struggles to mere acquaintances. And even if he did want to, it was hardly his place to do so.

"Juniper has been busy with her horticulture. You know she's rather obsessive about it? She's constantly trying to best herself and make finer ingredients for spells and potions," Oleander said, willing his face to soften. "In some ways, that greenhouse was the worst thing she's ever received; at least she used to stop working when fall and winter would come 'round. Now she works all year!"

"I admit I've been curious about that," Theo stated, still looking at his cards.

"About what?" Oleander asked.

"About why the daughter of a world-renowned combative sorcerer would settle for flowers and herbs." Theo set down a card on the table. "I'll start, I have the Ace of Coins."

All three of the other men at the table stiffened.

"Ah, careful there, Vervain. Don't speak ill of the girl, you're among her friends," Beckton stated a little warily.

"Some people don't want to follow in the footsteps of their fathers," Oleander said unsmilingly. "Juniper is a gentle soul. She yearns to create life, not destroy it." A second passed, and another. "Things must be quite different in . . . Kingsborough, was it?"

"Your move, Ambrose," Theo stated flatly.

Oleander's mouth tightened and he looked down at his cards.

"I'll draw," he said as he reached for the deck.

"I certainly wasn't implying that she should be among men on the battlefield. But certainly, her talents could be better used than for gardening," Theo stated as the flow of the game fell to

Dante. "As far as I know she hasn't even gotten her Sorcerer's Diploma."

Dante placed a Two of Coins and a Two of Swords. "That's a bit reductionist, isn't it? Herbalism is a vast field of study. And I know first-hand that you needn't go to Conservatory to be a talented witch. The whole concept of a Sorcerer's Diploma is younger than I am."

Theo's eyes finally lifted from his cards to look at Dante, they sharpened slightly. "Any self-respecting member of a celebrated family should do what they can to continue the legacy. It's practically a demand of duty."

"Not everyone is as obsessed with duty as you are, Theo," Beckton said, clasping a hand on his shoulder and giving him a friendly shake. "Let the poor girl be."

"I see, this is a concern of personal integrity," Dante cut in as Theo allowed himself to be jostled. "Certainly, even your father knows the values of seedling curses in his line of work? Explosive bulbs during the war *won* the Battle of Oblivion, or did you forget about that?"

"You know of my father, do you?" Theo asked, brushing Beckton's hand off his shoulder.

"I have even met him a few times," Dante said. "He heads the Chaos and Crime Department in the city, doesn't he?"

"So he does," Theo stated. "Is that what Juniper specializes in, then? Seed curses?" he asked a bit sharply.

"Miss Harlow actually provides medicinal herbs to the clinic in the village free of charge, even makes tinctures for them," Beckton stated as he set down a Three of Wands onto the pile.

"Among many other things, like making crops that don't die when the frost comes through," Oleander said as he set The Emperor on the pile.

"Drat," Dante said as he drew three cards from the deck.

Beckton set down a Five of Cups and a Five of Coins.

"I hadn't heard of that. That's bound to revolutionize agriculture," Beckton said with shock.

"She hasn't perfected it yet, but I ran into Hailey Connifer on the train, and she said Juniper's been working hard on it to help them get through the winter," Oleander said with no shortage of pride for his dear Juni's efforts.

Theo snorted as he placed down the Six of Coins and the Six of Swords. "Of course she hasn't perfected it," Theo muttered under his breath.

"You want to say that a little louder, *Vervain?*" Oleander spat as he reached over, picking a card from the deck without looking at it.

Theo's eyes rose from his own cards, and he leaned forward on his elbows. A sharp chin jutted forward, and indigo eyes narrowed at Oleander.

"I said, 'of course she hasn't,'" Theo stated in sharply clipped words. "What else can you expect from an uneducated witch?"

"She learned at home with tutors." Oleander said, thick brows knitting. His cards scraped together as the muscles and tendons in his hands tightened with restraint. "And she can probably cast circles around a pig-headed oaf like *you.*"

Beckton put his hands up and gave a pleading look to the two men opposite them, both now giving Theo a burning gaze. "Come on gents, let's change the subject. It's not proper to speak on a woman when she's not here."

Dante broke his eyes away from the blond-haired man at the table and gave a terse nod to Beckton. He set down The Chariot. "You're right," Dante said, willing to settle the matter.

Beckton's shoulders slumped with some relief but tightened again when he looked to Theo and Oleander. Oleander looked about ready to pummel the man sitting across from him.

"Ah," Beckton said, trying to jostle them out of their staring contest. "I draw, your move, Theo."

"Learned at home with tutors, did she?" Theo stated as he looked down at his cards and set down the Strength card.

"And what of it?" Oleander said, his voice dangerously low.

"Well, there's only two reasons a girl of her means studies at home instead of at Conservatory," Theo stated with the only genuine smile he'd given the entire night. "She's either hideously ugly or a bumbling idiot. So, tell me, which is it?"

Oleander stood to his feet, his chair toppling to the ground behind him. He reached across the table to grab the newcomer by his lapel but before he could make it, a strong hand reached out to stop him. Oleander started and looked down to see that it was Dante's hand that stopped his momentum.

Dante still sat, like an emperor on a throne. His eyes were lethal as they rested on Theo. Those golden eyes looked more like a dragon's than a cat's in that moment. His pupils were barely visible with how tightly they had constricted. "Do not talk about the young lady like that in my establishment," Dante said with terrifying calm. "Unless you'd prefer to patronize the pub down by the farms and stables, I suggest you shut your mouth."

A quiet yawned there between all three men for too many moments. Oleander gave quick, angry breaths through his nose as he stared down at Theo, who still looked entirely unbothered.

"It's your move, *Ambrose*," Theo finally said looking up at him tauntingly, putting strange emphasis on his family name.

Oleander's mouth twitched and a muscle flagged in his jaw. He pulled a bent card out of his balled hand and threw it angrily on the table.

There sat The Tower, card number 16.

"The Tower. You're out of this round, Vervain," Oleander said tightly.

Theo looked at the card, the depiction of a tower smashed in half by the fury of an angry storm. He gave a scoff of a laugh and rose from the table, smoothing blond hair from his face and straightening his jacket.

"Fetch me when you're done, Hawthorne." He stepped away without another word.

Oleander heaved a heavy breath through his nose and turned to right his chair. When he did, he saw the eyes of the entire room on their table.

"Show's over. Carry on, you rubbernecks," Oleander commanded as he sat back down, rolling his shoulders.

Dante stood and retrieved Oleander's hat, almost forgotten after it fell from the chair.

"I'm er . . . sorry about that," Beckton said with no small measure of embarrassment. He took Theo's cards and The Tower from the stack and began to shuffle. "I can't really do anything more. If I do, he'll complain to his father and—"

Oleander raised a hand and shook his head, "You don't need to explain, Beckton. We all know his type." He took a too big drink from his short glass of whiskey, "And at any rate, any person who knows Juniper even as an acquaintance knows how wrong he is."

"Still carrying that torch, are you?" Beckton asked with a touch of nostalgia in his expression. "I remember even when we were boys you would snub every girl who even tried to get your attention."

"Of course," Oleander said, expression shifting to show his fondness. "You don't simply move on from loving such a perfect woman."

"Good," Beckton replied. "She deserves a man like you."

Dante patted Oleander on the back and picked his cards up.

The matter seemed to happily drop after that, and the men finished out their game. Oleander just knew to keep Theo as far away from Juniper as possible. Men like Theo Vervain, men from the city, just found all the joy in crushing a tender heart like hers. And with all the strides she was making, with all the ways she protected him when he was just a boy, he would be damned if he would let anyone hurt her like that.

As far as he saw it, he owed her.

Now that he was home, he'd make sure that Juniper would never know hurt or discomfort again.

Delicate

"A party?" Juniper asked a few mornings later while at the breakfast table with her parents and Oleander.

In the few days that Oleander had been home, she had finally made herself comfortable with at least having conversations with him when others were present. The exchanges were usually short, and a bit timid, but it was an improvement. She had even managed to get comfortable with closer proximity.

Oleander had tested the waters a few times, mostly in tight quarters. He would ghost a hand on the small of her back or brush Juniper's hair out of her face when she was wrist deep in wet soil and a sneeze was threatening her.

"But of course," Mrs. Harlow said as she fashioned herself a cup of tea with a few deft flourishes of her hand. Sugar cubes, cream, and lavender syrup all danced their way into her flowery teacup. "It's only right after such an accomplishment don't you think? We should invite everyone to celebrate Ollie's recent graduation."

Juniper glanced at Oleander, who was already looking at her

with a soft gaze, but she could tell that he was gauging for her reaction. Her eyes fell to her plate while her father dropped a few pancakes there, pausing a moment to pat her head before moving on to Oleander.

"Perhaps we should have it here at the house?" her father asked.

Juniper grimaced at that, unseen to her father, but noticed by Oleander and Mrs. Harlow both.

"Why not The Cradle?" Oleander offered.

"No, that's far too small," Mrs. Harlow said as she gently tapped her chin.

"How many people do you plan to host, darling?" Mr. Harlow asked.

"Naturally the entire village will want to attend," she said.

"We do have plenty of room here in the house," Mr. Harlow offered again.

"Juniper wouldn't like that, though," Oleander said.

The way he said it wasn't unkind, but Juniper felt horrible about it anyway. Here she was, once again holding him back. She chewed on the inside of her lip as she distractedly smeared butter on her pancakes.

"We'll have it here," Juniper said quietly as she reached for the syrup.

She wouldn't dare meet anyone's eyes. She couldn't stand to see the shock and awe at such a simple solution. The silence stretched on a bit too long, however, and she eventually had no choice but to look up.

Oleander's face was one of concern, her mother's brows were nearly to her hairline, and her father looked a bit guilty. A feeling twisted in her gut, a bitter knowing. She was so far gone, so broken and useless, that even something as simple as this was a miracle to them. Juniper picked up her fork and dropped her eyes back to her pancakes.

"I can always just go to the greenhouse if I get frightened,"

Juniper finally muttered. "I don't want to ruin Oleander's celebration."

"It won't be ruined, Juni!" Oleander quickly insisted.

"No, of course not, something smaller and intimate can be nice," Mrs. Harlow added.

"This is your house too, after all," her father chimed in.

"All—" Juniper stammered. "All the same, we should have it here. It's Ollie's home; it would be strange to host it elsewhere. I probably won't attend anyway, large gathering or small."

Juniper cut a triangle off her pancakes and quickly took a bite.

She didn't need to look to know that Oleander dipped into a crestfallen posture. Another failure to add to the list of many. Another crack in the facade of the image he held of her in his head, she assumed. Better to be honest with herself now. Better to not give Oleander any idea that she was half the woman he thought she was. She cut through the pancakes again, this time a little more aggressively and took another bite. Her teeth clacked on the fork with the force of her movements. One restless hand balled up in the white napkin on the table. She was about to spiral into another fit of self-loathing when cool, calloused skin gently smoothed over her white-knuckled hand.

She looked to see Oleander kneeling next to her chair with a kind, knowing smile. Her hand unconsciously loosened, and he scooped it up between both of his. His skin was tepid with the chill of the autumn morning, but it wasn't off-putting. It was a little soothing even. This was the closest they had been since his return, but something about the way he knelt made it much less intimidating. He was even a bit shorter than her in this position. For some reason, it felt right, even if every other touch had been hard won or flustered her.

"Juni," Oleander said with a gentle tenderness. "I know that you had a hard time of things while I was gone. But I really do mean it when I say that I'd rather just do something small if it means that you'll attend."

Juniper tucked her lower lip and nibbled on it, a flush crept into her pale cheeks. She glanced at the other seats at the table occupied by her mother and father. They both watched with the same stillness one might watch a deer.

She looked back to Oleander who still knelt beside her. His expression was endlessly patient, and it broke her heart. She looked down at her hand, caringly held between them. "If we have a party, will you be cross if I hover near you the whole time?" Juniper finally asked quietly.

Oleander's eyebrows shot up and a brilliant grin grew on his face. He squeezed her hand between his.

"I'd have it no other way, Juni," he said with unbridled joy. "What man wouldn't want his best girl at his side on the night of celebrating his biggest accomplishment to date?"

"Alright," she breathed timidly. "Let's have a party."

Unseen to her, Mr. and Mrs. Harlow exchanged relieved glances.

Oleander rose from where he knelt and returned to his own seat. He was still beaming as he drenched his pancakes in an obscene amount of maple syrup and added two heaping table-spoons of marmalade atop them for good measure.

"So, shall we bespell some instruments or have live musicians come to play?" he asked.

For a fortnight, the party was all the family seemed to talk about during any shared time together. At dinner, they would discuss what dishes should be served to their guests. Oleander shouted what music should be playing during the party as he spun a giggling Mrs. Harlow around the living room and kitchen. When Juniper spent an odd afternoon baking cakes and cookies, he would politely request her creations for the dessert buffet.

When he asked her about her tension, she had told him that it wasn't so much that she was bothered by the planning of the party — she wanted to celebrate her dearest friend as much as everyone else did — but having no rest from the subject did start to wear on her nerves. For every lovely plan they made, Juniper could think of ten things she could do to accidentally ruin it. It was a mental feat to help her stop imagining every catastrophe that could ruin his night.

Oleander kept explaining that she could never ruin his night, just by virtue of being *her.* He wished he could find a way to convey how much he adored every moment he could have with her without making her want to run for the hills. Regardless, he could tell that she was doing her best to match his cheer and vibrancy as the day drew ever nearer.

A few days before the party, Juniper's mother had set an appointment for her at the tailors to be fitted for a new dress for the occasion. In all the planning they had decided on a theme for the event: A Thriving Garden Vista. It was a nod to Oleander's success in his studies and his new official status as Herbal Sorcerer. Best of all, the theme allowed her mother to buy one of her favorite things — new frocks.

Oleander, Mr. Harlow, and Mrs. Harlow had already gone for their fittings. All the same, Oleander was by Juniper's side to escort her to the tailor. Naturally, he wouldn't be able to stay with her while she was in her underthings being fitted, but he could walk her to and from the appointment.

He walked, keeping a respectful distance between them. Gloved hands rested casually in his jacket pockets. A knee-length cloak protected him from the cooling air, they truly would have the first frost soon if the descending temperatures were any indication.

Juniper was also bundled up, but in a few more layers. She

had always been much more sensitive to the cold than her family seemed to be. On her head she wore a knitted, wide-brimmed hat, pale pink in color. She wore a much thicker cloak than Oleander, also pink, and lined with fur. It was intended for the winter proper, rather than a frigid autumn day. Beneath her cloak, she wore a woolen pinafore with a dress made of heavy linen and woolen tights which only barely peeked through from the space between the hem of her skirts and the top of her boots. Her gloved hands held the cloak closed from the inside.

"It's freezing," Juniper mumbled through clenched teeth. "I don't know how you walk about with nothing but your usual summer clothes and a cloak."

"Are you still cold?" Oleander asked, his pale blue eyes looking at her from head to toe, as if looking for a missing puzzle piece. When his eyes fell on the bare column of her neck, he drew his hands out of his coat pockets and undid the scarf furled around his neck.

"Ollie, don't," she stammered. "We're almost there already."

"Pish," he tutted. "I'm too warm, anyway. Here, stop for a moment."

Juniper reluctantly slowed.

Oleander noted the faint flush that crept to her cheeks and wondered if it was the nip of the cold air that caused it, or if it was some other feeling all together. His chest felt tight as he turned to face her, lifting the scarf over the rounded point of her hat and bringing the warm fabric to settle over her shoulders.

He looked at her and found her eyes glancing pointedly away from him. He let out a little chuckle. "You look like a chastened child," he teased softly. "Is it so bad to be fussed over?"

She was quiet for long enough that Oleander thought she may not answer, but just as he finished a fashionable little knot at the front of her neck she finally said, "I don't always know what to do with myself when you fuss over me."

His gloved hands paused for only a second as he thought of how to answer that. Then he began carefully extracting her silken hair from where it had been looped into the scarf, entirely too aware of how near he was to embracing her as he scooped his hand back behind her neck to work the thick tresses out.

"Who says you must do anything?" he asked. "Indulge me in a bit of fussing. I like to take care of you."

"That's not what I mean," she answered quickly as he used his other hand to coax out the few remaining locks he'd missed in the back. "I mean . . . I mean that I don't know what to do with . . . with my hands, or my feet. Or with anything else."

He bit his tongue as some mixture of thrill and frustration burned through him. He desperately wanted to tell her how he felt the same — how the very act of being near her was enough to turn him into someone who had never actually used his own limbs before. How it had been that way since he was small. But the fact was, he had no idea if what she described was what he felt, if they were the same first signs of love he was experiencing. He didn't want to take that realization away from her — especially if there was a risk that he could be wrong.

"Don't think so hard about it, Juni," he finally answered as he smoothed his gloved hand near her flushed cheek and freed the strands of hair that framed her face. Moon above, how he wished he didn't have the blasted gloves on; he wanted to feel the softness of her skin, the silken drag of her dark hair through his fingers.

He cleared his throat as he quickly freed the last strands on the other side, careful to keep his mind from drifting to other dangerous ideas: Like curling that hair around his fingers, like kissing that soft swell of her cheek, like . . .

"Are you feeling alright about the appointment today, Juni?" he asked her somewhat abruptly, drawing his hands back and shoving them into his pockets. He nodded to the road ahead, a silent invitation to continue to their destination.

"I am, actually," she said as she turned and began walking again. "It's been a good while since I've gotten a new dress, not that I've needed any more clothes; I have plenty. But it's still fun to get something new."

Mercifully, she seemed unaware of his mental transgressions, and he was grateful that he didn't somehow shout them at her across the aether, mind-to-mind.

The tailor was one of the few people Juniper seemed to fare alright with when it came to her nerves, so she didn't seem to be feeling all too distressed about the visit, even with no one to keep her company or shield her from unwanted attention. Perhaps it was because the seamstress had been making clothes for her since she was small or maybe because she rarely tried to make small talk, but getting fitted was something she admitted even she could enjoy sometimes.

"I'm excited to see what Mrs. Harlow has picked out for you," he said as he strode next to her, pleased that the train of thought he'd been on finally seemed to quiet down.

"Is that right?" Juniper said, her words becoming tufts of steam in the air. "Are you finding my wardrobe boring now?"

"Of course not, daft girl," Oleander said with a warm, easy grin before flicking the rim of her hat with playful menace.

Juniper giggled a little, the sound tickling along the back of his neck.

In the weeks that had passed, Oleander had managed to get her to loosen up a little bit. The two years apart, he'd found, had dulled his sense for her. But once he was able to settle in and spend time with her again, he realized it was much like a veteran musician returning to his seat after many years; the memory had returned to his muscles like it'd never been gone. There were things that were different, but at least it was no longer a mystery, at least she wasn't running and hiding anymore.

"Mrs. Harlow always picks the prettiest things out for parties. She's always dressed us very well," Oleander continued, "and she does her best work when there's a theme involved."

"Mmh, yes, that's true," Juniper agreed. "You used to hate it when you first came; all her primping and preening."

"What? I did not!" Oleander protested.

"You most certainly did, do you truly not remember?" Juniper asked.

"I remember always going to the tailor with the utmost enthusiasm."

"You did around nine or ten, that's true, but when you were eight — no. You hated it. You would pout and fuss, you even hit her once."

Oleander gaped at her, aghast to learn that he had ever laid hands on a woman.

Juniper laughed warmly at his shocked expression and after a moment peered up at him.

"You really don't remember that first year?" she asked him.

Oleander's mouth closed and his teeth clenched. A muscle in his jaw worked a bit as his brow knitted. He gave a small shake of his head.

"No, I suppose I really don't," Oleander said. In truth, most of the years of his childhood were a swirl of foggy memories at best. He knew that his father was named Linden Ambrose, and his mother was named Liliana Ambrose. He knew that his father had fought with Mr. Harlow in the war. He knew that his father had died. But he knew these facts in the same way one might know facts about any historical event — they were secondhand memories at best — not something he experienced directly.

In many ways, his life *began* when he came to live with the Harlows.

According to Mrs. Harlow, he'd been found squatting in rundown houses in the city when he was eight years old. Mr. Harlow had been looking for him since Linden Ambrose had passed away but couldn't find him or his mother anywhere. When he finally located Oleander, his mother was nowhere to be found. Mrs. Harlow said the choice to take him in had been an easy one.

"It's okay, Oleander," Juniper suddenly said, jarring the young man out of his reverie.

Oleander blinked down at her with surprise.

"Mother's always said that sometimes we forget things that aren't worth remembering," Juniper continued. "They think you experienced awful things, and it's okay if you don't remember. There is nothing shameful about how you coped with whatever you had to go through back then."

His chest warmed and ached. Moon above, how he adored her. In being so well acquainted with *her*, he often forgot that she knew *him* just as thoroughly.

"Thank you," he finally responded.

"I'm sorry if I upset you—"

Oleander lifted a hand out of his pocket and motioned her to stop. "You didn't," Oleander said. "I suppose it just got me thinking about that time. It's strange to have a black expanse where the first eight years of your life are meant to be."

Juniper quieted at that, looking for something to say, but Oleander saved her the trouble.

"I'm also horrified to know that I ever hit your mother," he quipped.

"Bah — you were a child! And a mute and half-starved one at that! How else could you have communicated?" Juniper insisted frantically.

Oleander laughed warmly. "I suppose I had better drop the matter before you fight me to defend my own honor," he said through his mirth.

"That's quite right!" Juniper said, lifting artlessly balled fists out of her cloak. "Don't think I won't use — oh, Moon above, it's colder than the afterlife outside," she said as she bundled herself up again.

Oleander gave a mirthful chuckle as his feet slowed. They had arrived at the tailor's shop. He looked past her, squinting to see if he could make out who was inside. The tailoress hardly ever cleaned the windows and always had a fire going to keep the ache in her old joints away. The fabric was always pristine, of course. But he supposed her focus on keeping that tidiness spell going left her windows terribly neglected.

"I see someone inside there, Juni. Do you want me to walk you in?" he asked.

Juniper looked over her shoulder and shook her head, "I'm sure it's just the tailor bustling about, preparing. You know how she gets flustered at the beginning of an appointment."

That he did. Usually because the older woman used any moment as an excuse to munch on a handful of butter cookies or lemon-scotch candies. Not that he could fault the woman for such a thing with his own voracious sweet tooth, of course. Still, he hesitated, loathe to leave the comfort of this strangely intimate walk he had stolen with Juniper.

A cool breeze rushed by, and she shivered against it. He moved his body to shield her from the worst of it, placing his hands on her upper arms with gentle care. To his great surprise, she came closer to him, angling her body just enough to hide from the bitter chill. She didn't quite lean into him, didn't throw herself into an embrace with him, but for once, it really felt as though he was protecting her the way he'd always wished to.

"You really are a delicate little flower, you know that, Juni?" he admired.

Juniper looked up at him and he could have sworn he watched a fresh flush break across her face again. He once again had to stop himself from making the flawed assumption that it had anything to do with him. It was just the cold . . . it had to have been.

Unconsciously, Oleander wet his lower lip with a quick swipe of his tongue, wishing potently in that moment to kiss her. It would be so easy, just a bit of a tilt here, a slide of his hand up her arm to cup her cold cheek, a slide of his other hand to the small of her back.

Instead, though, he dropped his hand and tucked it back into his jacket pocket. "I'll be back to pick you up in an hour."

Juniper blinked and looked behind her as if suddenly remembering why they were walking in the first place.

"Oh— r-right," she breathed.

"No spoiling the surprise, alright?" Oleander teased, doing his best to sound normal and not let the timbre of desire darken his voice.

Juniper huffed and looked back at him. "I wouldn't dream of it."

Oleander gave her a tip of his hat before turning to stride down the road, pulling his pocket watch to check the time.

He wondered if he could convince Dante to serve him something stiff to drink, even with the early hour.

Stranger

Juniper watched him for a time, surprised at how keenly his absence was felt. When she remembered herself again, he was almost out of sight. She started and turned, hurrying to open the door to the dressmaker where she was met by the sight of an impossibly beautiful, golden-haired man.

Across the threshold, two pairs of dark eyes met. One set indigo, one set gray. Juniper stood frozen for a long moment, her eyes widening. His eyes were wide, too. As if he hadn't been expecting anyone to be on the other side of the door. Oh no. She'd somehow made a mistake. She was here during someone else's appointment. She was going to cause distress to the tailoress and then this man was probably going to argue with her. She promptly turned on her heel to stride away.

"Wait," he said a bit forcefully, he almost sounded a bit frantic.

Juniper's shoulders tensed and lifted as she froze. She didn't want to be rude to the stranger, but she also couldn't bear to look at him. Not without losing all ability to string words into sentences, or, well — breathe.

"I uh . . . didn't mean to startle you," he said, clearing his throat once. "I'm Theo Vervain, I'm just here to mend a seam. I split it trying to keep up with Beckton Hawthorne on a besom."

"Oh — I thought I got my appointment time wrong," she said turning to look at him sidelong.

He narrowed his eyes, his gaze roving over her once, before meeting her eyes again.

"Wh-what is it?" she stammered.

"You smell of soil," he said quietly.

In only seconds, Juniper felt her ears blaze with her flush. Beneath her cloak she squeezed her fingers, trying to think of something to say. Luckily, he filled the silence for her.

"You . . . wouldn't happen to be Miss Juniper Harlow, would you?"

"Uhm," she started, voice as small as a mouse's. "Yes, that's correct."

He let out a gust of breath and looked up at the sky above them, shaking his head once before smiling down at her.

"You know, I almost got into a fist fight because of you," he stated with amusement. "Now that I'm meeting you properly, I have no trouble understanding the reasoning."

That piqued Juniper's interest enough that she turned to look at him properly.

Chin length hair the color of wheat just before harvest was tucked effortlessly behind one ear. Indigo eyes faintly curved along with his lips. Moon above, he was like a painting.

"A fist fight?" she asked.

"It's not important, and certainly nothing to concern a lady with," Theo stated easily with a shrug of indifference. He stood aside from the door and gestured her within with an elegant hand.

He looked perfect in his billowing shirt, with its seams and subtle embroidery; it was incredibly fine. Finer than anything she had ever seen. He had to be from a family of means and probably from out of town if he had access to such artisanship, and that he would wear those clothes so casually.

"Where did you come from?" Juniper found herself blurting.

Theo's pale brows rose in almost affronted surprise, and she remembered herself. "Wh-what I meant was—" she started, "I haven't seen you around the village before. Are you visiting?"

Theo seemed content enough with her correction. His hand dropped to his side, and he shifted his weight to one long leg. "I am. As I said, I'm a friend of Beckton Hawthorne," his own hands now gesturing to shake hers. "Theo Vervain." He repeated.

"Vervain . . ." the name had a familiar ring to it, but she couldn't place where she had heard it.

"I hail from Kingsborough," he clarified.

"The royal city?"

"The very one," he said easily with a charming smile.

A moment later the young man drew his hands up and rubbed them together. "As engaged as I am talking to you out here, Miss Harlow, might we move inside? I fear I'll catch my death out here."

"O-oh! You don't have a coat! I'm so sorry!"

Juniper hurried to run inside the establishment as Theo smiled. He followed in after her and shut the door behind himself. It was much warmer inside with a fire crackling in the hearth. Juniper scanned the room for the seamstress and didn't find her.

"She's in the back," Theo said, his voice just behind her ear.

Juniper's heart leapt into her throat, and she yelped. Theo laughed.

"You really are as delicate as a doe," he said, taking her hat for her and hanging it up on the stand not far away. "Forgive me, Miss Harlow. I didn't mean to startle you."

She felt her cheeks grow pink; she convinced her mind to unpink-ify them but to no avail.

Perhaps even more baffling than the fact that this beautiful, graceful man was talking to her was the fact that she found herself able to speak to him as well. There were people she'd known her whole life in the village that she couldn't do that with. There was something about him that was hard to avoid. Something that made her want to know him despite the very present apprehension that made her muscles pull taut.

"Easy now," he said as he reached up to right a few disheveled strands of hair. "I don't bite. You're as still as a doe found during a hunt."

Juniper's face and ears warmed as she swallowed tightly. The reflexive reaction caused a sound to come from her throat, which seemed to amuse Theo even more.

"Do you intend on being fitted in that cloak?" he said, teasingly.

"N-no" she stammered.

"Then allow me to take it for you," he crooned, placing that elegant hand once again in patient expectancy.

It was all so uncomfortably intimate. She didn't even know how she was existing so close to this man without spontaneously combusting or evaporating into the aether. All the same, Juniper somehow managed to pry her balled hands open. She unclasped the cloak and drew it off her shoulders, placing it in the waiting hand.

"Good girl," he said as he took it and carefully hung it on the coat hanger near the door, "Was that so hard?"

Something about that little phrase, something about hearing him praise her made her stomach flutter and tingle.

"No—" she said, the word coming out heavy and stilted.

He smiled calmly down at her, his eyes deep pools of night that sparkled and seemed to laugh at some private joke. That moment extended for some time and Theo laughed, the sound warm and bright. "Are you just going to stand here in the foyer staring at me, Miss Harlow?"

She turned quickly to sit on one of the plush chairs in the showroom. Her steps were about as smooth as a scarecrow's might be when cast with an animation spell. Theo continued to laugh behind her. She couldn't describe it but there was something strangely enticing about the stranger. Sure, there was the obvious charm of his good looks and worldly countenance, but there was something else too. She quietly watched him stride across the room and up to the counter. He bent over it, as if trying to spy the seamstress wherever she had disappeared to.

He straightened after being unsuccessful and looked sidelong down toward Juniper. "Miss Harlow," he said in a low singsong, "It's not proper for a girl of your standing to stare . . ."

Juniper balked and looked pointedly away, drawing another laugh from Theo.

"I only said it wasn't proper, not that I wanted you to stop," he teased.

"O-oh," she said quietly, hesitantly bringing her eyes back up to him.

"Something about you," he breathed as his eyes searched hers. "Inspires the most unlikely sort of mirth in me. It's rare I find myself smiling so much in the presence of . . . well . . . anyone."

Again, Juniper felt that sparkling tingle within her. There was something about Mister Vervain, something easier than the others in town. It was almost like she knew what was expected of her, like she knew the way she was supposed to respond. She so rarely felt that with anyone else; social interaction was always such a frightening enigma, like walking across a frozen lake and hoping you won't find a weakened spot on the ice and fall through to your death. She inhaled to speak, but before she could, the seamstress walked out with Theo's jacket.

"Master Vervain, your mending is done. I did my very best to follow the stitching of your tailor in Kingsborough, but I'm afraid you will have to send it to him to have it repaired properly," she offered the young man, along with the garment.

"I assumed as much; this will do for now though. Thank you for going through the trouble, anyway," he said as he pulled the coat on. He produced three golden shards from his pocket and held them out for the tailor. "Here you are."

"Thank you kindly, Master Vervain," she responded.

"It was a pleasure meeting you, Miss Harlow." he said glancing at her. "I hope we'll be afforded the opportunity of spending more time together before I make my way back to Kingsborough." And without much more of a thought or regard for Juniper's reply, he turned around and strode with steady purpose out of the small business.

Juniper found herself watching the door for a few moments after he departed, feeling a sort of . . . curiosity about him.

"Miss Harlow," she heard the tailor say, jarring Juniper out of her stupor.

"Oh, yes?"

"Are you ready for your fitting?" she asked.

"Yes, please, thank you," she responded and rose to her feet.

She followed the seamstress into the back of the shop.

Every Cost

Oleander returned about an hour later to retrieve her, as promised.

Juniper, for her part, was still a bit shaken from her interaction with Theo Vervain. She seemed mildly distracted as they resumed their journey back to their shared home.

"Juni, did something happen while you were getting fitted by Mistress Cordelia?" he asked gently. He was not overly worried or overbearing; he asked in the same curious manner one might ask another what they ate for lunch.

Juniper's brow furrowed, and she nibbled on the edge of her lip.

"Oleander . . ." she started hesitantly, "You didn't . . . try to fight a young man named Vervain, did you?"

Oleander's face answered the question well enough. His eyes grew wide as saucers and a flush rose to his pale cheeks. He offset the brim of his hat as his hand went to the back of his head in embarrassed surprise.

"I mean — those aren't quite the words I would—" There

was a sudden shift on his face, the embarrassment fading and morphing into potent concern and worry.

"Juniper, you didn't encounter that sorry lout, did you? What did he say to you?"

"I did. He was actually very polite," Juniper said. "I take that to mean he wasn't as polite the time you encountered him?"

Oleander sighed with relief and shook his head. Thank the Moon that he hadn't been cruel to Juniper, that she hadn't been ridiculed and ostracized on one of the very few times she ever left the house.

"He wasn't," Oleander said. "He was a bit haughty and said some things that I felt disparaged you. But considering that liquor was flowing that night, I'll give him the benefit of the doubt and assume that he was too deep in his cups to think with any sense."

Oleander, of course, had no intention to give that poor excuse for a man any benefit of any doubt. Regardless, repeating what was said about Juniper in her absence would only cause her harm and heartache, and he was more concerned about that than getting points for being willing to relieve Mister Theo Vervain of his teeth on Juniper's behalf.

"I see," she responded.

It bothered Oleander to no end that she seemed so unsurprised by words against her.

"Ollie, you mustn't get into trouble on my account," Juniper pleaded. "You're so beloved in town, and there's no reason you should go hurting your own reputation for a few silly words said about me."

"What could you possibly mean, Juni?" Oleander looked down at her with abject consternation.

"The cost isn't worth the benefit," she said as if it was the most obvious thing in the world.

Oleander reached out for her arm to stop her mid-step. She looked up at him with bright surprise.

"It is worth *every* cost, Juniper. It's worth everything to defend you from any words that impugn your honor and worth as a young lady," he insisted. "I would put my life on the line to protect that, Juniper."

His pale eyes were so heavy on hers, endless sunny skies instead of the pools of starless night she had been drowning in only moments ago. These eyes burned with the blazing heat of the summer sun. At those words, Juniper's heart thudded painfully in her chest. The idea that Oleander would ever risk his own life for her sake was not something she could bear to think about. Not to mention that she could never live with herself if Oleander ever did indeed *die* defending her. She would simply collapse in on herself like a dying star.

"Don't you ever put your life on the line for anyone, Ollie. Especially not me."

"I would do it happily."

"Why would you ever do something so foolish?"

Oleander finally released her arm and sighed. The fire in his eyes extinguished into something somber and tired. There was no impatience there, just the face of someone who had long struggled with carrying a heavy burden.

"Juniper," he finally said. "You know why. You've known for some time now."

Oleander had not brought up his vow or his feelings since his return to the village. After being made aware of Juniper's newfound discomfort, it felt unkind to do so. This was the closest he had gotten to bringing it up, and in this moment it felt necessary. Had Juniper already forgotten that he loved her deeply? Had she already forgotten his stalwart dedication to one day being her husband?

The shift in expression on Juniper's face made it clear that she had not forgotten, or that she was at least selectively remembering. Her head tilted down where she looked at the silver gleam of Oleander's jacket buttons. It felt much more serious coming from this grown version of Oleander.

What was once a precious, endearing vow, was suddenly much more real.

"I was certain you would have grown out of that since your time at school," Juniper mumbled.

"Well, I regret to inform you, Juni, that I haven't," Oleander sighed.

A quiet fell between them that began to feel awkward. Oleander lifted a hand and patted Juniper's shoulder.

"You don't need to worry or think about that right now, Juniper," Oleander said. "Suffice to say that I will put my life on the line where your honor is concerned. And you needn't feel any guilt or shame for that. Because you *are* worth every ounce of that, my feelings for you notwithstanding."

"I suppose we'll have to agree to disagree," Juniper said.

Oleander scoffed derisively and shook his head. The sound drew her attention, making her look back up to him. He could feel her eyes on him, feel the subtle shift in her playful banter to something a little more hesitant. A little more worried.

"Have I made you cross?" she asked very quietly.

"It isn't you that I'm cross with," Oleander said. "It's this damned village that has forced you to feel like you aren't worthy of the most basic modicum of care and respect." When he turned his gaze back to hers, his countenance changed to one of tenderness and melancholy. "I will make sure you see it, Juniper," he quietly promised as he lifted one of his gloved hands to cup the curve of her cheek. His thumb drew a tender line beneath her eye, as if to wipe away invisible tears. "I'll help you see yourself the way that I see you."

Juniper's heart squeezed in her chest again and she found herself at a loss for words and air alike. Her own gloved hand went over his own and squeezed in affirmation. "Well . . . if you won't avoid a fight for your own sake, will you avoid it for mine?" she asked him.

"Yours?" he asked. "You're the one I'd be fighting for."

"I couldn't bear the idea of you getting hurt for me," she said. "Whether we disagree on my worthiness of it or not, if you were harmed I would be beside myself with worry. You always hear about duels gone wrong. Sure, they're supposed to be gentlemanly, but you never know what could happen."

His eyes scanned hers, a tightness hurting his throat at the idea of losing his life in a silly fight. Because she was right. There were tales from all over the world of sparring swords being swapped out for real ones. Of combative magics rebounding on the caster. Of women weeping as their lovers or brothers or fathers stared unseeing into the sky above. He couldn't bear the idea of causing Juniper the pain of grieving for him.

"Alright," he said. "I'll do my best to control my temper when it comes to the matter of your honor."

She smiled up at him with such care that he wanted to kiss her again. But he didn't. He merely dropped his hand from her face and offered her a bent arm to hold onto.

"Shall we head home?" he asked her. "Or should we make a stop at the sweets shop first?"

"That's a trick question isn't it?" she said.

"Naturally," he said. "Of course we're stopping by the sweets shop first."

Her laughter had him forgetting all about Theo Vervain.

Thank the Moon for *that*.

Stealing Sweets

Juniper grew more and more anxious over the impending party with every passing day. Autumn was in full thrall outside, the beginning of the winter frost starting to threaten its conquest over the land. Every time the first frost came, Juniper thought she would be better prepared for the strange grief she felt as she watched once-lush leaves crackle with ice or dull into a painful-looking brown hue. Yet, every year she found herself saddened by the barren quality of the estate grounds. Her only comfort in those moments was the greenhouse and Oleander's presence in it. He had started assisting her in her work on the seeds for the Connifers.

The work was taxing. Not physically, but emotionally. All there was to do was let the plants sprout and place them outside overnight to see how they fared. And each morning Juniper would wake to the desiccated corpse of those plants.

As the party drew nearer and nearer, she found herself more and more prone to fits of melancholy. It became so severe that one morning after a particularly grueling night of adjusting the magic in the seeds, she came out to find the sprouts in even worse shape than the prior trial.

Despite years of going through the same seasons over and over again and dealing with the same frustrations over and over again, she found herself shedding heartbroken tears over the umpteenth failure, dropping to her knees and curling the small pot into her arms, as if she could warm it up herself and bring it back to life.

The poor sproutlings didn't deserve this. They didn't deserve her continued failure. She sniffed, wishing that Oleander wasn't so preoccupied with the party; wishing that he was there to comfort her as she had once again grown accustomed to. And following that silly wish came a wave of fresh guilt that seemed to plague her so often these days. More than ever, Juniper was feeling like an unnecessary burden to Oleander.

There were so many ways in which she was holding him back, and she was becoming increasingly aware of this. She felt guilty that she had prevented him from realizing his full potential. She felt increasingly compelled to reprimand him for being overly concerned with her convenience and her feelings. She didn't though. She was far too cowardly to face the possibility of losing him forever; at facing the possibility that she could be truly and utterly alone in her experience of the world. Juniper was genuinely fearful that he might finally see what's been in front of his face the whole time and scorn her as he should have for quite some time now.

And so, here she was, cradling another dead sprout. Weeping over another inevitability that she already knew was likely to happen. And she couldn't tell if it was really the arduous work she was crying over or if it was more the fact that this party she dreaded was growing ever closer.

She forced herself out of her wilted posture and smeared her tears away from her face with one hand, still cradling the pot in her other hand and she thought about the conversations she'd been having with others lately — Oleander's insistence on her seeing her own worth, and Dante encouraging her to allow others to support her while she learned how to be brave — and she made a decision.

She was going to take a bit of a rest.

While Oleander was gone at Conservatory she'd found so much comfort in her books when she couldn't make it to the social gatherings in the village. Something about a good book could get her through the most frustrating of times when it came to her nerves. Escaping to a new world and being able to imagine herself as someone as bold and capable as many of the heroines in these novels gave her a sort of relief from the daily nightmare of her life. At least in this way, she could be brave. She could be brave through the eyes of someone other than herself. Wasn't that sort of what Dante had encouraged her to do?

She walked into her greenhouse, still sniffling softly. As her mother had become more of a nightmare with obsessive planning, Juniper had found solace in the fact that she had so much work to do. It allowed her to escape the menial tasks Oleander had been conscripted into. Unfortunately, it also led to this fumble into distress she found herself in. But no one needed to know that she was taking a break. She could take a moment for herself, couldn't she?

She set the failed seedling on her desk and picked up her most recent read, a romance between a faerie king and his court magician. She slid her shoes off and put her feet in some slippers she kept in the greenhouse before settling in on a worn-out chaise positioned below a bough of wisteria blooms, her magic keeping them in perpetual bloom.

And much to her surprise, as she got lost in the narrative, she found herself forgetting about the nausea that seemed to constantly churn in her gut at the idea of the upcoming party and the heartbreak over her failure with the seeds. She even found herself enjoying her day.

She'd reached the final act of the story when she heard the door to her greenhouse scrape against some dirt that had been tracked in on the bottom of mud-caked shoes. An unavoidable inconvenience during the autumn months that had its own brand of nostalgia to it. Juniper tented the book on her chest and lifted her head to see Oleander standing there, smiling. Her heart kicked up in pace as she looked at him and she did her very best not to be too relieved to see him. But she couldn't deny the instant wave of comfort that accompanied any moment she found herself sharing a space with him.

His charcoal-colored hair was tangled and messy with a few unnoticed cobwebs hanging off from this lock or that. He wasn't wearing his jacket. He merely wore one of his less precious shirts, one in a creamy hue. The fit was imperfect, billowing from the top of his trousers and his gray suspenders. The too-big sleeves were rolled carefully to the crook of his elbow. She took him in, his casual state strangely intimate in a way that was unique to their friendship.

"Almost done with it already, hm?" he asked about her book as he came to sit at the foot of Juniper's chaise. "When did you start that one?"

"A day and a half ago," she answered, pulling her feet closer to herself. "I'm surprised that you managed to escape with how mother has been."

"Only by the skin of my teeth!" Oleander crowed. He slumped back on the seat, back sliding so that his head lay almost on the cushion of the seat. "You know, you'd think that since it was a party in *my honor* that I wouldn't have to work so damned hard."

Juniper laughed a little bit, her eyebrows playing up as she tucked her skirts beneath her feet, making a tent of her garments.

"My, such language around a lady?" she joked.

Oleander didn't move from his slumped posture; he merely placed a hand on his chest and bobbed his head once in a teasing bow of sorts. "May the lady forgive this sorry excuse of a gentleman. I fear my time in fraternity amongst men my own age has corrupted my good manners."

Juniper laughed, a little more freely this time. She dog-eared her novel and set it on a nearby table. Her arms wrapped around her knees, and she placed her chin in the space between them. In moments like this one it almost felt like he had never left, like he was still the sweet Ollie that he was when he left those two years ago. That was the crux of it, she supposed; he still was that Ollie. He just had a taller, more handsome packaging these days.

She looked at him for a long time as he seemed to glance around the greenhouse, surveying her work. His eyes went all around the space before finally landing on her own. "I've missed you today, Ollie," she said softly. "Almost as much as I missed you while you were off at Conservatory."

"And I you," Oleander replied without a single thought. He paused for a moment and then looked at her, sobering somewhat. "You've no idea how much our letters got me through some of my worst homesickness, Juni."

"They got me through some of my worst loneliness, too," Juniper replied. She looked down at the hems of her skirts, her toes wiggling faintly beneath. "I wish sometimes . . . that I could be more like you and Mother," she whispered.

"You don't need to wish to be like anyone but yourself, Juni. You're perfect just how you are."

It wasn't becoming for someone to refuse a compliment. She didn't want to seem like she was trying to milk her childhood friend for pity or kind words, so she just remained silent. Perhaps it was better this way. After all, she was doing her best not to be such a burden to him. Oleander was a kind boy that would do anything to help anyone feel better about themselves, even if it was a lie. He just did what he could to make people feel good.

"So, what shall we do next week?"

The question from Oleander broke through the silence and drew Juniper out of her own distraction.

"Next week?"

"You'll be turning twenty-three; we have to do something," Oleander said as if it were obvious.

"No, we don't. At this point in my life, the years mean nothing more than a string of digits."

Oleander sputtered a laugh. "When you talk like that, you sound like an old spinster. Come now, Juni, we must celebrate the day of your Solar return *somehow*."

"I don't want to have a party."

"No, no, no. Not a party. An outing. Just you and me, hm?"

Juniper blinked.

Actually, that sounded quite nice. She tilted one ear onto her knee and looked up toward lush leaves swaying from drafts that made their way through the windows. She had no idea where they would go for this outing, though.

As if reading her mind, Oleander continued. "We'll take a train to the town a couple stops over — Faeridge, it's called. I've heard there's some faerie rings over there. We can go foraging for mushrooms," he said, "and there's supposed to be a really excellent bakery out that way, also!"

"Oh, *I* see how it is," Juniper teased.

"What?" Oleander said, perking onto his elbow to look at her.

"You just want some company to go get some cake!"

"W-what? I do not!" Oleander retorted.

"I see, I see," Juniper continued tapping her chin. "A young man going to a faraway town just to get some cake does seem a little strange, after all. You have to have some kind of lady you're escorting."

"Juniper!" he cried in exasperation.

Juniper broke out into giggles and flopped back onto the chaise, letting her legs fall and extend off to the side.

"I jest," she said breathlessly. "Worry not, I would not begrudge you even if it were true."

"So . . . we'll go then?" Oleander said.

"Hmmm," she hedged.

Oleander gave a little growl, and before Juniper could respond, he got up on his hands and knees and he climbed up the chaise like a stalking predator. The young man poised himself above her, bracketing her in with his hands on either side of her head.

He seemed to think nothing of it. Why would he? They used to do things like this all the time when they were children. Tease each other. Rough house. Play.

He looked down at her with a sort of impatient expression, mouth quirked to the side, one brow lifted and one low.

"Juni . . ." he warned.

Juniper's breath caught in her throat and her hands balled up where they rested on her stomach. Her legs were left hanging askew, tightened and crossed at the ankle. Above her, a few stray locks of Oleander's hair fell forward, making him look attractively disheveled. His shirt billowed in such a way that his collar bones and the musculature of his shoulders were tantalizingly displayed. He really did have the build of a man, now. Juniper swallowed dryly as her eyes flicked from his shoulders up to his face. The impatient expression had been replaced by a wryly amused one.

"Should I move?" Oleander asked.

"Wh-what?" she stammered.

"Am I too close?" he clarified.

Her mind swam with a cacophony of dissonant thoughts. He

was very close; he most certainly was. She ought to feel uncomfortable, shouldn't she? Or should she be comfortable because this wasn't any different from the ways they used to play as children? It was untoward of a young man to be so liberal in occupying her space, but Oleander wasn't just any young man. He was Ollie.

"I-I don't know—" Juniper fumbled finally.

Oleander huffed and lifted a hand from where it rested near her face. He brought that hand closer to her and hesitated for a moment. Hooded eyes searched her face before his voice sounded, a low rumble in his chest. "I'm just going to fix your hair a little bit, Juni," he uttered.

Juniper's heartbeat was ringing in her ears, but she managed a small nod. Those hands were so gentle, so delicate, as they carefully pushed some stray strands of hair off her face. Calloused fingers caringly tucked them behind her ear.

"Please, Juniper?" he breathed.

Juniper shuddered out a breath, her long lashes fluttering softly as the trace of his touch tingled on her skin in an unfamiliar way. Some distant part of her wanted to feel more of that, wanted to surrender to this little stolen moment of intimacy.

"Please?" he repeated.

She swallowed again, mouth paper dry.

"Juniper—"

"Hmm?" she asked on a breath, fully distracted by her traitorous heart lodged in her throat and the butterflies in her stomach.

Oleander laughed again, the sound a warm and syrupy chuckle. "*Your birthday?* Remember, we were discussing your birthday?" he teased.

Juniper choked a bit on her words, flustered by how close Oleander was. It was almost as if he knew precisely what he was doing to her.

"O-oh, right . . . s-sure. We can go . . ."

It was a far too fast mumble as Juniper's foggy senses were suddenly flooded with fresh mortification.

Moon above, what was she *doing?*

Just as she was about to say something there was the noisy grind of the greenhouse door and the familiar quick cadence of her mother's footfalls. Both Juniper and Oleander leapt from their positions on the chaise. Juniper righted herself to a seated position, and somehow Oleander had managed to place himself almost across the room from her. He was leaning against the desk where she'd set the failed sprouts and was flipping through her romance novel that she'd been reading.

"There you are, you naughty boy," Mrs. Harlow said.

Both youths drained of color at that greeting.

"Wh-what did I do?" Oleander asked, sounding far too guilty.

The tone made the woman stop mid-step and look between them. Mrs. Harlow was no idiot and read many of the same books that Juniper did. She even saved a few of the saucier ones for herself to enjoy privately. She saw, plain as day, two young adults caught in the middle of something they shouldn't have been doing. There was a moment — much too long of one if you asked her daughter — where she looked between their two faces; Juniper's was downcast and flushed scarlet, Oleander's with eyes as wide as when she had caught him stealing sweets past midnight as a boy. She hummed a single, satisfied sound and then raised a manicured finger to Oleander.

"I'm not done with you yet, sir," she said. "You're nearly a head taller than Mr. Harlow and there are things that need grabbing in high spaces. Unless you'd like me to risk breaking my hip," she retorted.

"N-no, of course not," he said quickly, his voice an octave too high. "Let's get back to it then, shall we?" Oleander's voice cracked and he ran a hand down his face. He shut the book with an emphatic thud and cleared his throat. He approached Juniper and held the book down toward her, intercepting her line of sight.

"H-here you go, it's good so far."

"A-ahm, yes, I'm . . . glad you think so," she said stiffly.

Oleander awkwardly rubbed the back of his neck. He looked to her mother to find her staring them both down.

"S-see you at dinner, then," he mumbled, and then he hurried out of the building before Juniper could respond.

Juniper's eyes followed him outside and then fell upon her mother, who merely beset her with a pleased smirk. And then she walked away.

Leaving Juniper to stew in . . . whatever it was she'd just gone through.

The next day arrived in short order and if the night before the party was chaos, now that the party was finally upon them, it was worse.

In many ways, Mrs. Harlow was insufferable when she was playing hostess. The way she poked and prodded and changed her mind repeatedly was enough to drive everyone in the house mad. Juniper couldn't get away with hiding as much on this day. Mrs. Harlow would periodically call her down from her room to ask opinions on some form of decor or taste some fancy cocktail. She finally resigned herself to one of the sofas in the living room to limit her trips up and down the rickety stairs of the cottage home.

At least Mr. Harlow had gotten sweet relief being the liaison between the household and the vendors that were supplying goods and services to the party. He'd left early in the morning to talk to caterers and pick up last-minute items that Mrs. Harlow had deemed absolute necessities for the party.

The celebration would begin at dusk, which only left that

morning and afternoon to prepare for their guests. Juniper supposed she was to blame for her mother's obsession with this event. Mrs. Harlow was an exceptional hostess, but with her daughter's lack of social graces and her reclusiveness, she never really got to have people over for more than an afternoon tea or a small luncheon. Juniper did what she could to indulge her mother as much as she could and not be sour about it.

Still, when the sun started to dip low outside and everyone was dismissed to get ready in their separate rooms, the worst of it began to hit her. It started small and niggling. A pinch behind her ear, a tickle in the throat. She was fine all through her bath. She used oils of her own creation to help calm and soothe her fearful, fluttering heart. Lavender, eucalyptus, and a bit of vanilla.

It only helped a little.

When she sat down at her vanity, her towel wrapped about her and her hair draped in dripping tendrils, that's when it hit. A crushing weight settled somehow on both her shoulders and her chest. She struggled to get her ribcage to expand all the way when she inhaled. Her breaths *in* became much shorter than her breaths *out* and she began to feel sick.

"Twenty-one people. It's only twenty-one people," Juniper whispered to herself through panting breaths.

Only twenty-one? Moon above, what was she saying? It might as well have been a ball, or a gala, or a festival! She wouldn't be able to do this. There was no way. It would be better for her to stay in her room. She couldn't embarrass herself that way. She couldn't do something foolish to bring more shame and ridicule to her family.

To Oleander.

It's not as if anyone would miss her, anyway.

Juniper rested her head on the surface of her vanity and wept silent tears. In her head danced dark and distorted visions of the future ahead. People whispering over cupped ears. Eyes pointed in her direction. Her mother's apologetic glances. Her father changing subjects and trying to move attention off of her. Ollie—

Ollie.

Juniper winced and sucked in a shaking breath before sobbing it out again. Her mind went back to that night at dinner. His roughhewn but gentle fingers cradling hers. His easy smile. The way his words came soft, unintrusive, and kind.

Juniper sniffled quietly and lifted her head. She met her own gaze in the mirror, seeing tear-pinkened skin and puffy features. She opened a drawer in her vanity and brought out a worn handkerchief to clean up her face a bit.

Her breaths were still coming too quickly, but she did what she could to move past it. Her mind went back to her last episode of nerves when Oleander had first arrived home. Back to the forest clearing with Dante.

Name five things you see.

She sniffed and looked to her vanity. She saw the enchanted hairbrush that Oleander had sent her for her last birthday. Juniper gave a little flourish of her hand; it sprang to life and began combing through her tumbling hair.

One.

As it worked through the gnarls, she looked about her room and noted her windowsill cast in the slanted orange light of the fall evening. There, tumbling in and climbing with vines was the very first seed she ever planted with Oleander. Before he felt comfortable speaking with anyone in the house. Some sort of philodendron plant variety.

She spoke a quiet incantation, and a tiny spot of sunlight hovered like a ghost over the plant, granting it the sun it would lose in the fading daylight.

Two.

Beginning to feel clearer, she looked to her mirror and saw in its reflection the photographs she had taken with Oleander hanging on the wall near her bed. One when he was eight, one when he was twelve, and one when he left for Conservatory at age sixteen.

Three.

The brush finished its fastidious work of combing through her tangles and floated back down to its resting place, its work done. Juniper looked to her toiletries where she spotted the botanical cosmetics on the tray. She picked up some rouge made of crushed rose petals and began to gently brush some on the apples of her cheeks with the tips of her fingers.

Four.

Finally, she turned toward her wardrobe where a fine dress hung. Finer than anything her mother had ever ordered for her before.

When it arrived, she wondered if she was even worth such a beautiful thing. It looked more like a ball gown than a dress for a dinner party. Regardless of it being made to her exact measurements, she doubted she could fill out such a lovely garment.

Five.

Regardless of her hesitation and her skepticism when it came to her dress, she stood from her vanity and reached for it. She still wasn't sure if she could avoid making a mess of tonight. She wasn't sure if she would be able to make it through the party without making a fool of herself.

But she could try. For Oleander, she would try.

Uninvited Guest

The guests had finally started arriving at the Harlow cottage around a quarter past five.

Dante, naturally, was the first to arrive, bringing a small bottle of something fine and dark. He wrapped it with a simple black bow and a large brass bell. A sort of private joke in regard to his history of being, well, a cat.

Then came Mrs. Harlow's luncheon regulars, mothers of this or that person who grew up with Oleander and Juniper in the village.

Of course, some of Oleander's acquaintances from past parties or rites arrived, having been invited during cards and drinks at The Cat's Cradle. Some of Mr. Harlow's colleagues even came from out of town, eager to see how the Ambrose boy was getting on under the guardianship of the Harlows.

By six, the sun had finally taken its leave behind the horizon and the party was in full swing. There was only one person unaccounted for.

Juniper.

Oleander nursed a short glass of the whiskey Dante had poured for him as he nervously checked a pocket watch.

"That's the third time you've done that in ten minutes," Dante drawled from where he stood next to him. "I'll give you a tip. If you check the watch in five minutes, it will be five minutes from the time you just observed."

Oleander gave his friend an unimpressed glower. "You know why I'm checking the time," he grumbled.

"I do. She said she would be here, didn't she?"

"Yes."

"Then she'll be here."

Oleander took another sip of his liquor. He had to fight the urge to pace around the room like a caged animal. The obvious tension and anxiety in him made Dante huff a quiet laugh and give a pat on his shoulder in fraternal comfort.

The crowd was all clustered in different spaces, depending on who they were mostly there to see. Oleander and his friends were all together in the living room area, with drinks or finger foods in their hands. Mrs. Harlow was with her friends in the dining room, gossiping about this and that. Mr. Harlow stood with his colleagues in his library with the door open to not make anyone feel unwelcome. They puffed on herbal cigars and discussed business in Kingsborough and other far away towns that Oleander had never heard of.

Oleander checked his watch again, frustrated to find that only three minutes had passed since his last check.

"I'm going to go check on her," he said.

Dante merely lifted a finger in response. "That won't be necessary," he said.

Just when Oleander was about to ask why, he heard the tell-tale squeak of that one rickety stair on the staircase. His gaze immediately went to the steps to find his childhood love standing awkwardly on the last steps.

Juniper was a vision.

He had never seen her look so wonderfully resplendent in all his life with her. Not at any ritual or rite, not even at her debut. He didn't know why Mrs. Harlow spent particular attention on her clothes for this party, but Moon above did he thank her for it.

Her gown was a beautiful dusty shade of green, like sage sprigs or eucalyptus leaves. The bodice of her gown hugged every delicate shape of her and was speckled with pale white embroidered flowers. The sleeves, constructed of fine lace of the same white color, elongated her slender arms by coming to a point where they met at her middle finger which connected to a pretty, silver ring. Her skirts were layers and layers of gossamer fabric that looked as if she was wearing a dress made of airy cobwebs with more of the delicate bulbs and blossoms peppered throughout.

This wasn't a dress from the tailor in town. No, the fitting must have been for something that Mrs. Harlow ordered from one of the finer clothiers in Kingsborough.

Every eye in Juniper's line of sight was on her and Oleander could see that it was starting to make her fearful. He wordlessly handed Dante his drink and approached Juniper at the bottom of the stairs. They met eyes, nearly at the same level with her slight elevation a couple steps up.

"Everyone's staring, Ollie," she said with a warbling, tiny voice.

"Because you look exquisite, Juniper," he said quietly enough that their words could not be overheard.

Juniper's rouge pinkened face flushed a bit further and she put her hand into his, which was still outstretched. His fingers curled around hers and he gave them a reassuring squeeze.

"I won't leave your side tonight, Juni," he said.

"Promise?"

"Promise."

Oleander led her to the group of their peers. Dante gave her a knowing nod by way of greeting; he was the only one who didn't openly gawk.

"Am I meant to be the person minding your drinks all night, Ambrose?" Dante asked wryly.

"Only if you wish to, darling," he said mockingly with a laugh.

This drew a laugh from the others in the room, releasing some of that tension that had spooled during Juniper's arrival. Oleander's hand released Juniper's and moved instead to the small of her back. "You all remember Miss Harlow, I'm sure," he said with proud mirth. He wouldn't kick up a fuss about her being here because there was no reason for it. The best way to scare Juniper off from future social engagements was to make this one horrible for her, after all. "She's been busy at work in her greenhouse lately."

"Oh wonderful, I heard from Hawthorne about the seeds you'd given to the local farm folk," one girl said. She was short and full-figured with blonde curls to her shoulders; a daughter of one of Mrs. Harlow's guests in the other room. "It's incredible to ride past their fields and still see life sprouting out of the ground!"

"I-it's not perfected yet; they will probably fade with the coming winter frosts, I'm afraid."

"Still, it gives what, at least a few weeks longer for them to fill their pantries and larders, no? You should be very proud of your work."

"Thank you, you're very kind," Juniper mumbled.

"Shall we join the others in the dining room?" Oleander asked, mostly looking at Juniper.

Juniper met eyes with him and inhaled to speak.

Just then, a knock came to the door, stalling the conversation. Oleander looked to the door with a perplexed expression. "Suppose someone decided they would arrive very fashionably late," he said with all the ease and grace of a perfect host. "Excuse me."

Dante came to her side as Oleander left it. Oleander strode to the heavy wooden door and opened it. He was grateful that no one could see the way his face fell when he beheld who stood on the other side of the door.

Standing there, looking as smug as a cat with a fresh kill was none other than Theo Vervain.

"Vervain," Oleander said tightly.

"Ambrose!" Theo said loud enough so that Oleander wouldn't be able to refuse him and claim that he was just some wandering beggar or salesperson. "Beckton is feeling under the weather and has sent me to attend your little soirée in his stead. He sends his best wishes."

Indigo eyes wrinkled with too much satisfaction at Oleander's irritation. Still, he couldn't very well turn the man away. Not without risking the Harlows' good standing in the village with gossip about slamming the door in the face of an esteemed guest. Oleander mastered his expression and opened the door fully, allowing the young man to enter the family home.

"O-oh, Mister Vervain," Juniper said in surprised recognition.

Theo seemed mildly taken aback when he finally laid eyes on Juniper. Oleander fought the twist in his mouth when he saw the very same expression that was probably on his own face at first seeing her tonight. A protective flame burned in his belly and his hands itched. Moon above, he'd never known a man more deserving of violence in his life.

Theo's stunned expression mastered itself into a charming smile. He approached Juniper and paid no heed to Dante's amber eyes as they bore into him. He took Juniper's hand up on his own, cradling it with precious delicateness. He bowed over her hand like one might do with a lady of the court. He then drew up her small hand and graced her ringed finger with a gentle kiss. "Miss Harlow, you're a vision from the Moon herself tonight," he said in sweet earnest.

The gesture was enough to make Juniper flush scarlet and begin to stammer awkwardly. Oleander's eyes tightened faintly, stomach churning at the public display, especially after their first encounter at The Cradle.

"Th-thank you, Mister Vervain," she finally managed to say.

"Before you arrived in such a timely manner," Oleander interrupted, "we were about to move to the dining room with Mrs. Harlow and her friends."

"Of course, don't delay on my account then," he said.

The group started milling about, trickling into the other room. Theo released Juniper's fingers bidding her to go. Juniper hedged a bit, looking from Theo to Oleander.

And then much to Oleander's surprise — she went.

Juniper specifically requested his presence at her side the entire night and now she was just doing as this fool bade her? It wasn't that he was bothered by her independence, that was a wonderful thing. Something about Vervain had her acting . . . differently.

When the group was out of earshot Oleander set Theo with a sharp glare. "What are you doing?" he hissed.

"Whatever could you mean?" Theo said with far less volume control.

"I thought she was wasting her birthright. I thought you had no interest in Juniper," he spat.

"Oh, she is. And I didn't. At least not until I learned she was beautiful." He reached over and patted Oleander on his lapel. "I have to hand it to you, Ambrose. Your taste in wives is impeccable. She'll be sweet and obedient and come with an impressive dowry. She won't kick a fuss about having to stay home with the children, since she prefers it there anyway."

Oleander's face drained of color, mouth going paper dry.

This bastard of a man was intending on courting Juniper. *His Juni.* And locking her up like a bird in a gilded cage.

"You stay away from her, Vervain—" Oleander warned.

"Or what?" Theo stated with far too much amusement. "Miss Harlow seems more besotted with me than with you. Would you block her from her happiness?"

That question shut him up and shut him down. He went silent.

Theo huffed a haughty laugh and then looked Oleander from head to toe.

"Better get a move on, *Ollie,*" Theo cooed. "Your adoring public awaits."

The party was a miserable time for Oleander after that. He stayed by Juniper's side, as she had requested. But he had to watch with quiet respect as Theo made his first nauseating attempts at enticing Juniper. The bastard even had the gall to compliment her on the work he had been dismissing only weeks before.

But Oleander couldn't deny what Theo had claimed. Juniper was actually talking to this man, even having quiet, stilted conversation with him. He could tell that Juniper wasn't comfortable, but he couldn't deny that it was an improvement on the usual way of things. It wasn't right for him to try to stand in the way of that, not when she loathed herself so deeply for being the way she was. Even if that insecurity of hers was misguided, he couldn't stomach standing in the way of Juniper's newfound bravery. He would find time later to talk to Juniper and warn her away from Theo Vervain.

He found himself acting as a chaperone between Theo and Juniper, watching from the sidelines for most of their conversations. Periodically he was able to get a word in edgewise, but again, he didn't want to get in the way. Really it was Theo that did most of the talking anyway, he didn't seem to care much for Juniper's input. And he definitely didn't seem to feel any embarrassment for waxing on and on about his many positive attributes and accomplishments.

There was finally relief when Theo was summoned by Mrs. Harlow and her friends to discuss life in Kingsborough. Oleander was on his third glass of whiskey by then.

"Ollie, are you okay? You seem tense," Juniper asked him as he took a cranky sip of his liquor.

"Wh-what? I do?" he choked in response, coughing on his liquor.

Juniper only looked at him with curious expectancy.

He rubbed his neck, hedging. "I'm just not sure about our new guest," Oleander said. "I didn't get the greatest first impression of him, remember?"

"Perhaps he was just having a bad day that time. I've been trying to navigate the conversation toward you but . . . well, I'm not very skilled at it."

Had she been? Oleander scanned over the conversation that had happened so far. He had been so deeply focused on guarding Juniper from potential insult that he didn't notice those little asides and misdirections, but they had indeed been there: Juniper mentioning Oleander's penchant for the Tarot, comparisons of Theo and Oleander's love of besoms and horseback riding. He felt like a fool. Here he was, trying to protect Juniper and he couldn't even hear her conversational cues because he was so focused on the bastard in the room.

"Forgive me, Juni," he said with remorse, "for I've been distracted ever since he arrived."

Juniper reached up to adjust his pocket square. "This is your party, Ollie," she said. "Don't let anyone ruin it for you. Not even *Theo Vervain*," she said with teasing warmth.

Oleander reciprocated with a gentle adjustment of a stray

lock of her hair. His heart warmed looking down at her, soothed by her gentle encouragement.

"You're right, of course," he said. "And being that it's my party, I would like to humbly request your attention for the rest of this evening."

"You *are* the man of the hour, who would I be to deny you?" she lilted.

Following their little exchange, Juniper obliged him with his fair share of attention. It seemed a moot point, however, seeing that Theo found some way to deftly insert himself in every conversation the two were having.

Oleander supposed he couldn't begrudge his rival for trying. Juniper was a beautiful girl and full of compassion and kindness. He could, however, begrudge him his motivations for showing interest in her.

Every smile and laugh that Juniper deigned to give the stranger of a man bit and nipped at the back of his mind. If he'd had any sense, or if he wasn't so worried about how it might affect Juniper's already fragile reputation, he would have just kicked the bastard out. This was *his* party after all, and he didn't understand why Theo even showed up in Beckton's stead. Must be some sort of arrangement they worked out. Beckton wasn't usually the type to stir the pot.

The party came and went without any more dramatics. Theo was the last to take his leave, taking every possible moment to bug and pester Juniper, it seemed. He did eventually go, thank the Moon, leaving Juniper and Oleander standing in the foyer. As soon as Theo was halfway down the gravel drive, Juniper deflated with a breath.

"I'm exhausted," she said quietly. "I don't know how you and Mother do it."

"What?"

"Socializing," she said.

"You seemed to be doing a fine job of it to me, you held plenty of conversations with me and Theo."

Juniper's mouth quirked to one side, and she looked up at Oleander, meeting his eyes. "I feel like . . . when I talk to Mister Vervain, I'm doing a dance I know the steps to," she said. "He says one thing, and I know I'm supposed to respond a certain way."

Oleander pressed his lips, not liking to hear her describe interacting with him with any kind of pleasantness. Still though, he understood.

"Everyone else is harder to pin down," he offered.

"When people in the village talk to me, I feel like I'm trying to avoid quicksand," Juniper described. "Half of the time I freeze up so bad because I am so afraid that I'll misstep and wind up with people thinking me even more odd and tactless than they already do. With Mister Vervain, I think I can tell how I'm supposed to answer his questions."

Of course, she would find comfort in that. Of course, she would be charmed by a man who helped her understand how she was supposed to respond. Especially one as princely as Theo Vervain. *Of course.* But he loathed it.

"I'm still so tired though, I feel like I was stumbling to keep up the entire night," Juniper mumbled.

Oleander reached over toward her and smoothed a hand down the back of her head. The touch drew her attention, and she lifted her gaze to his once again. She stared at him enigmatically for a moment, for once unreadable even to Oleander.

"Juni?" he asked quietly.

"M-may I—" she said in a tiny voice. "May I have that hug now? I think I'm ready for it."

The abruptness of the request startled Oleander. He blinked down at her with a quiet stare. The silence carried on for one moment too long and Juniper stepped to move away.

"F-forget I asked. It was stupid," she said.

Oleander's body moved faster than his mouth could. His hand grasped her wrist, and he tugged her back towards him. The sudden movement triggered a chain of events. She was on uneven footing when he pulled so she stumbled slightly. Oleander quickly compensated for her lack of balance by catching her under her other arm. He then hefted her slightly, bringing her off her feet for just a moment and into a firm, supportive embrace. The hand on her wrist lifted to slide into the back of her hair, cradling her carefully as he let her back down to her feet once again.

The feeling of her arms snaking around his waist was complete bliss. His eyes shut as he soaked in the pressure of her squeeze and the soft touch of her hand smoothing up the planes of his back. He let a sigh escape him and felt a warm breath leave Juniper, dampening his shirt slightly.

"Welcome home," Juniper said quietly into his chest.

Oleander could have wept, but instead he heaved a wet, shaky huff of laughter.

"It's good to be home."

Faeridge

For days afterward, Juniper reflected on that embrace.

That hug was like the ones she'd shared with Oleander before, but also very different. She had never felt so caringly enveloped by an embrace before; his enormous arms were wrapped around her, pulling her close as if to protect her. He had lifted her off her feet so tenderly; as if he were picking up a newborn infant, as if they were dancing, as if she were his bride. The feeling of his fingers tangling in her hair still tingled on her scalp, and warmth radiated through her body like tropical sunlight at dawn.

His musk haunted her like the ghost of a departed lover. She puzzled herself on the differences that interlaced that familiar smell of honey, sage, and firewood. Was it whiskey? Aftershave? She often found herself wishing she could hold him again to determine the answer, only to bring such a flush of embarrassment that she would have to hide her face in her hands or under her blanket. She imagined having his scent in a little bottle for her personal use.

Outside, the air began to get colder, and the lush, fiery colors of fall gave way to the muted palettes of winter. The trees shed their leaves, their forms becoming crisp as the morning air before melding in with the damp, dark clay that made up the floor of the forest. Blue-gray foliage bloomed with white, star-shaped jasmine flowers. The witch hazels Juniper had planted many years prior flecked with yellow, feathery flowers that smelled somehow floral and peppery all at once. Fires in the hearth became all the more common and left the estate with the smell of burning pine and sage brush as the first frosts fell outside, covering the property with an almost pearlescent quality in the mornings before the midday sun melted it away.

Despite the cold, Juniper warmed up to Oleander again. The final bits of distance faded, and she felt an almost inexplicable draw to him that he seemed more than happy to oblige. Naturally, neither party admitted to feeling any attraction to the other. She had no idea how she could ever even broach such a subject. She had been feeling distressed over her frost-resistant seeds, but only a few days after the party, Juniper had managed to perfect them when Oleander had mentioned some obscure theory about the life force contained within a seed.

Juniper spent three days sleeping in her greenhouse after that. She'd become almost obsessed with the idea and he fussed over her, begging her to get some sleep in her bed. She couldn't abide it, though, not when she was so close to the answer. So close to saving the Connifers from a barren, hungry winter.

On the morning of the fourth day, she threw stones at Oleander's bedroom window and held up a happy sprout, untouched by the frost that surrounded the estate. He opened the window and leaned outside, peering down at her as he rubbed sleep out of his eyes. "Juni?" he asked, before balking at her shivering form. "Juni! What are you doing standing out there in nothing but your pajamas!"

Her teeth chattered as she danced between her bare feet. "We did it!" she said breathlessly. "We've made seeds that not only grow in the winter, but they grow *fast!* The Connifers should have almost fully grown plants in a matter of days!"

She watched his conflicted expression, like he couldn't decide if he should cheer or shout at her. In the end, he closed his window. Moments later, he came around the side of the building, wearing his own pajamas and a too-large cloak that he immediately wrapped her in.

"Congratulations, you daft girl," he'd said as he immediately steered her towards the house. She almost slipped on a patch of ice, and he quickly caught her, scooping her up into his arms. "You are going to be the death of me, Juni. Either from worry, or from catching my death trying to save you from yours."

They were both sick for nearly a fortnight following their exposure to the cold of the early morning.

Even after delivering the successful seeds to the Connifers, Juniper was spending more time than ever in her greenhouse, protecting her precious friends from the cold outside and supplying the delicate plants with some much-needed sunshine charms in lieu of the real thing. Winter was always a much more demanding time for Juniper. Her plants required more gentle care and observation.

A few times in seasons past, Oleander had gone to check on her when she didn't come down for breakfast only to not find her in her room. As a child, when she'd finally made it to the table in the morning, Oleander would poke fun at her as she rubbed her eyes and stretched. He would tell her how he had discovered her at her greenhouse desk, her face propped up on her hand, her work neglected in front of her, but the plant in question content simply to be in her company and receiving her loving care.

But now that Oleander was a young man, things had shifted a bit. Now, when Juniper's final conscious moments were spent in the greenhouse she would often awaken in her bedroom, not sure how she'd gotten there. She would still be fully dressed in her work attire from the previous day but with her shoes removed and carefully stowed by the door while she lay tucked into her bed in perfect comfort.

She knew, of course, that it was Oleander moving her. Her father hadn't been able to carry her to bed since she was thirteen. But whenever she joined the breakfast table, nothing was ever said about the matter. She would only catch the odd teasing glint in Oleander's eye as he smiled into his tea.

Her birthday arrived in due time. It was one of those rare winter days when the persistent cloud cover had finally broken, revealing a clear blue sky and a pleasant chill in the air. It was the kind of day where breathing in the fresh air would leave you feeling revitalized and refreshed.

Too eager to wait for Juniper to get up on her own, Oleander came into Juniper's room to wake her. While in any other relationship this would have been considered rude or inconsiderate, these two had spent their entire childhoods rousing each other for various reasons, so despite the shifts in their dynamic, it still felt normal to them to do it now.

Juniper protested, in an effort to recover from her late night of plant care and begged to stay in bed. Yet Oleander was having none of it. He woke her up with the promise of breakfast and bergamot tea and hurried her out of bed.

She begrudgingly acquiesced and managed a smile despite her exhaustion. Feeling rather content, she soon bade Oleander farewell so that she could get dressed, and she strongly suggested that he do the same.

Juniper, once left to her own devices by a skeptical Oleander, dressed in some of her more casual clothes. A simple black skirt, a threadbare laced blouse with billowed sleeves and a pair of spelled tights to keep her warm. She put a very old-fashioned black woolen pointed hat on her head and left her bedroom.

In many ways, this birthday outing was reminiscent of old outings together, though the roles had changed. Juniper was the one who often woke little Oleander and nudged him toward getting dressed when he was a boy.

They drank tea and ate thick slabs of toast that were so slathered with butter and honey that it could only be classified as dessert, just as they did back then. Honey clung to the corners of their mouths as they grinned at each other in the absence of Mr. and Mrs. Harlow, who were still soundly sleeping in the master bedroom.

They ransacked the kitchen and made off with some dry fruits, crusty bread, and hard cheese. Oleander carefully folded them into a tea cloth and then a burlap sack along with a jar of dried tea leaves, two worn teacups without handles, and a kettle large enough to boil just enough water for two cups of tea.

A moment later, they were standing in the entryway and Oleander was helping Juniper into her warmest woolen cloak. It was a charcoal gray, and when combined with the rest of her outfit, she looked like a genuine hedge witch from days of old.

"You sure you're going to be warm enough?" Oleander fussed as he straightened her cloak. "Positive you won't need gloves?"

"If I wear gloves, I'll bruise the flesh of the mushrooms. It's safer to just not wear them so that I can control the amount of pressure I apply."

"I'm bringing an extra pair anyway," Oleander said.

Juniper scoffed and shook her head with sweet amusement. "Since when did you become such a mother hen?" she tutted.

"Since always — you wilt like a flower in the cold," he said as he drew a pair of fur-lined gloves from the basket where they kept them by the door.

"You make me sound fragile," Juniper retorted.

"I make you sound *delicate*, because you are," Oleander said with a flick of her nose. She made a little pained sound and rubbed the affronted spot, wincing one eye. In answer, she swatted at him playfully, only for him to dodge it.

"You know I'm right, Juni."

"Perhaps. But that doesn't mean I have to like it," she retorted.

Oleander gave her a hearty chuckle and opened the door, gesturing outside with a hand to allow her to exit first. "After you, milady," he said charmingly.

Her cheeks were chafed as cold air rushed into the room, despite the warmth of the fire in the hearth she shivered and grimaced. She turned to watch Oleander exit and instead was met with that pair of gloves, directly at eye level.

Oleander lifted a single brow expectantly.

Juniper's mouth tightened and she begrudgingly took them, sliding them on with a bit of fight and aching pride.

"That's what I thought," he announced.

"Not another word. It *is* my birthday after all," Juniper said, swatting at him again and landing the blow this time. She crossed the threshold of the cottage home.

Oleander laughed warmly as he followed her and closed the door.

On their journey to the railway station, the sun had just begun to peek above the horizon. Talk on the walk was light and upbeat. They discussed anything from books to mycology to which baked good was the greatest (they determined it was birthday cake, without a doubt). It was the fact that they were having so much fun talking to one another that separated these exchanges from those they had with people who did not share their special bond. Oleander and Juniper enjoyed each other's company and could have a serious conversation about anything from the growth of grass to the drying of paint. Since his arrival, it had been that way, albeit one-sided initially, but it was always pleasant.

Juniper snuggled into the wool cloak and gazed up at her dearest friend. Moon above, was she grateful for him. Grateful for all the ways she felt so incredibly special thanks to his tender care and attention. The two- or three-mile walk was a welcome delay from the train station, both of them knowing that the distance meant more time afforded to converse with each other.

All the same, in quiet moments together Juniper found herself reminiscing on past excursions. Memories flooded back to her about other trips taken with him, like the one when she was seventeen:

Oleander was thirteen years old and had been fussily insistent on joining her for a trip deep into the forests. It wasn't the first time he had insisted but being that he was freshly a teenager he was much more persistent in being allowed to join. He grumbled and argued that now that he was older, he was properly man enough to escort her on her supply runs.

Juniper always treated Oleander with a touch of overbearing preciousness when he was a child. She felt compelled to shield him from harm because of how frail he appeared to her. She didn't want him to make the same clumsy mistakes she had out in the wilderness. Oleander, on the other hand, was adamant that he come with her. After his eyes began to fill with frustrated tears, she gave in, unable to maintain her resolve.

Juniper never told him about how she adjusted her plans that day, opting to collect four-leaf clovers instead of the poisonous bulbs she had originally intended to find. It was a good thing too; Oleander found no less than five of them. She had only managed to find one.

Remembering that day, she looked back up at him. He looked so different, but he was still her Ollie. Stubborn, kind, and effusively bright. There was an unfamiliar pang in her heart. Something like pain, but different. She couldn't quite place a finger on what it was.

She was reflecting on it when Oleander seemed to feel her gaze upon him. He looked down at her and gave her a heart-breaking smile. It was the kind she'd always imagined on the love interests in her romance novels: Tugged a little higher on one side, perfect teeth barely showing, a bit of a curve present in his angular, beautiful eyes. She inhaled quietly, chest feeling tight, but not in the same way as when she was afraid. This feeling was new, and it didn't push her away from him. It made her want to get closer.

"Shard for your thoughts, Juni?" he asked.

"Ah," she said quietly, breathlessly. "Nothing really, I just am already having a really nice day," she said.

"Me too," he said as he shifted the burlap bag from the shoulder closest to her to the one farther away. He bent his arm in a casual way and offered it to her. It was not an intrusive or aggressive offer. Like a stranger offering a carafe of cream at a tea party, it was placed on the table for her to take if she wanted it.

She looked at the offered limb for a moment or two, and then she just — did it. She reached out and rested her gloved hand on the bend in his arm. His arm drew closer to his body, and she followed along with it, their upper arms almost flush against each other. Her heart rate spiked, but she made no effort to move away. Again, it wasn't the same as in other circumstances, this was different. She just didn't know what it was called.

Oleander continued to stare ahead of them as they walked down the street, as though he were pleased with their current level of interaction. Juniper imitated him, sharing his inner peace. The pair continued their travel in companionable quiet mostly, especially once they reached the sleepy village. Many people in the village were still asleep and neither one of them wanted to cause a fuss or raise eyebrows by sneaking off together.

They arrived at the train station without incident. In reality, they had seen no one else while walking through the village's dew-dampened cobblestone streets. On this day, it seemed as if the entire globe was theirs for the taking. This day, without the worries and stresses of Juniper's life, could have been a gift from the Moon above.

Oleander and Juniper sat together on the train platform. It was small, only a single building with an attached post office that remained closed in the early morning. It faced out across a section of forest that Juniper knew was well-supplied with hanging moss. Before the chilly winter sun chased it away, the morning mist always appeared to linger longest in that thick greenery.

"Remember all the hanging moss we would collect from there, Juni?" Oleander said as if reading her mind.

"I was actually just thinking about that," she said with a soft laugh.

"I think that was the only time you ever yelled at me," Oleander recalled.

"You were running towards the train tracks, and I heard the whistle of the approaching train." She groaned. "Of course, I yelled at you."

"And then I cried," he said with a sidelong smirk.

"Which, in turn, made me cry," she offered. "Thanks for that."

They both heard the distant approach of the train they were waiting for.

"That feels like a lifetime ago," Oleander mused. Juniper squeezed his arm gently in agreement. His other hand gently rested over hers and he looked down at her. There was something unrecognizable in his gaze, something she couldn't read.

"That was the day I saw — for the first time — that I finally had a family that cared about me," he admitted. "I don't remember much about the time before I came here, except feeling alone in the world . . . until you shed tears for me."

His voice hardly rose above a whisper, yet she made out every word. She felt the urge to cry again, but instead tightened her grip on his arm. "We love you, Oleander," Juniper said softly. "Every year I thank the Moon above for bringing you into our lives. It-it's hard to imagine my family without you there," she said in a similar near-whisper.

"I can't imagine my future without you, Juni," he replied.

There was something potent in the words he had said, something that took on a different meaning than her words, though the sentiment was similar.

The train whistled closer, and Oleander's gaze lifted from her to see it appear.

"Come on, Juni," he said. "Train will be here soon."

Juniper looked over her shoulder to where it was starting to chug along closer to the platform. Oleander rose to his feet and held out a hand for her, which she took and stood beside him. There was a subtle jolt of electricity in those gloves. With his free hand he delved into his pocket and produced two parchment train tickets, which he handed to her.

"You give our tickets to the inspector, and I'll carry the bag, hmn?"

Mentally she rehearsed the moment in her head a few times as the train pulled to a wheezing stop in front of them. Performing routine tasks like handing over tickets or placing an order proved challenging for her, but not impossible. She knew it was silly to rehearse for such small tasks. It wasn't that she didn't know it was a few seconds of her own day that would likely not matter a few hours from now. It was only a few seconds of the ticket inspector's day too, she didn't doubt.

But still, she had a hard time going about her day without spending at least a few minutes mentally preparing for tasks.

Here you are.

Thank you, sir.

Same to you.

Here you are.

Thank you, sir.

Same to you.

She mentally experimented with many tone variations, trying to determine which would be the most diplomatic. The most normal.

Finally, it was time.

Oleander offered her his elbow once more which she was happy to take. The gesture was like a tether to this plane when she felt she might just evaporate into thin air.

They stepped onto the train and the inspector stood there. A white-gloved hand was held open to her, the wielder of the tickets.

"Your tickets, miss?"

"Here you are," she said, handing them over. He tore the stubs off in a practiced way and handed them back to her.

"Thank you, sir," she said.

"Anywhere in the cabin is fine, have a nice day."

"Same to you," she said. As they walked to their seats, Juniper exhaled a gust of air as if she had been holding it.

Oleander chuckled to himself a bit and leaned closer to her. "You did fine, Juni," he encouraged.

She looked down at the torn ticket stubs, perfectly severed at the same spot on each one, despite them not being perforated like they often were in larger cities. When she was a girl, her father took frequent trips to Kingsborough and whenever he returned, there was a tradition of sorts they had. He would come into the house, kiss her mother and then "accidentally" mistake Juniper's little head for a coatrack, shucking off his jacket and draping it over her with a dramatic sigh. This would be followed by her father inevitably realizing his error with a wholehearted apology.

"Tell you what," he would always say after correcting his error. "Why don't you search through my pockets. Anything you want in them is yours to keep."

This was always the method her father used to deliver her souvenirs from his travels, usually some small piece of jewelry or a unique, regional pastry or candy. She would always find his torn ticket stub with the gift and she liked to drag her fingernail against the neat divots in the paper until they softened and the ink eventually wore off onto the tips of her fingers.

"I think I'll save these," she said.

"Oh?"

"This is the best birthday I've had in a while," she told Oleander looking back up at him, "I want to remember it." Oleander gave an endeared laugh.

"Nothing has happened yet, Juni."

"Still, I'm having a nice day. I missed you."

"I missed you too, Juni."

The cabin was empty for the most part, both due to the hour and the fact that they were so far removed from what most people called "civilization." It gave the trip its own special feeling, like a train had come specifically to transport only them to their outing.

They opted to take a seat on a bench smack in the middle of the train car. While Juniper chose the seat by the window, Oleander stowed their bag in the overhead compartment and then walked over and sat down next to her.

"Should only be an hour or two out," he said easily.

"I love train rides. I haven't been on one in so long."

"I thought you'd like a little jaunt," he said sweetly. "I remember how much you loved staring out the windows when we would go to the festival for Ostara."

Juniper laughed softly. "That's the only part I liked," she said moving her gaze from the forest outside to him. "I was so relieved when I debuted and wasn't bound by obligation to go anymore."

"I know, I remember," Oleander teased with a wink. "You ran around your empty greenhouse on the day of Ostara screaming about how you'd never do an egg hunt again."

"And so I never shall!" Juniper proclaimed.

Oleander laughed and elbowed her a little. "Come on, they weren't all bad."

The whistle sounded somewhere from the front of the train and a great sigh exhaled from the steam engine, as though a beast was waking. The train began its slow churning and chugging into locomotive movement, pulling away from the station. The excitement of travel flitted and fluttered in her stomach, and she beamed over at Oleander.

Oleander returned her effusive expression. "Off we go," he said warmly.

Juniper was a joy to observe during the ride out to Faeridge. Oleander had always thought that if Juniper could get past her own nerves, she would be somewhat of a globe trotter. Her eyes always seemed to inhale the scenery wherever they went. He remembered as a foul-tempered little boy that he used to get annoyed with all the questions she would ask Mr. and Mrs. Harlow when they traveled. The girl constantly pointed out windows to ask what this or that building was when her parents couldn't possibly know.

It was fortunate that he was still largely mute at the time, as he never said anything to dampen her enthusiasm for travel. He was perhaps even grateful, since it ensured he got to see this side of her now. It certainly would have been a thoughtless thorn he would have had to spend years prying out. The joy on her face as they took in the sights made all his efforts worthwhile.

"Ollie, look!" Juniper said, pulling him out of his reverie.

Oleander followed her gaze to the outside, where, despite the desolation all around, a single crop was emerging from the ground on a farm some distance away. It was the land owned by the Connifers, bursting with verdant life despite the cold outside. Over the crops he could see the faint shimmer of a ward keeping the frost from falling onto the plants while still letting what small amount of sunshine the day offered reach the seedlings.

"That's the first batch to make it through the frost." She pressed her face against the glass of the window with a sweet laugh. "I knew they would work, but it's so different to see them cover a field like that."

"You worked really hard on them, you should be proud of yourself," he told her with a warm smile.

"*We* worked hard on them," she said. "I wouldn't have been able to figure it out if it wasn't for you."

Oleander looked outside and saw the dilapidated barn and farmhouse across the field from the still-thriving plants. He wondered if Hailey was inside, or if she was working her route to Kingsborough today. He wondered if the turn of good fortune would allow her to stop working to help support her family. He hoped so.

"Moon above, look at them all. They might even be able to turn a profit this year, don't you think?" Juniper said happily. "We'll have to make more seeds for them! Wouldn't it be amazing if we could get them back on their feet for good?" she said looking at him again. "Finally nip that salted field's curse right in the bud?"

Centuries ago, an old blood curse was cast on the Connifer's land. Every season, some disaster or pestilence swept through and ruined their crops. After seven generations of this, the blood curse was not the only thing that the Connifers would pass down their lineage — the new generations would also inherit the poverty caused by the curse. The Connifers were kind though, and the community usually pulled together during the harshest months to ensure the family's survival. The Harlows had even paid for a roofing repair a couple of winters back when a blizzard caused it to cave in.

Oleander chuckled softly. "So eager to jump headfirst into the frustration of doing that process again with other seeds are you?"

"Well, I have you to help me. We'll figure it out in no time, I'm sure."

It was something wonderful to see the person you loved overjoyed with their life's work. Juniper so clearly wanted to be of service to her community, even when she couldn't actively take part in it. He wondered if he would be the same way if he felt as ostracized as Juniper did. Honestly, Oleander didn't know if he would be capable of showing the same level of care and kindness as Juniper did — he didn't know if he would still make the effort. Hell, he'd probably just leave the village altogether and be done with the blighted place. It was one of those beloved dichotomies of Juniper — she was delicate and fragile but also very resilient. She was like a winter-blooming flower, staying bright and beautiful even under the harshest conditions.

"Ollie, do you have your little notebook with you?"

"Hm? I do, yes." He'd often carried a little bit of parchment and a pen, an old habit from before he was ready to speak and communicated with written missives instead. He retrieved a pamphlet about the size of a cigarette box out of his inside coat pocket. The book was bound with fine stitching but lacked a cover. He then took out a fountain pen that had been a gift from Mr. Harlow before he left for Conservatory.

"Thank you," Juniper said as she took the pen and notebook from him.

He watched curiously as she jotted down a few neatly written notes.

Root vegetables seem to respond better – incubated by soil?

Try Carrot, Beet, Turnip, Parsnip, Radish, Yam, Sweet Potato, Onion.

Maybe Cabbage?

"How about rhubarb," Oleander suggested. "I know their little one likes rhubarb pies."

"Oh, that's good," she said as she scribbled it down. "Maybe some varieties of chard as well?"

"Careful, there may be one or two plant species you left out," Oleander teased.

Juniper flushed and closed up the pen, handing it back to him along with the notebook. "Well, that will certainly keep me busy for the remainder of the winter, I suppose. I'm sorry if I'm being too eager."

Oleander smiled as he placed both items back in his pocket. "You know that I love your enthusiasm, Juni. Don't apologize for it. Especially with how much you're helping people."

"It isn't right that they've had to put up with that silly blood curse for so long," Juniper said.

"I imagine it's never too late to have a generational curse circumvented, Juni. Their daughter will thank you when she comes of age and wants to marry."

"Well let's hope we can make it happen, right?" she said with a wink.

He beamed, his heart warming. "It would be my honor, master teacher," he said with teasing deference.

"Oh, stop," she said, swatting him with the back of her hand. "I'm just Juni."

He laughed and shook his head. *Just Juni.* As if that wasn't more than enough.

A hush fell between them as Juniper turned her gaze back to the passing landscape. They were starting to get to the outskirts of the village, the scenery becoming more unfamiliar and thus, more interesting to Juniper.

As Juniper watched the horizon, Oleander watched her. He observed the gentle flick of her long lashes as her eyes drank in everything. The gentle roundness of her profile cheek. That sweet little upturn at the end of her adorable nose. Once in a while, she would lean forward and follow something they passed with her gaze or point out an odd little animal here or there as the train worked its way through the wilds that separated one village from the next. It was times like this that Oleander really remembered what it was he fell in love with. Juniper was full of gentle, excited whimsy when she wasn't bogged down by fear of the people and places around her.

Oleander propped his elbow up on the seatback behind her and crossed his legs, resting an ankle on the opposite knee. He rested his face on his propped-up hand and continued to watch with delight. Even though the change in posture brought him nearer to her, it wasn't something she seemed to notice. Or at least, if she did notice, she didn't mind.

The two sat in companionable quiet as they traveled, with only a short conversation starting here or there, about this or that. About an hour after leaving their first stop, they pulled into a slightly larger village to pick up passengers. There was only a handful that got on; luckily, none in their car. Oleander thanked the Moon for her magnanimity in allowing him the joy of experiencing more of Juniper unimpeded by her nerves around strangers.

"I think this is as far as I've been," Juniper noted as the train once again pulled away from the station. "The Ostara festival always was at the village in the opposite direction."

"I saw this place on my way out and on my way back from Conservatory. I had a couple of classmates that lived in the area, and they sang its praises. On the way back, I was too busy thinking about you to consider it much at all, but it came to mind again when I realized your birthday was approaching," he informed her.

"You should have said something to your classmates. You could have paid them a visit," Juniper said.

"I can come to see them another time. Today I wanted to be focused on you and me." His hand that wasn't propping his face lifted from where it rested on his knee and tapped the tip of her nose by way of emphasis.

She laughed softly. "I suppose that's just as well," she said. "Hopefully you can see them soon."

Oleander shrugged again as if to say he wasn't worried about it. He wasn't.

The remainder of the ride returned to that companionable quiet, at least until the last few minutes when Faeridge came into view. Juniper sat up from reclining in her seat to get a look at the approaching city.

"Ollie! It looks like something out of a Faerie story!" Juniper said.

"Doesn't it? I knew you would like it," he said, giving her a mirthful grin.

Faeridge was truly a hidden gem in the countryside. According to his peers, this is where all the posh Kingsborough folk came to spend their springs and summers. It was known by the locals as the "Old Faelands," and they were careful to honor the legacy of that. In addition to celebrating holidays marked on the standard calendar, they also observed old Fae holidays. It was the observance and respect of the Fae that many Faeridge residents credited with the beauty and success of their small town.

The train pulled closer towards the station and was quickly enveloped by the town. Even in the winter, there was a sort of spring-like brightness to Faeridge. Pastel pinks, blues, and yellows colored every house, cottage, and shop. While most properties had roofs thatched with golden straw, some of the more upscale ones also featured attractive coral-hued shingles. Any parts that were not painted a myriad of pretty tones were bedecked in murals of mushrooms and flowers and toadstools. Juniper's eyes glittered as she pointed them out on stone walls and pleasantly worn on the streets beneath the residents' feet.

"The Fae can't make art, so the people here make it as an act of devotion to the old Fae spirits. A lot of artists keep studios out here, saying their genius seems more apt to pay them a visit while they're working," he intoned.

"What a beautiful tradition," Juniper said, staring outside as the train once again wheezed to a stop.

Oleander stood up as the distant voice of the conductor announced that they had arrived at the Faeridge stop. Before extending his hand to her, he lowered the burlap bag from overhead and slung it over his shoulder. Her hand found a comfortable place in the crook of his arm; the two of them fit together naturally. They parted only once when Oleander stepped off the train first to ensure she made it across the gap safely, only to be reunited once again. They looked very much the part of a young couple in the throes of love as they made their way through the bustling platform. For once, Juniper was too focused on the pleasant environment around them to worry too much about her nerves. Besides, having Oleander there, having him available to steady her, was its own grounding force.

When they exited the train station, Juniper gasped with delight. It was like a fairground, or a village straight out of a storybook from her childhood. Despite the cold, there was quite the crowd milling about. People were shopping and selling their wares. The sweet smell of confections wafted from several stands along the moss-addled brick roads. Bespelled flowers near a tidy florist filled the air with the smell of roses and jasmine.

Identical twins stood outside of a perfumery offering spritzes of fragrance that took on the perfect scent for its wearer. Juniper and Oleander indulged them by offering out their wrists, receiving a spritz, and leaving it to dry.

Oleander offered his upturned wrist to Juniper first.

"Chocolate and whiskey," she said after an appraising sniff. "How fitting."

"And yours?" he prompted.

Juniper lifted her wrist and he bent a bit at the waist to sniff it.

"Tea and hazelnut," he said softly. "We'll have to get you some of that."

"You think so?" Juniper asked as she brought her own wrist down to sniff again, "It is nice; I think Mother would like some too."

"So, we'll get two bottles then," he said.

It was nearing breakfast time and they were both feeling a bit peckish. While they had been eager to get out to enjoy the Faerie circles, now that they had arrived it felt appropriate to take their time and enjoy all the attractions available during the brighter parts of the day. Oleander led her to the famed bakery that he'd mentioned when trying to coerce her into celebrating her birthday. It was a stroke of luck that it was both a bakery and a cafe. Inhalations of wistful anticipation accompanied their entrance, prompted by the aroma of freshly brewed dark roast coffee and steamed milk.

"Oh, it smells heavenly in here," Juniper said.

"Doesn't it? Where shall we sit?"

She pointed to a small, round table by a window that was tucked away. He led her to it and pulled out her chair for her, taking her cloak as she sat.

The cafe was a marvel. The interior was painted a sunny yellow with murals displaying jasmine vines and bluebirds strategically placed in every cranny and nook. Some corners held other surprising creatures, like rabbits and even a Faerie floating about.

Oleander sat across from her as she marveled at the decor. She wondered if she could get a mural like this in her own room.

"It's nice, isn't it?" Oleander questioned.

"It's incredible! I'm so glad you dragged me out here!"

"Dragged you? Am I so much of a bore?" Oleander retorted with feigned outrage.

"Please, you couldn't be boring if you tried. Indeed, the problem is actually quite the opposite, isn't it? I can hardly keep your pace most days," Juniper said warmly.

"Well, you must be having a good day, then," he offered.

As they bantered, a young woman wearing a dress the same color as the walls approached the table. Her hair was arranged flawlessly atop her head and was bespelled to be the most enchanting color of pale, bubblegum pink. Her cheeks were rouged in the same color and swelled pleasantly with her smile.

"Welcome to Ridge Rest," she said as she offered them menus. "Today our specials are an egg and cheese tart with peppers and mushrooms. And for those with more decadent palates, we have a white chocolate trifle served with a raspberry jam, and coffee with frothed milk."

Oleander's eyes became wide as he looked across to Juniper, causing her to laugh wholeheartedly.

"I think we'll have two of those, miss," she said to the waitress. "Would it be possible for me to switch the coffee for tea instead?"

"But of course. Do you have a preference?"

"Do you have a bergamot black?" she asked.

"Yes, I shall have it prepared for you posthaste," she said and hurried off. Juniper watched her for a moment as she disappeared behind a curtain and then looked over at Oleander. When she met his eyes, there was an interesting crinkle to them, an unreadable expression. He had his hand cupped slightly over his mouth like he was deep in thought.

"What is it?" she asked.

Oleander inhaled deeply as if he was considering not saying something. As he examined her, she watched him and felt her nerves start to fray. But then his hand relaxed and rested on the table, and he spoke what was really on his mind.

"Juni, you just put the orders in for the table without a thought."

The realization seemed to startle her, as if she herself hadn't even noticed that she had done it and, well, she hadn't.

"I . . . well . . . suppose I did," she said. A sort of self-consciousness immediately started to encroach on her pleasant mood. Did Oleander think she had been faking her nerves on the train? Could he have been annoyed that she didn't let him peruse the menu before ordering? Perhaps, despite her confidence, she should have deferred to him and—

"Stop that," Oleander said, the words dropping like an anvil. "I can see those little wheels churning through those pretty eyes, Juni. There's nothing wrong. I was just surprised is all. Pleasantly surprised, not unpleasantly."

Juniper couldn't help but give a weak little laugh and shake her head. She wasn't laughing because he was overbearing but rather because he really could read her like a book. He could tell she was worried, even knew that he needed to specify that he was *pleasantly* surprised and not affronted.

"I guess I'm just having such a nice day that I'd forgotten my own nerves," she finally admitted with chagrin.

"That's a good thing, Juni," Oleander told her. "I'm glad you're enjoying your day. You should be enjoying it. It's your birthday, after all."

Conversation ebbed and flowed as they waited for their meals. They talked about the book Juniper was reading (she had finished the one about the Faerie king and had moved on to a romance between two brothers-in-arms in a hundred-year war). They talked about Oleander's losses in cards at the hands of Dante, and about what they wanted to have for dinner. The mood remained light and jovial as they spent time together.

Quick conversation led to the arrival of their pastries at the table. Oleander's face lit up as he examined the artfully presented delicacies on the dish. He dove right in, taking a bite, and then slouched back in his chair like he'd been turned to jelly by the food.

"Oh, Moon above, it's perfect," he said, taking another bite from his slackened position. "The chocolate flavor is so rich without being overpoweringly sweet."

"Yes, yes, go on," Juniper indulged. Oleander gave her a bit of a withering look but decided to play along. He sat up straight and flourished his tiny fork in a considering twirl. "The whipped cream is clearly sourced from cows that have been read bedtime stories and given massages daily." He took another bite and tapped his tongue about in his mouth like Mr. Harlow did when his whiskey tasting friends came over. "Mmm, yes, vanilla bean and a touch of lemon."

Juniper almost spit out her tea but managed to swallow it before bursting into laughter. Oleander beamed the way a young man does when he's impressed the girl he holds a flame for.

"And how do you find your tea, milady?"

"Oh, yes, very refined. Like the bergamot was expeller pressed this very morning, and the tea harvested" — she took a sip — "yes, the tea was harvested during a Pisces new moon." Oleander feigned serious consideration, his chin and mouth cupped in his hand. "A revolutionary time to harvest." The two then both laughed, sighing out at the same time.

"I know I keep saying it but—" Juniper started.

"I missed you," Oleander finished for her with so much warmth in his gaze that it made Juniper's heart hurt. But it was a different three words tingling on the tip of her tongue. She just wasn't sure which ones.

"We should probably actually eat our breakfast, I suppose," Oleander said. "We have so much left to see before we head out to the forests and the Faerie circles."

"I'm looking forward to it," Juniper said, taking a generous bite of her own treat.

They finished their breakfast and stopped at the counter to place a sizable order of pastries to take home, which they would pick up upon their return after seeking out their bounty of mushrooms.

After leaving the establishment, they stopped here and there before finally making it to the edge of the small township and started to make their way into the copse of trees that hemmed in the town.

As they did, Oleander glanced over to Juniper to observe her.

She placed a hand on the trunk of a massive, old oak tree.

And she smiled.

River of Blooms

he hum of magic in Faewood was tangible, tingling beneath her fingers. Despite having seen many enchanted forests, this one was unlike any others. She had read the notes of many witches that say they could feel the pulse of their favored element the same way a healer might feel a pulse with a thumb on your wrist. It was Juniper's nature to doubt her experiences similar to those written in the books, but at this moment she couldn't deny any longer that she had that same sense.

Juniper loved plants because of their grounding, steady nature. There was something uniquely calming about the weight of damp soil in your hands; something cathartic in the way you could place seeds in a safe home in the warmth of sunbaked ground. The feeling of this forest, though, was different. It was jovial, playful, ecstatic. The trees and the weeds and the flowers all linked together in some kind of energetic dance, swaying like an inebriated ingenue on the night of her debut — giddy with champagne and attention.

"I think the Faeries still wander the earth here," she said finally, looking over to her friend and escort. "Can't you feel it?"

Oleander looked at her with an unreadable, warm expression. He shook his head. "No, Juni, you know that I can't," was his answer. The words weren't scolding, but rather, sweetly affectionate. "Tell me what it's like," he requested in a near reverent murmur.

"It's like . . ." Juniper started as she moved from one tree to another, fingers smoothing over silken eucalyptus bark, "like the trees have been fed cakes, and milk with honey."

Oleander hummed and came to join her by her side. "Sounds like my kind of party," curled his wry tease.

Juniper reached down and took his hand. "There's singing deeper in the forest. Let's follow it," she suggested, smiling up at him.

"Lead the way, Juni."

She did, leading through densely growing tree trunks, ducking under spider silk with clinging morning dew untouched by the rare sunny winter day. The sound of packed dirt was muffled beneath their feet. They didn't slip or slide or move about; it was more like they were walking across down blankets than compacted mud.

They smelled them before they found them.

There was a lovely perfume to the air, like the wafting of the first blooms of early spring. Through the dark network of trees they wandered, and they could see a vibrant clearing ahead, the comparative brightness blinding her eyes to what her nose could already sense.

Juniper started to run, her little boots carrying them faster through the thicket, her hand squeezing Oleander's tightly, not wanting to lose him. One moment they were beneath the dense, dark canopy of ancient trees and the next they stood in the middle of a sea — no — a river of brightly blooming wildflowers. Poppies, peonies, posies. Yellow, pink, and white. Covering a swathe of land as thick as snowfall after the solstice. Juniper released his hand and spun around in it all, laughing.

"Flowers! Even during the frost!" she exclaimed joyfully.

Oleander watched her dance with a hearty chuckle. Seeing Juniper act so wild and carefree was a real treat. It had only been on these kinds of excursions that she seemed at ease enough to be like this. He was reflecting on his wish to always see her this way when he watched her trip and disappear beneath the blooms, as if gobbled up by the earth itself. His joy sharply tapered off into concern as he hurried for her.

"Juni, are you alright?" he fussed.

He heard the airy giggle of her and took another step to seek her out. Two small, gloved hands seized his ankle, causing him to topple beneath the surface of the blossoms as well.

He moved a bit to find Juniper on the other end of those hands, smiling at him. Oleander laughed softly and started to adjust. Juniper relinquished his ankle and propped her chin up on her hands as he did. He came to mirror the same posture just inches away from her.

"You seem like you're having a nice time down here," he said teasingly, lifting a hand to draw an errant flower petal from her hair. Her hat seemed forgotten in some unknown place, perhaps spirited away by changelings or imps.

"I would say the weather is quite fine, wouldn't you?" she said, eyes nearly closing with how brightly she beamed. That expression took his breath away. And his words along with it. It was all that he could do to just stare at her and take her in. He would build her a house with his own hands right here if it meant she could always be happy like this.

Juniper picked up one of the broken blooms from the ground and tucked it behind Oleander's ear.

"There must be a Faerie lord that lives nearby," she said softly. "The processional has been through this way, that's why the flowers are here. They're Fae-touched."

"I see—" Oleander answered. "Is that why you're so silly right now?"

Juniper shook her head.

"No, I just—" she heaved a sweet sigh. "I'm happy, Ollie. It's been a long time since I've felt the freedom of being away from the scrutinizing eyes of the village."

Oleander's smile remained, but his eyebrows softened and lifted in that kindly worried way. "You should be allowed to feel this way every day, Juni. You shouldn't give a damn what the people in the village think or feel about you. This is *your* life."

Juniper's eyes fell back to the ground, and she picked up another flower, spinning it between her thumb and forefinger. "I know. I wish I could be more like you and not care," she said quietly.

Oleander watched her for a moment, spinning and spinning that flower the same way she spun her thoughts into nightmares. His hand reached out to hers and stopped the fidgeting movement.

"Who says I don't care," he said. His thumb smoothed over the sensitive belly of her index finger and gently coaxed it away from the bloom. Her finger obliged him, and he carefully cradled the bloom in his own hand. A pink peony bud, half open. He reached with his opposite hand to smooth some of her hair back behind her ear. He lifted the flower and tucked it behind her ear, mirroring the way his own ear had been graced with one from her hand.

"It's only . . . that I've learned that there are only certain people whose opinions matter to me," he finally clarified. "I can deal with Emelia's scorn at the clinic or Ethan Frond's misplaced dislike of me because he doesn't get to dance with you . . . because at the end of the day it is you, Juni, that I care about. And if you're happy, and you're with me, nothing else matters."

Juniper's mouth quirked to the side as she considered his

words. Her lashes fluttered as he tucked the flower behind her ear. The cover afforded them by the flowers gave her a feeling of safety in expressing her fears and doubts.

"But I want everyone to like me," she finally admitted. "I mean, I think everyone's opinion matters."

"How come?" Oleander asked.

The question wasn't asked in a way that challenged or criticized her. It was genuine and respectfully curious. Juniper had never really quantified it or thought about it before, so she had to get quiet for a few moments and really give it the time it deserved.

Oleander started collecting other blooms and arranging them in a flower crown, allowing her the time to think about her answer without the pressure of his gaze upon her.

It was a few minutes later when Juniper finally felt ready to speak. "I think—," she started cautiously, "I think I just want to know that I'm doing the right thing, always. And when people have a poor opinion of me, I worry that I'm not doing the right thing."

"Do you think that it's realistic to always do everything right?" he asked as he weaved in another poppy.

"For me, I think it should be."

Oleander laughed a bit and looked up from his little project.

"And why are standards so much higher for you?" he asked.

"Because I've already wasted so much time, and if I'm going to turn it around, then I need to compensate for all that time," she said as she fiddled with a small pebble on the ground. Oleander watched her busy fingers for a moment before grabbing another flower and incorporating it with the others.

"Do you remember reading *Memory of Love*?" he asked finally.

"Of course I do. I loved that novel," she said.

"Remember when Matthew was still suffering from amnesia,

but wanted to return to work as a carpenter? Remember how horribly it went?"

"That's what I'm trying to avoid," she winced.

"But remember, returning to carpentry is what allowed Matthew to start unearthing his forgotten memories. It's what allowed him to fall for his wife all over again. Those errors gave her a capacity in which to support him," he said. "Isadora never shamed him for not remembering his clients, or where a certain tool was, or forgetting how to make basic things. She merely found the ways that he could learn again. Then, through learning how to be a carpenter again, he gained access to the memories of his beloved wife."

Juniper picked up a new pebble.

"Juni," he said. "You're not going to be able to sort everything out in a vacuum. You can only grow and change by challenging yourself."

"But how can I challenge myself without falling to pieces? I can barely function around most people," she said.

"You lean on the people who love you, the people who have been supporting you anyway. You lean on me and your father and your mother. You let us help and protect you. You see yourself through our eyes until your own eyes adjust to the lighting."

Juniper looked down at the pebble between her fingers, mouth working.

Oleander let her stew on his words as he continued adding poppies and peonies to his project. He'd added four before Juniper spoke again.

"I had thought—" she started, her voice almost too quiet to hear, "I had been thinking about possibly—" she trailed off and Oleander's eyes lifted to her.

She was still staring down at the ground. He could tell that she was working through something, working up the nerve to speak some truth that she'd carefully locked away. His eyes remained on her, ever patient. Never daring to rush her.

"There is no storefront that sells seeds to the farmers," she said so very quietly, as if someone would hear her and berate her for even daring to have the idea. "I thought that I could serve the village and the farmers on the outskirts of town by selling seeds. That way they don't have to send for them, and they know they won't be getting any duds."

Oleander knew how much bravery it took for her to even think of sharing that with him.

"You want to open your own shop?" he said with sweet surprise. She timidly shrank at his tone, humbly looking at her fingers.

"I don't know that I would be a good shopkeeper," she said. "Right now I still fumble in most social situations, but . . . if you're there . . ." she trailed off.

Oleander grinned, his heart aching and thumping in his chest. The joy of acknowledgment from the woman that he loved warmed his face. What a wonderful feeling it was.

"I'll be there, Juni," he promised. "Let's open the shop."

Juniper's eyes flicked from the ground up to him.

"You really think we should?" she asked.

"Of course, we should," he told her emphatically. "If that's something you want to do, I'll support you, and I know Mr. and Mrs. Harlow will want to support it as well."

"There's a vacant storefront in the village," Juniper mentioned. "The one with the leaded windows—"

"Oh, you're right. Across from The Cat's Cradle," Oleander remembered.

"And if you or Mother and Father are too busy to help, then I could ask Dante," she said softly. "Not so often that it becomes a problem, of course . . . but I just thought . . . since you said to lean on your friends . . ."

"I'm sure Dante would be more than happy to assist when the situation calls for it," Oleander said.

He picked one final flower and finished off the crown with

it, only to place the creation on her head; it made her look the part of the May Queen of winter. She smiled at him in turn, gray eyes warm in the diffused light.

"So, we'll do it?" Juniper asked.

"We'll get started right away," he promised. There was a pregnant silence between them for a few long moments, the two witches basking in each other's company. After a time though, Oleander inhaled and patted the ground. "Shall we continue on to the Faerie rings?" he asked.

Juniper seemed to consider it for a moment, surprising Oleander with her hesitation. "Why don't we save it for another time?" she asked. "I want to go look at the stores back in Faeridge for inspiration for the nursery. I think it'd be nice to emulate some of the mood of it out in the village."

Oleander blinked, taken aback.

Juniper, reading him, shrunk a bit.

"Unless it would ruin the trip for you," she said.

"No, no, of course not. It's your birthday and we'll do what you'd like," he said quickly. "I just suppose I didn't realize how keen you were about this."

Juniper looked at him with a bit of tender shyness. "I didn't want to say anything about it for fear of making you feel obligated and tied to me," she said softly. "But, I have honestly looked forward to you finishing Conservatory and having the legitimacy to work with me. I'm still worried that it's my fault that you'll face ridicule for what you chose to study, and it's not as if you can go back in time and change it . . ."

Oleander shook his head and lifted his arm from where it supported some of his weight in the dirt. His hand rose to cup her cheek and his blue eyes once again rested on hers. Juniper's lashes fluttered softly as she looked at him, not shying away from the touch for once — not set on edge by it. She even came to enjoy these little stolen moments of intimacy.

Oleander seemed to sense this because the moment lingered.

His hand drifted gently to the tender spot where her neck met her jaw, and his thumb grazed the line beneath her lower lip. The touch caused the faintest parting of her mouth, and her eyes hooded slightly as she gazed upon him, allowing him this brazen exploration — this closeness. Again, Juniper thought of how this moment might be described in one of her beloved romance novels.

His roughhewn thumb traced the line of my lower lip, and my mouth answered the call, parting for him. My eyes gently shut, and I exhaled against his skin, feeling the cloying dampness of my breath collect there. At that moment, I desperately wanted to feel the softness of his lips upon mine.

Unbeknownst to her, Juniper's eyes really had shut.

Oleander peered at her, thumb tracing that line once again and observed the little opening of her lips, the flutter of her eyelashes, and the shifting of her eyes beneath her lids. Moon above, he wanted to kiss her. Well, he had always wanted to kiss her, but now the urge was so palpable that he thought he might just combust if he didn't.

His curiosity was piqued, being as inexperienced in the matter as he knew his Juni was. All he had to go by was the books that Juniper read; the books he'd read in the hope of understanding what she daydreamed about. He had read every single one she said she'd liked, hoping to find a common thread between them, hoping to make her as happy as possible.

He wanted to say words that made her stomach tingle with the flutter of butterflies. He wanted to give her the perfect first kiss. He wanted to feel her melt into it the same way that the heroines did in her books. And one day, when they were wed, he wanted to express his love for her in the way a proper man would only do for his spouse.

It could all start right here, right at this moment.

And one day he could tell their children about the day beneath the Faerie flowers when he kissed their mother for the first time. These thoughts all spun through his young mind in the space of seconds as he traced the soft curves of Juniper's lips.

The delicate touch had acted almost as a metronome, pulling Juniper into what she could only describe as a trance state. She stood on the edge of something, the precipice of a moment. Her breaths were steady, almost meditative. She exhaled again against the pad of his thumb which had come to a stop on her lower lip. A distant part of her mind heard him exhale a shaky breath and inhale tightly. Her mind was aware of a movement, a drawing of his body closer to her. Her brow faintly tensed, and she too inhaled a tight breath through her nose. An accommodation for the obstruction that was sure to follow, lips against lips.

His hand gently slid into the hair at her nape, cradling her head. She tilted her chin back, seeking him. Her eyes closed. She felt his lips finally press . . .

Against her forehead.

She gusted out a nasal exhale as her eyes fluttered open, feeling as if the earth had been pulled out from under her feet. Or, perhaps it was more apt to say that she had made a crash landing to the ground after flying through the air.

Oleander held the kiss there for just a few more moments before parting, the faintest hint of moisture clinging to her skin. Her eyes fluttered softly, a dim ache of something pulsating in her chest.

Disappointment?

Yes, that's what it was.

Oleander placed his forehead against hers and exhaled softly, his breath brushing across the sensitive skin of her lips. It made her ache deep in her belly.

"I think all this pollen is getting to me, Juni," he gusted.

His voice was unlike she had ever heard — raw and breathy — and something else she couldn't quite identify.

"Shall we head back into town then?" she asked. Her voice was airy and dreamy, something she had also never heard from her own lips.

"I think so," he said.

Oleander parted from Juniper slowly and negotiated his body back up to his feet. Once there, he reached down and drew Juniper up with him, supporting a fair bit of her weight as he did.

Her body was tired. Loose. She looked up at him with a dreamy gaze, the likes of which he had never seen.

"Off we go then," she breathed.

And the two went to gather their things and head back into Faeridge.

The Shop

If the King's Council in Kingsborough was filled with carbon copies of Mrs. Harlow, the crown would never be called inefficient ever again. Of this, Oleander was absolutely certain.

Only five days had passed since Juniper's twenty-third birthday and she and Oleander were already standing at the door of the dusty, old lead-framed building, a worn brass key in her gloved hand. Behind them was a horse-drawn coach, the horse and the coach both new to the family — they couldn't very well carry all the necessary supplies back and forth on foot, Mrs. Harlow explained. It had been entirely downhill from there.

Juniper and Oleander, luckily, had been able to convince Mrs. Harlow that they would not need a full staff of carpenters and handymen on their payroll. The building was sound and, truth be told, after the two had spent the rest of Juniper's birthday looking at quaint little shops in Faeridge, both parties were wary about having too many cooks in the kitchen mucking up their vision for the place.

Oleander, bucket of paint in hand, stood in his most worn-out shirt and his most tattered trousers. Juniper swiveled to face him, and his eyebrows arched in confusion.

"Nervous?" he quietly intoned.

"Terribly so," she responded.

Oleander looked at her, his expression warm and reassuring.

"You got this, Juni," he said. "Today is the beginning of the greatest adventure of your life."

She finally slid the key in the lock and turned it, the old mechanism clunking as the latch released. The door squeaked open and the stale air that had been locked inside wafted out over the pair. As she stepped inside, she gave Oleander the same smile she had given him when he left for Conservatory all those years ago.

The place was in a state, having been abandoned by its last lessor and unoccupied for years after. It seemed the landlord hadn't paid much attention to its upkeep. A wall at the back of the room that supported a worn flight of stairs was covered in mold, which gave the room a musty smell. The source of the grimy growth was apparently a dripping skylight that spilled light and water into the place.

Another wall had wallpaper that looked as if it had been there for a century. It was curling at the seams and where it was lifted, the remaining glue was patchy and yellowing. There were a few mouse droppings on the floor and a few mouse traps that were empty of cheese and bread but still ready to pounce on an unsuspecting rodent. Juniper saw visions of Oleander trying to disarm them, only to become their prey.

Yes, their work was cut out for them, indeed.

Despite that, Juniper found herself with that breathless excited quality, the same way she felt when she opened a new book.

"Where shall we start?" Oleander asked.

The process was long and arduous but rewarding.

The shop came together bit by bit as they worked on a different section every day. Dante had come to help when he saw the beast of the task, and he and Oleander peeled wallpaper and painstakingly scraped off the glue beneath it. Forgotten for some time, but still visible from the outside, was a hearth connected to a chimney. Both Oleander and Juniper had assumed it was for superficial reasons, but they agreed that fixing it up and revitalizing it would be a good idea to add some cozy warmth to the space.

After thoroughly cleaning and treating the moldy wall, they cast a spell at the site to prevent the sludge from returning and causing further issues in the future. The skylight was repaired by Dante — after Oleander nearly fell to his death when climbing the ladder by himself. It was a smarter choice, being that Dante could quickly assume his feline shape and catch his own fall. Juniper had been fetching more paint during this almost-mishap, and Oleander had been glad she was spared the worry it would have caused her. He did not have as much luck in escaping Dante's unimpressed chastisement, however.

It was when the place really started to come together that they began to get oglers and unexpected visitors. The visitors always came with this or that reason: a few sandwiches for lunch for the hard-working trio, a couple of houseplants to spruce the place up. Juniper wasn't always sure how to react to these surprise visitors, but after watching Oleander handle the first two or three, she began to at least attempt it.

Even with everything going on in these densely packed days, Juniper had found time to make a new friend, a nomad painter by the name of Daisy Floriana.

Daisy started as a visitor and stood in the space, looking

quite like she belonged there. She was a riot of color herself against the room's new coat of white paint. Her hair was vibrant copper beneath a raspberry-hued beret, her face pleasantly freckled, with deeply tanned skin, and she wore a strange frock of worn blue and green and red fabric. Daisy turned about in place, taking it in the way one might a landscape. Her eyes landed on the staircase with a bit of a curious raise to her eyebrows.

"What will you be doing with the loft upstairs?" she asked.

"As of right now," Juniper said looking to Oleander for confirmation, "we don't have plans for it." Oleander and Juniper had discussed ideas for the space but had decided to leave it as a half office, half storeroom. Neither was fully necessary, of course. They had more than sufficient rooms in the cottage that could serve the same purpose, especially now that they had a horse and carriage to take them to and from expeditiously.

"Would you allow me to occupy it as an artist-in-residence in exchange for murals on your walls and help in your store?"

Juniper blinked, eyebrows curved upward at the shorter girl in surprise. She was so used to the people in the village that danced around the things they wanted or needed. Never had she experienced such a direct request like the one Daisy made.

"Let me talk it over with Ol— er, my assistant," she said. "Do you have a place to stay tonight?"

"'Fraid not, miss," she answered.

It wasn't said in a pitiful manner, just a statement of fact.

"Well, then you'll stay with us at the cottage tonight, in one of our guest rooms if you're not opposed to it," she said.

"I couldn't impose, miss," she said.

"It's not an imposition. Mother would love to have a guest overnight, and I can't leave you to sleep on the floor here when we're uncertain that the chimney is clear. You'll catch your death sleeping on the floor in winter," Juniper insisted.

Daisy's face was friendly in a subdued way, and she took her hat off respectfully to thank her. In some ways, the small artist reminded her of Dante.

Daisy explained she had been paying the Connifers a nominal rent to stay with them, but after a bumper crop of their miraculous winter harvest, the small shed she had been staying in had been relinquished as storage for their food.

"I'm so sorry to hear that their success has put you out," Juniper said with no shortage of worry.

"Not at all. The Connifers were kind to me and, as a traveling artist, I am used to the changing of the seasons," she said.

"I have a few things to do still, why don't you make yourself comfortable somewhere and we can return home together with Oleander when he returns from picking up fabric from the tailor's shop," Juniper said.

"Would it be alright if I started to sketch ideas for your approval?" the young artist asked.

"Oh, please do. I just put a chair in the back; it's a little threadbare, but it should keep you comfortable while you work."

"Thank you, Miss Harlow," she said.

"Oh, you can just call me Juniper." The corners of her eyes crinkling.

Daisy was warm in her response: "Juniper, then."

Juniper felt, as the three of them made their way back to the cottage that day, that she must finally be doing something right. She thought that the Goddess was finally rewarding her for getting on the right track with her life. After years of stagnation, she was finally blooming, like *jasmine nudiflorum* in the winter. While she wasn't exactly sure where she was going, the fact that she was going anywhere was nothing short of a Moon-given miracle.

And one she was eternally grateful for.

Daisy

Daisy started working on the mural straight away.

She was a remarkably intuitive artist. The night that Daisy came to stay with them, she and Juniper spent most of the night in her greenhouse, talking about Daisy's travels and Juniper's experiences while Daisy sketched the rosemary sprigs and monstera leaves that were growing inside.

Juniper was so surprised when, after losing track of time talking, Daisy showed her the plan for the murals in the shop. Daisy had been sprawled out on an old blanket on the floor and climbed up onto the chaise joining Juniper there who was cooling off with a cup of tea. The work was incredible, like nothing she would have ever hoped for or even imagined in her own mind's eye: Starry nights and a beautiful earthen maiden with hair made of vines, whose hand bestowed upon the landscape a multitude of stylized flowers and leaves.

"It's beautiful," she gasped.

"It's what I see when I talk to you," Daisy replied as she looked from the sketchbook in Juniper's hands to her face. "You have a very kind heart, Juniper. You have a — how do I put this — uncommon gentleness about you that I think is what gives you your way with plants."

"Oh, it's not all that hard," Juniper dismissed quickly.

"It is, though, Juniper," Daisy insisted. There was something unobtrusive about the way Daisy delivered her insistence — something kind. "Plants are fickle, sensitive creatures. They don't have voices, so all that you can do is observe them and hope that you understand their plight — empathize with them. There is a reason there are so few herbalists anymore."

"Because it's not as valuable a skill," Juniper informed her.

Daisy laughed as if that was the silliest thing she had ever heard. "Moon above, *no,* Juniper," she laughed in frustration. "There are fewer herbalists because there are fewer people who have hearts like yours. Hearts that feel deeper. Truer. The heart of an artist." Daisy put her hand on her own heart then, drawing a comparison between herself and Juniper.

No one — outside of Oleander — had ever related to her. No one had ever opened their heart to her the way that Daisy did. The realization hit Juniper hard. To suddenly be seen, to be *acknowledged*, by someone other than her family was something powerful.

Not that she didn't value the approval of her loved ones; quite the contrary. It's true, she did care deeply for each and every one of them. But this moment, the fact that she was able to talk to someone who seemed to understand how she experienced her life's passion, even though it wasn't shared between them, was its own special kind of magic. Daisy understood it in a way that only someone who had experienced it personally could.

It was *everything* to Juniper.

Juniper felt a familiar tightening in her throat that comes when she is profoundly affected by something. In a genuine moment of affection, she extended her hand to Daisy's. "It would be my honor if you created this in our store," she said, throat a bit thick with her emotion. "And it would be my honor to host you as an artist-in-residence with your own gallery in the loft, should you like it." The offer seemed to take Daisy aback, dark citrine eyes blinking with wetness of her own.

"You would allow me to show my work in the space?"

"If you'd like. It must be hard to have the creative intuition you have and limit it to a little leather-bound book," Juniper urged. "We need more art in the village. I would be happy to help you for as long as you'd like to remain here."

Daisy gave her an emotive beam and squeezed Juniper's hand. "Thank you, I'll take on the task with steadfast commitment," Daisy told her. "I will make myself worthy of your patronage, trust on me on that."

Juniper smiled and squeezed her hands a little tighter, stemming the flow of tears that threatened to accompany her gratitude. "I think I'll make us some tea, if you're amenable to the late-night burst of energy," Juniper said.

"Why don't you let me make you a drink from my home country?" Daisy asked. "It's less likely to keep you up late into the night and it's delicious."

Juniper tilted her head in consideration. "Well, that sounds lovely, I admit. But I also must tell you I almost wanted the help staying up. I find myself not wanting to end our time conversing. I've never had another woman to talk to like this . . . I mean . . . aside from my mother, of course."

Daisy smiled, her tan, freckled cheeks deepening in color slightly. "Don't worry, it's got enough sugar in it to give us just enough energy to keep the conversation going, Juniper."

"Oh? What kind of drink is that if it isn't tea?"

"I'll show you. Can we make use of your kitchen?"

"Yes, of course."

Daisy reached into her bag and produced a small parcel of something wrapped in brown paper that had clearly been opened several times before, judging by the wrinkles in it. The two young women scurried into the house and into the worn kitchen.

Daisy requested a heavy-bottom pot and a carafe of milk or cream, which Juniper happily provided. When Daisy finally opened the paper, Juniper was surprised to find a small, circular brick of chocolate divided into triangular subsections, two of which had already been broken off. Next to the brick of chocolate, there was a small sachet. Daisy opened it and produced a hard lump of what seemed to be brown sugar shaped like tiny pointed hats. Dusting the top of the chocolate was a generous sprinkling of what looked and smelled like . . .

"Is that ground cinnamon?" Juniper asked.

"Yes, and a bit of clove and allspice, too," Daisy said as she took the milk from the counter where Juniper had placed it within reach. She poured the milk into the pot and then placed the sugar-hat into the milk.

"I've never seen a sugar cube like that before," Juniper said. "They're adorable."

"Where I come from, these are called *piloncillo*," Daisy said. "But my mamá and I always called them little hats. They're made with raw sugar and poured into molds to get this shape."

As the sugar melted into the warm milk, Daisy started to break up the chocolate into segments, dropping each one into the simmering pot. In the moments that followed, the pale milk darkened and bloomed with clouds of rich chocolate. The smell of cocoa and aromatic spices filled the small room, and Juniper could see why Daisy suggested it as an alternative to tea at the late hour.

For a while, the house was quiet except for the rhythmic stirring of the wooden spoon. Then, from upstairs, there came the sound of a door opening and quietly clicking shut. Soft foot-steps followed and after a few moments, Oleander appeared in the doorway, wiping sleep from his eyes.

"Are you baking at this hour, Juni?" he asked sleepily.

"You have a nose for sweets," Daisy said, amused.

"You have *no* idea," Juniper quipped.

"Do not tease a poor man when he is only half-awake," Oleander said through a yawn.

"Well, at least you're an optimist, seeing yourself as half-awake instead of half-asleep," Daisy teased.

Oleander chuckled and looked past their guest to the pot she was stirring.

He approached, standing between both women. Juniper did what she could not to think about the heat radiating from his sleep-warmed body — or the angles of that body evident beneath his threadbare night shirt.

"What is this you're making?" he asked.

"Hot chocolate," Daisy said. "It's a drink from my home country. Juniper wanted something warm to drink and I suggested this as it wouldn't keep her from sleep."

Oleander's brow tensed slightly. "You're telling me there is a drinkable form of chocolate and I've not been made aware of it until this very moment?"

Juniper couldn't help but laugh at his affronted expression.

Daisy smiled. "I take that to mean you'd like to try some?"

"Naturally," Oleander said. "Please," he added as an aside, as if remembering his manners.

"Of course," Daisy said. "There's plenty to go around."

A few moments later, Daisy used a metal ladle to pour generous helpings of the liquid into three mismatched teacups, serving Juniper and Oleander their cups first before picking up her own.

Juniper blew gently on the liquid, watching it ripple before taking a sip. The flavor was creamy and rich, yet somehow light. It felt as if the warmth of a fireplace in winter had been captured into a beverage.

Oleander took a sip of his not long after Juniper and let out a little sound from his chest. "That is *obscenely* good," he said, sighing dreamily. "I still can't believe I've never heard of it."

"It's very popular in the southern half of the world."

"Where exactly are you from, Daisy?" Juniper asked.

"A small nation in the tropics called Isla Estrella. We grow huge groves of cacao trees in many regions of the island. It's where most of the world's chocolate comes from."

"We must go visit, Juni." Oleander said, his expression fervent.

Juniper sputtered a laugh as Daisy gave him a calm smile.

"It's much hotter than it is here, but I admit I do love it there," she said. "It's quite the lengthy boat or zeppelin ride, but if you can handle the strain of travel, it's well worth it."

Juniper didn't have the heart to say she wasn't sure she could, especially with how excited Oleander seemed by the idea. Daisy looked at her and Juniper looked away quickly, almost nervous that her hesitance would be obvious to the attentive artist. She felt Daisy's eyes linger on her a bit longer before the visitor turned her attention toward Oleander.

"Have you ever left the country Oleander?" Daisy asked.

"I've not had the pleasure of doing so yet, no," he said. "I'd like to someday, though. If fate allows."

Juniper imagined Oleander dressed in a fresh set of traveling clothes, seeing sights in other lands. She pictured him greeting strangers, becoming fast friends with them, and eating fantastic and unfamiliar foods enthusiastically. The thought of it tugged at something in her gut. The idea that fate would undoubtedly take him so very far away once he broke free of his idealized view of her.

"What about you, Juniper?" Daisy asked.

"Ah, no. I haven't," she said, hoping the subject would drop from there.

"Well, I hope you both have the opportunity to do so," she said.

"Tell us about Isla Estrella, won't you? Tell us about things other than your lovely groves of cacao trees."

And so she did, telling them tales from her childhood and explaining the matriarchal structure of Isla Estrella. She talked about the traditions around death and how they celebrated Samhain — a time when the veil was thin between the living and the dead — by staying up late to commune with the spirits of their lost loved ones and making altars covered in bright marigolds and sweets to entice them back home.

And for some reason, the more Juniper heard about, the more melancholic she felt.

When their cups were empty of the sweet chocolatey drink and the conversation had petered out, Daisy finally addressed Juniper again.

"You've been quiet," she said.

"Oh!" Juniper said a bit too loudly. "I uh— well, just lost in thought I suppose."

She glanced over to Oleander and found him looking intently at her face, his eyes flickering as he searched her expression. She wondered what she had written on her face, wondered if he would say something about it. But just as she was starting to feel the urge to speak into the quiet, Oleander stretched his arms above his head and yawned.

"Well, it is late, isn't it?" Oleander said. "Allow me to leave you ladies to your conversation. I fear I've overstayed the invitation I'd granted myself when I smelled chocolate."

"N-not at all," Juniper insisted. "You're always welcome, I didn't mean to make you feel—"

"Easy, Juni," Oleander said with a grin. "Only teasing. I know you love my company. I just want you and Daisy to get some time to yourselves as well. It's hard to talk about matters of the heart when a man is around."

"Oh — well, alright," Juniper said, deflating slightly.

"I'll see you both in the morning when it's time to break our fast," he said, reaching over to gently right an errant hair on her head. "Sleep well, you two."

"Sweet dreams," Daisy said, smiling cooly.

"G'night," Juniper sulked.

Juniper watched him vanish up the stairs again and heard the quiet click of his door shutting.

"Are you alright?" Daisy asked her.

Juniper startled again and looked toward the artist. "Yes, why?"

"You seem sad," she said. "Come, let's go back to the greenhouse and we'll talk about it. If you're willing to, of course."

"A-alright," Juniper said. "Let me just get a few things. It's going to start getting a little chilly in there at this hour."

Daisy waited patiently as Juniper gathered up a few pillows and blankets from a trunk in the den, and gathered some of them into her own arms when it seemed Juniper may trip on them. They quietly wandered back out to the greenhouse and made themselves comfortable by pushing together some of the mis-matched furniture in a sort of make-shift, oversized daybed.

With the mountain of blankets and cushions, it felt sort of like being in a bird's nest made of linens, and as they settled in to relax with a belly full of hot chocolate, Juniper found herself unspooling some of the tension she'd picked up in the kitchen while Daisy and Oleander had been talking.

"So," Daisy said. "Tell me everything."

"It's alright if you don't wish to talk about it," Juniper said. "I know that it can be a cumbersome task to listen to someone moan about their lives. Especially someone who has been so fortunate in life."

"If I didn't want to talk about it, I wouldn't have asked, Juniper," Daisy promised, reaching to take one of her hands in both of her own. "Why did you get so sad?"

"Am I so transparent?" Juniper asked, feeling her face warm with embarrassment.

"Only to those who know where to look, my friend," Daisy answered. "I've trained myself to observe the finer details of emotion on someone's face."

That did make Juniper feel at least a little bit better.

"Well, I suppose I was just worried that Oleander fled so quickly from the kitchen," Juniper said.

"Fled?" Daisy asked. "It didn't seem that he was fleeing to me. Being a bit over-courteous perhaps. But not fleeing."

"I thought he ran off because I made him feel unwanted," Juniper said. "Since I'd gotten so quiet. I was only stuck in my own thoughts. I didn't mean to make him feel like he wasn't wanted."

"I didn't get that impression, for what it's worth," Daisy said. "I know I've only recently met him, but he said himself that he just wanted to give us privacy. It was an effort at kindness, I'm sure."

"I hope you're right. I fear I was feeling so melancholic that I made him think he wasn't welcome to spend time with us."

"What had you feeling melancholic?" Daisy asked. "Was it all that talk about death? I apologize, I know that's not a subject everyone is comfortable with over here."

"No, no. Not at all. All of your stories were so wonderful and charming," Juniper insisted.

"Well then what upset you?" Daisy asked.

The question was one of genuine curiosity, not at all defensive or annoyed. She just wanted to know what bothered her. "Well . . . Oleander mentioned going to Isla Estrella," Juniper said. "And I just realized that . . . well . . . I'm such a fearful person that I could never dream of spending weeks or months at sea. And I most certainly can't ride a zeppelin or a broom. I'm terrified of heights. And . . . and I just . . ."

As she spoke, the reason for her melancholy became clearer

and clearer in her mind. As the thought crystalized and made its way to her lips for her to speak aloud, she found herself choking on the words. Choking on the shame they brought with them.

"It's alright," Daisy said as her words halted. "You can speak it out loud."

Juniper swallowed the pain in her throat as it tightened. "It just . . . sounds terribly selfish."

"Juniper, as of yet, you have been one of the most generous people I have ever met," Daisy promised. "No person is immune from a selfish thought or two, myself included."

"But . . . I don't want you to see me that way," Juniper said, pressing her lips.

"Would it help if I shared a selfish thought of my own?" Daisy asked. "Then we will both be a little selfish and neither of us will have to feel bad about it."

Juniper considered for a moment, wondering if that would actually be helpful. "Well, I suppose it's worth a try," she said, finally.

Daisy didn't hesitate. "I was disappointed when Oleander came down from his room to have hot chocolate with us," she said. "I was enjoying having your company to myself and I even felt a little annoyed that his presence seemed to result in your deflated mood."

"O-oh," Juniper said. "Really?"

"Really," Daisy said with a smile.

"It's not his doing, it's just my foolish mind," Juniper said, feeling the need to come to his defense.

"I know," Daisy said. "So, tell me what's on your mind, so that I can enjoy being of help to you."

Juniper remembered her conversation with Dante; how he'd said that it could be fulfilling for others to be of help to their friends when they were in need. How he'd said it was okay to lean on one's friends. Was that what she and Daisy were?

Friends? Perhaps this was the way people became friends. They opened up to one another.

"I don't want to hold Oleander back from his life," Juniper said. "But I don't want him to be far from me either . . . a-at least the selfish part of me doesn't want that." A moment of silenced passed between them, and Juniper inhaled deeply before whispering, "I've never even told Ollie about feeling that way."

"It's a perfectly natural way to feel about someone precious to you, if you ask me," Daisy said. "I'm certain you're not the first person to feel it and you won't be the last."

"But it isn't fair," Juniper asked. "I can't make him stay here."

"Would you?" Daisy said. "Try to make him stay here?"

"No, of course not," Juniper said.

"Well, there you go, you're not selfish, then." Daisy said.

"It isn't that simple."

"Sure it is," Daisy promised. "Selfish people behave selfishly. Wishing to be near Oleander doesn't make you selfish. Do you think of me as selfish for wanting to have your company for myself?"

"No," Juniper relented.

"And why not?"

"Because you weren't unwelcoming to Oleander even though you thought that way, I suppose," Juniper said.

"See?" Daisy said squeezing her hand again. "Juniper, it is not selfish to have unhappy feelings. That isn't something you can control. What matters is how you act based on those feelings. I'm sure Oleander would be overjoyed to hear that you don't want him far from you."

"Moon above, I would never *tell* him. He would throw his dreams of going to your country out of his mind," Juniper said.

"And that is the very thing that makes you selfless," Daisy said. "Because you know this about him and yet you keep your sadness to yourself so that he won't alter his dreams for your benefit."

There was some truth to that, Juniper thought.

"I do wonder, though." Daisy continued. "Why is it that you think you could never travel to Isla Estrella?"

"I don't really ever leave the house," Juniper said.

"Well, that isn't true," Daisy said. "You're opening a shop, aren't you?"

"Well, yes, but I'll probably only go there," Juniper said. "Going into town isn't the same thing as traversing the ocean."

"No, but no one says you must do that tomorrow," Daisy pointed out. "Just because you can't do it now doesn't mean it won't ever be possible for you. Mountains are scaled one step at a time, Juniper."

"I don't see how I could ever make it up that particular mountain," Juniper said.

"Well, why don't we talk about the things that hold you back, then?" Daisy asked, "I've been all over the world, maybe I can help things feel a little less scary for you."

"Oh . . . that's a clever idea!" Juniper said. "So much of what frightens me is what I don't know about traveling."

"Perfect. One moment," Daisy said, letting go of Juniper's hands and reaching for her sketchbook and pencil. "Let's make a list."

And so, they did. For hours after Juniper brought up every concern and worry, even the smallest, most insignificant sounding ones, and Daisy fought each fear with her depth of experience. They talked so long that before she realized it, Juniper had become a sleepy puddle in their makeshift bed, slurring through the intricacies of her fears of boats.

Daisy was slowly crumpling into a sleepy heap herself, bundled in blankets against the cold of the wee hours of the morning. She was the first to succumb to the pull of sleep, falling quiet after a hoarse question from Juniper. For a few moments, Juniper considered getting out of the blankets and climbing up the stairs to her own bed. But the blankets she wrapped herself in were so very warm, and the pre-dawn air was so very cold. Instead, she helped Daisy lie down more comfortably and settled in next to her. Daisy woke just enough to take Juniper's hand in her own and mutter a sleepy "Sweet dreams, Juniper."

Juniper smiled as she squeezed the hand of her new friend. Yes, she was sure she could call her that now: Friend.

"Sweet dreams," Juniper replied as she slipped into deep sleep. She dreamed of the spray of salty sea air.

And Oleander right by her side.

The following morning, Mrs. Harlow was so ecstatic about being the patron of a true *artist* that she sent Oleander and Daisy to Faeridge to stock up on all the paints that she could possibly need for the mural and any other creations she planned to make as an artist-in-residence.

Oleander offered to bring Juniper with them, but she still had plenty to do in the greenhouse; start cuttings to root, sort seeds, and get them packaged into small sachets for customers. All tedious tasks that were not very well suited for Oleander's particular brand of focus, and thus, had been put off in favor of other pursuits.

"You two have fun. Daisy will love Faeridge," she said happily.

"I'll bring you back a souvenir, Juniper," Oleander promised.

"I'll look forward to it!" she said.

Juniper worked for some time in her greenhouse and started to load materials into the carriage to transport them to the shop in the village. It was risky business, transporting the seedlings from the comfort of their greenhouse to a new location entirely, so it did require a fair amount of her focus. As she worked on getting the cart loaded, she kept a sunshine charm running near the cart, warming the spot where it stood and melting the snow into water nearby. It was taxing to do both at once, causing a bit of sweat to bead on her brow, even in the cold.

After getting nearly all her goods loaded, she strode towards her greenhouse to shut the door, lest the winter chill get in. The short walk to the greenhouse was lined with frozen dirt, and she slipped when she stepped from the watery muck onto the frozen path. She did her best to right herself, arms flailing as she tried to catch her bearings on even icier stones. In the end, she lost her footing and fell forward with a jolt towards the ground.

Only, she didn't hit the earth. Instead, she was caught with elegant hands, bracing her forearms from behind.

"Easy there, Miss Harlow," a voice said, cool and quiet as fresh snow. There was a familiar curl of amusement in his voice that told of a smile.

Juniper craned her head back to see Theo Vervain had been her savior from what would have been an awful spill.

"O-oh, Mister Vervain!" She tried to get back onto her feet, only to cause even more chaotic slipping.

His hands tightened on her. "One moment, Miss Harlow. Allow me."

Theo didn't look like a particularly strong man. His nature was more like that of a polished dancer — more grace than strength. Despite that, however, he easily maneuvered her weight, getting her shifted back onto her center of gravity.

By the time Juniper could properly turn to face him, she was pink in the face.

"Apologies, Mister Vervain."

"No need to apologize," he intoned. "I'm glad I caught you."

Juniper laughed at the joke and looked sheepishly down at her shoes. She felt Theo's gaze on her and brought her head back up to see the man smiling down at her. The way he acted around her was so contrary to how she felt internally. There was always this feeling of needing to rush when he was around. Meanwhile, he seemed entirely unhurried.

"M-mister Vervain," she mumbled. "What brings you by today?"

"Ah," Theo said, as if remembering himself. "Right, I apologize. You looked so enchanting in your work clothes that I nearly forgot."

The compliment brought some fresh heat into her face and ears. How did he say such things so casually? She felt like she needed to fan herself even in the dead of winter.

Theo reached into his overcoat and produced from it a small, wrapped parcel. It looked about the size of a small almanac. It was wrapped in indigo paper, the color of Theo's eyes, with a silvery ribbon.

"I neglected to bring you a birthday present. I hope you'll forgive me for not bringing it on the actual day."

Juniper accepted the gift delicately, looking up at him with genuine surprise on her face. "I didn't even know that you knew."

"Open it, won't you?" he urged.

Juniper carefully untied the ribbon and methodically undid the folds of the paper. She was never one to just tear into wrapping parchment — she liked to save the paper. Opening it revealed a wooden box, stained a deep mahogany, though feeling too light to actually be mahogany. Her mouth dried out as she looked at it. Suddenly, she feared that the man had spent an exorbitant amount on jewelry for her, which just wouldn't do at all. There was a tremble in her hands as she opened the box and peered nervously inside. Inside, on a bed of indigo satin, was a pair of finely made leather gloves; white, with pale green embroidered vines of ivy snaking delicately up the fingers, as if they grew from a soil bed within the gloves.

"Oh!" Juniper exclaimed, "They're lovely — For riding?"

"For your little garden," Theo answered.

Juniper looked down at them again. She took her hand out of her dirty glove and slid it into the new one. The inside was lined with the softest fur.

"They're very lovely, too lovely to ruin with dirt," she told him. "Thank you so much, what a kind gift."

"Feel free to ruin them. I could always just send for another pair," he said nonchalantly.

Juniper came from an affluent family, but she was starting to see that Theo came from an entirely different class of wealth. Accessories like this, she thought, shouldn't be ruined when it was so clear that the artisanship that went into creating them was so painstakingly done.

Theo looked past the top of Juniper's head to see the carriage being packed behind her. "Are you getting ready for a trip out of town?" he asked.

Juniper didn't understand his meaning at first until she looked over her shoulder. "Oh no! The charm!" she cried. Juniper hurried over to the cart, almost slipping again on the mud around the cart. In absence of her sunshine charm, the wet mud had frozen over again.

She once again focused her energy and called forth the energy of the sun from her own memory of the feeling of summer. It took some doing, what with all her flustered mood from Theo's surprise visit. The miniature sun sputtered and popped a few times as it tried to gather in her hands, but she gave it some more determined focus and it finally stabilized. Juniper lifted her palms, as if sending a carrier dove to deliver a message and the sun-spell floated back where it was before her clumsy near-fall. She looked down at her plants, some of her more spoiled specimens had already started to wilt in the freezing air. She quietly spoke to them, coaxing them out of their malaise.

"Come on now. You're alright. It's back," she encouraged.

She heard quiet, assured steps approaching from behind her.

"That really is something, Miss Harlow," Theo said looking up at the miniature sun. "It feels like a Beltane fire," he said, cupping his chin in his hand.

"Thank you, I read about it in some old tome. Took me almost three years to master it. It's a pain to keep it going, though. Requires pretty focused energy," she said.

"Hm—" Theo said, still staring at it.

"I just have to go grab a few more things from my greenhouse. Would you like to stay here by the warmth?" Juniper offered.

He shook his head as he looked at her.

"Allow me to aid you, Miss Harlow. No need to risk any more spills," he said.

Juniper gave an embarrassed laugh and carefully made her way back to the greenhouse. Theo took the liberty of holding one of her forearms to offer the required stability. He followed her into the glass and metal structure and glanced around as she gathered her last few goods.

"Where are you taking all of these things?" He asked

"I'm opening a storefront in the village across from The Cat's Cradle," she said with some exerted breathing. It was much harder to keep a conversation going at the same time as moving her wares *and* keeping up the charm. "I'm going to be selling seeds and seedlings there."

"Ah, so that's what's been going on there," Theo mused. He moved out of the way as Juniper approached with a tray of rosemary starts.

Juniper loaded them onto the carriage and looked back at her unexpected guest. "I have to get these over to the shop before I run out of energy for this sunshine charm." She hesitated a bit, dusting the dirt off her new glove. "You could . . . join me . . . if you'd like?"

Theo gave her an approving, closed-mouth smile.

"I would love to," he said.

He climbed into the driver's seat of the carriage and Juniper saw to having the horse properly hitched to the cart, patting it on the side of the neck. Theo watched her with surprise as she did so, his brow tensing slightly. When she climbed up to the seat beside him and he took the reins he looked at her for a long moment.

She shifted uneasily in her seat at the glance. "What is it?" she asked.

"You don't have a stable hand?"

"Oh, well — no. Ollie and Father are quite skilled with horses, and I know enough to get by," she said. "Besides, she's a gentle mare."

"Gentle she may be, but you're a lady," he said as he started the horse on the road, "You need to be careful, as delicate as you are."

"Ah. Well . . . I suppose," she muttered in a mixture of defeat and flattery. She didn't realize it was a problem for her to handle the horses. She did suppose they could be dangerous though. Father always told her so.

"I'll ask my father to do it next time," she promised.

Theo smiled sidelong down at her with approval. Something about that validation made her feel the tug of her own lips.

They arrived at the empty shop shortly before dusk and Juniper unlocked the creaky door, stepping in first at Theo's insistence. The musty smell of mold had been replaced with the smell of fresh paint and handcrafted soap. He gave the area a quick glance before nodding.

"Coming together," he said.

Juniper heaved a few tired breaths but gave him a warm glance.

"Just have to get the plants in here and start a flame in the hearth," she said. "Shouldn't be long." Again, Theo watched her work, leaning against one of the counters with his legs crossed casually at his ankles.

It took about half an hour to get everything inside, during that time Juniper stoked a fire in the fireplace to keep the shop toasty. She was more than happy to let the sunshine charm down and start sorting through things as Theo quietly watched her work. He watched her with the same disinterest a cat might, blinking slowly and holding utterly still.

The sun had fully set when she finished her tasks. She wiped the sweat off her brow with the back of her dirty glove, smearing dirt there in the process. Theo clicked his tongue softly and pushed off from his place at the counter.

"That won't do," he tutted as he pulled a silk handkerchief out of his jacket pocket and approached her.

"What?" she asked as she turned towards him.

Theo approached, encroaching into her personal space as if he belonged there. Juniper's stomach did flips as he took a firm grasp of her chin, lifting it. Her mouth pressed and her shoulders tightened, hands fisting in her skirts.

"There, there, you silly girl," Theo soothed. "I'm just going to clean you up a bit."

"Oh—" she said, exhaling a bit but not quite deflating.

"You'll have to be more mindful of things like this, Miss Harlow," he drawled with easy correction. "You're a lady of means."

"I'm sorry," she stammered.

How different from the time she stood in a similar spot with Ollie, when he brushed her hair out of her face with that handsome smile of his and referred to her as "delicate as a flower." All the same, her chest was as tight as it was then and just as hard to breathe, with him so close.

After wiping off the grime from her forehead, Theo's eyes focused above her head, narrowing slightly. She was going to ask what was wrong when she heard the door open behind her, bell tingling.

She turned to see who entered and saw Oleander storming in, a bewildered Daisy following closely on his heels.

"Get away from her, Vervain," Oleander commanded.

"Hello to you too, Ambrose," Theo mocked in response.

Oleander ignored him, placing down the bags full of paints that he carried. He hurried to Juniper's side, placing a hand on her shoulder and moving himself in the space between the two. The blond man clicked his tongue and was forced to take a step back, lest he wanted mud on his fine leather shoes.

"Are you alright?" Oleander fussed.

"I am. Theo was just cleaning some dirt off of my face," Juniper said. "How was Faeridge?"

"Oh, it was a dream! Come look at all the things we found!" Daisy interrupted, coming to seize Juniper by the arm and pulling her away. She glared at both men as she did — only Oleander shrank from it.

"If she's got dirt on her face, she's more than capable of cleaning it off herself," Oleander hissed under his breath.

"Just like she's capable of hitching a horse to a cart? Do you make her muck the stalls too?" Theo countered.

"If you're so concerned, why didn't you just do it for her?" he spat.

"Because I'm not poor enough to *have* to."

Daisy cleared her throat pointedly and glared again as Juniper started to look through the day's spoils.

Oleander shot Theo a look and walked over to watch her.

Juniper glanced at the paints with delight. "This is amazing, I can't believe you found herb-infused paints!" she said as she looked up at Oleander from where she knelt before the bags and boxes of supplies.

"We thought it was the most appropriate," Daisy said with sweetness. "Would you be willing to consecrate them for the paintings?"

"Oh, of course!" Juniper rejoiced. "It would be my honor! I'll do it tonight!"

"You don't have to tonight, Juni — you're looking pretty pale. Did you do extended sunshine charming again?" Oleander asked her.

"Ah, well it took me longer to load up the cart on my own, but I feel alright," she offered with every sincere assurance.

"Next time take a half-full cart, or just wait until I can help you," he insisted.

Daisy watched Theo as Juniper and Oleander interacted, seeing his face go sour and the slightest line appearing between pale brows. "Why don't you go across the way and ask Dante for tea for Juniper, Mister Vervain?"

"I actually have to head back up to the Hawthorne estate, I'm afraid," Theo remarked with a flourish of an elegant hand. "It's getting late."

"Oh, well, thank you for the birthday gift and for coming to see the new place," Juniper said in sincere gratitude.

"Of course. I'm sure this will be a stimulating diversion for you, Miss Harlow," the departing guest stated, patting the top of her head. He leaned over a bit and Juniper thought he might whisper something, but instead, Theo planted a kiss on the top of her head.

Oleander inhaled to retort as Juniper's face flushed crimson, but he couldn't say anything before Theo interrupted.

"Good night, Juniper," he trilled, already heading for the door with his long legs.

"Um . . . good . . . good night," Juniper warbled.

Oleander Ambrose had never wanted to hit a man more in his life. Each successive time truly seemed to trump the last. If it took much longer for that blighted man to finally slither back to whatever viper's den he had been birthed from, Oleander truly believed that he very well might lose his temper and give himself the satisfaction.

Our Job

They spent a fair amount of that night working on the shop.

Daisy got on a ladder and began the underpainting for the mural on the giant, white-painted wall.

Juniper got to work consecrating each tub, tube, and bucket of paint. It was a lengthy process, requiring her to meditate with each one and call on the spirit of the herb it was infused with, request a blessing for each, and charge it with a little bit of her own energy.

Oleander went and got that tea for Juniper, asking Dante to include a good tincture for focus and meditation, but even with the energizing properties in the tea, Juniper still wound up depleting her energy. Luckily, the task wasn't particularly temperamental spell work, and thus, didn't carry the risk of some kind of rebound.

Oleander glanced over to her while watching Daisy work on the painting and found Juniper asleep against the counter she was sitting at; her hand was opened loosely at her side, still half-holding a tube of paint. She had probably fallen asleep mid-meditation.

"Ah, Juni . . ." he chided in a murmur.

Daisy glanced over to where he looked and huffed a quiet laugh, "Well, isn't that darling?"

"She's probably going to feel wretched tomorrow. I wish she'd give herself a break sometimes," he said, keeping his voice low so as not to wake her.

He walked over and gently took the tube of paint out of her hand. It was the last one that she had to do it seemed. Of course, she tried to push through the exhaustion of the day to finish it.

Oleander removed his jacket and folded it strategically, ensuring the buttons were placed on the bottom of the bundle of fabric as he set it down on the floor. He was gentle as he coaxed Juniper's sleeping body into a lying position, cradling the back of her head carefully as he set it on the makeshift jacket-pillow. He straightened her still-bent legs and righted her skirts to avoid any embarrassing wardrobe mishaps. Once done, he grabbed his cloak on the wall and returned to drape it over her body. In her sleep, she tugged the comforting fabric closer to her and turned onto her side, heaving out a sleepy exhale. Oleander sighed looking down at her, feeling that crushing pang of affection for her.

"How long have you loved her, Ambrose?" Daisy asked nonchalantly.

Oleander spooked and turned to face her, almost forgetting she was there. He didn't shrink from the question though, only looked back down at Juniper.

"Let's see . . . must be . . . eight years now? I vowed to marry her when I was ten," he said with an almost somber seriousness.

Daisy looked up at a rose she was painting. "You need to be careful how you handle things with Vervain," she said.

Oleander rolled his eyes and gritted his teeth.

"I hate that bastard," he said.

"I don't like his aura, but he's not showing those unsavory aspects of himself to Miss Harlow. If you set yourself too far his opposite, you will make him look rational and make yourself look like an ass," Daisy said.

He had to admit that she was right, but it was difficult to control his reactions when dealing with a spoiled prince. "I just know that his intentions aren't genuine," he said.

"You will have to trust Juniper's ability to find that out for herself, don't you think?"

Oleander's jaw worked as he clenched his teeth. He reached his hand up to the back of his neck and rubbed the muscles there, turning from Juniper and going to hold the ladder steady. "Do you think he'll charm her?" he asked, without meeting her eyes.

Daisy didn't look away from the leaf she'd started painting. "No, I don't. That said, I think interfering will cause problems for you. I have the feeling that Vervain is a soul bond of hers."

"A *what?*" Oleander snapped.

"*Relax*, Ambrose. It's a soul bond, but not how you're thinking. Sometimes we meet the same soul over and over again, life through life, because they teach us a lesson we must learn."

Oleander audibly ground his teeth. The idea of Theo and Juniper's souls being bound through lives made him want to hurl the man off a cliff. Vervain could try his luck again in the next one, and if Oleander had anything to do with it, he'd be there to hurl him again. There was some catharsis in imagining himself chucking the smug cretin endlessly to his doom for the rest of time.

"Easy," Daisy soothed, dabbing her brush and making another stroke. "They're not *romantic* soulmates. You need to read up on soul bindings, Ambrose. You're insufferable."

"You're telling me they're soulmates. How else am I supposed to take that information?"

"Not soulmates, soul *bound,*" Daisy said. "It's more nuanced than you're thinking. Being soul bound it less a romantic thing and more like the Moon giving you just enough of a challenge to teach you a lesson. Well . . . an opportunity at a lesson. Some people don't actually *learn* the lesson and fall into a mess of a friendship or romantic partnership."

"I'm going to vomit," Oleander said.

"Such dramatics," Daisy said with a roll of her eyes.

"What could such a beautiful soul like Juni have to learn from a condescending twit like *Theo Vervain?*" Oleander asked.

"It may not be Juniper who is learning the lesson," Daisy said. "It may be the condescending twit who needs to learn the lesson. Maybe it's a soul like hers that can teach someone how to relax, or how to be kind, or even how to love."

Oleander's stomach twisted at the thought of someone like Theo Vervain learning to love through his interactions with Juniper. If he was learning how to love, he sure had a funny way of showing it.

"Well, I would prefer it if someone other than Juniper would provide such a lesson," Oleander grumbled.

"If only we were able to choose such things," Daisy retorted.

Oleander pouted and looked at Juniper through the rungs of the ladder as she slept peacefully. She looked so calm and at ease when she slept, and downright adorable with his coat folded up under her head as a pillow. His expression was still troubled, though now with more worry than crossness. "I just worry that with how she sees herself, she'll take anyone's mistreatment because she feels it's all she deserves."

"And it's our job as people who carry a flame for her to help her see the lie in that. But we can't force her to see another person for what he is. We can only be the ones to show her the differences by embodying them ourselves."

Oleander looked up at her with a quirked brow.

"Our job?" Oleander repeated. "Don't tell me I have to compete with you, too."

Daisy looked down at him with a wry grin.

"I'm an artist. It's my job to see the unique beauty in everyone and fall in love with it enough to paint it," she teased. "But don't worry, she's not interested in me."

Oleander grunted and shook his head. "That's the secret, isn't it? The Goddess made her too damned perfect, so they had to make her afraid of people, to make sure she doesn't break every heart in sight."

Daisy laughed warmly and returned to her work. "You know, I think that's a pretty accurate interpretation of the Goddess creating Juniper," she said.

Oleander laughed too and shook his head, looking once again at Juniper sleeping as the hushed sounds of Daisy painting mingled with the periodic crackling of the hearth. He thought, as he watched her slackened face and the steady rise and fall of her chest, that he wasn't sure at all if he would make it through this winter without Juniper breaking his heart in one way or another.

Feverish

Juniper did, in fact, feel wretched the next day, and for a few days after that. Over-exerting energy was similar to overindulging in alcohol; it could lead to headaches, light sensitivity, and a lack of appetite.

Because of this, Juniper spent a couple of days in bed while Daisy and Oleander worked on the shop on their own. Oleander focused on creating shelving and organizing products for display while Daisy made progress on creating a mural for the previously blank wall.

Once the shelving and displays were built, Oleander set about organizing the products in an orderly and appealing manner. He then made his way around the building where he cast warmth-retaining sigils to ensure that the warm air stayed trapped inside the store even when it was unoccupied and over winter months.

In the afternoon, Theo arrived with a bundle of flowers in hand and stepped into the tiny establishment. The two gentlemen met eyes across the room.

"We aren't open, Vervain."

"Obviously," he responded. "I came to see Miss Harlow."

"She's home in bed after overdoing it yesterday," Oleander grumbled.

"Ah, I see," Theo said. Then, just as easily as he arrived, he turned to leave.

Oleander sputtered, taking a few steps after him. "You're not going to the house." It wasn't so much a question as it was a directive.

Theo set him with an irritable look.

"And why shouldn't I?"

"I just told you, she isn't well," Oleander seethed.

"Surely, she can't be so bad off that she can't sit for tea," Theo said with a roll of his eyes. "Really, what kind of homemaker can't deal with a little spot of spell fatigue? She's going to have to be a little tougher than that."

Oleander clenched his fists at his side, his mouth screwing. Theo's eyes fell on his hands, and he gave a haughty huff.

"Are you going to fight me, Ambrose?" Theo provoked. "What will the villagers say? Will anyone come to a shop run by a violent madman?"

"I'm not going to fight you unless you give me cause to, Vervain," Oleander spat.

"Good. So, Juniper and I will see you tonight when you get home." Theo turned on his heel with irritating smugness as Oleander choked on outrage.

Oleander looked as though he was unsure what to do with himself, hedging between pummeling the man and staying in place to get the necessary work done. As much as he hated to admit it, Theo was right. If Ollie chased after him, yelling in the streets, the gossip in the village would close the shop's doors before they had even opened. Even so, Vervain was possibly the most arrogant, selfish, repugnant weasel of a man he had ever met. Oleander found himself praying for an opportunity for violence. He rarely got angry or lost his temper, but something about Vervain had the power to ignite rage in him — as white hot as a blade being worked in a smithy. His fury seemed to rouse the moment he had to endure anything relating to the man.

He stood in place long after Theo disappeared, breathing heavily through his nostrils, his body still tight and tense. His ears were practically ringing with the urge to break things.

"If you quit huffing and puffing long enough to get your work done, you'll be able get home sooner and intervene," Daisy lazed from somewhere behind him.

Oleander forced himself to draw in a long inhale and, after holding it for a few moments, released the breath in a steady gust.

"Right," he uttered, turning back to his work.

"Ah, how fortunate. It seems the bull that wandered into the shop has made his way out. You know what they say about that, after all," Daisy quipped.

There was a bit of a derisive roll of his eyes, but as much as it stung his ego, it affirmed he needed to keep his head on his shoulders. Vervain just . . . made him feel a much more indelicate man, merely by existing in the same space, let alone when that deplorable dandy opened his fool mouth. His mouth that would look far better, in Ollie's opinion, with at least three less teeth.

Back at the Harlow residence, Juniper rested in bed and read through her most recent romance novel. This one was a dark romance between a captive and her captor — a pretty damsel and a dragon lord that hoarded her affection as he did his gold. She was just getting to a flush-inducing scene when there came a few quick raps at the door.

Juniper about bolted out of her skin, smashing the book into her chest with a yelp.

"C-come in," she said.

"Juni, dear, Mister Vervain is here for a visit, would you like to come down?"

Juniper's expression shifted into one of slight consternation. *What was Theo doing here?*

"He said he'd stopped by the store to bring you congratulatory flowers and heard you were dealing with some spell fatigue. He wanted to come check in."

"Ah. Well . . ."

If that was true, that meant that Theo had traveled clear across town to come and see her. The Hawthorne's residence was up in the hills on the other side of the village — a stately, beige mansion — it had probably taken him close to an hour to make it to the cottage.

Juniper's mouth worked a bit; she really didn't have the energy to do more than rest, but she didn't want to put the man out.

"Give me a moment to change and I'll come down . . ." she finally relented.

"Are you certain?" Mrs. Harlow said.

"Yes, I'll be right down."

Juniper dog-eared the page she was on and closed her book. As she heard Mrs. Harlow go back downstairs to keep Theo busy, Juniper let her body slump like a rag doll and stared at the ceiling. She gave a low groan, careful to keep it quiet enough so that no one in the house would hear her.

"Okay, Juniper," she told herself. "Get up."

She did not get up.

It took another several minutes for her to negotiate her tired body out of her comfortable bed. Her muscles and bones ached in protest as she walked to her wardrobe and opened it. She knew it wouldn't be ideal to dress less formally for their guest, but she just didn't have the energy to fuss with stays and corsets and multi-layered skirts.

He was coming to see her to check on her well-being, wasn't he? Surely, he would understand if she was a little more casual today.

Juniper selected a simple cotton dress in a light gray color and a slip to go beneath it. She put on the dress and added a plain white apron to wear over it to guard a bit more of her modesty without running herself ragged.

Once she had her clothes on, she quickly brushed through her hair and braided it loosely over one shoulder. She put on house shoes — some satin slippers with soft soles — and made her way down the stairs on slow, achy feet.

She found her parents and Theo in the sitting room. Her father and the young man both rose to their feet as she entered and only sat when she did. She winced slightly as she joined, the exhaustion still actively present in her bones. She watched Theo's eye rove over her once when she joined them before his focus returned to Mrs. Harlow.

Juniper's mother, being the social butterfly she was, kept Theo occupied for some time with talks of Kingsborough and the Chaos and Crime, or CAC, department there. They chatted a bit about the senior Vervain's time with Mr. Harlow in the war and how they went back so far but were too busy to keep up much with each other.

Theo fielded all the questions and conversations with perfect politeness and charm while Juniper hid behind her mother's eager chatter. She was relieved not to have to calculate the nuances of social interaction while she was feeling so fatigued. Unfortunately, the conversation did naturally ebb, giving Theo leave to once again glance at Juniper from head to toe. Sensing his change in focus, Juniper looked his way, finding a peculiar expression on his face that she couldn't quite read.

It almost looked like disgust.

"How are you feeling, Juniper?" he asked.

"Tired and a little sore, but generally alright," she responded with a tired but earnest assurance. "Thank you for coming to check in on me. You really didn't have to do that."

"Of course, I've come to check on you — I suppose Ambrose and that woman are working you ragged?"

"Heavens, no," replied Juniper, laughing as though the idea were preposterous.

"In fact, Oleander gave her quite the talking to when he served her a tray of breakfast this morning," Mr. Harlow teased.

Juniper flushed and smoothed her hands over her braid. It was true that Oleander had given her a warmly exasperated lecture about the importance of pacing oneself. They went back and forth with cranky bickering about whether it was worth it to lose out on several days of work.

"I tend to agree with him," Theo said, looking first at Mr. Harlow and then at Juniper. "It's a lovely thing that you're so passionate, but clearly your ambition has impaired your ability to see to your daily tasks."

Theo made a nod towards Juniper — well — more towards her choice of clothing.

"I can't imagine making myself so tired that I couldn't get properly dressed for the day," he tutted. "You must be miserable."

Juniper shifted slightly in her seat, tight hips straining.

Mr. and Mrs. Harlow met glances before looking over at Juniper.

"I am quite fatigued, yes . . . I didn't want to keep you waiting," she mumbled.

"Very thoughtful of you, Juniper. I imagine it must be difficult to get dressed in a full frock without someone to aid you," he remarked. "I do appreciate you coming down to meet me in spite of your condition today."

"Of course," Juniper mumbled.

"Mister Vervain brought you some flowers, Juni," Mrs. Harlow said, quite satisfied to get away from the topic of Juniper's choice of clothing for the day.

"Oh, thank you, Mister Vervain."

"Of course," he responded. "Anyways, how has your day been thus far?"

"It's been fine. I've mostly just been in bed reading," she admitted. "It's nice to catch up on my collection of books I've been meaning to get to."

"Oh, and what is it you like to read?" he asked.

"Mostly romances. It's a nice way to pass the time," was her lightly given answer.

"Ah, I suppose that's a worthy diversion," he said with no shortness of condescension.

She, as ever, found herself swept away in the tide of Theo Vervain's opinions. Something about him made her feel the need to perform. Perhaps it was just the challenge of finally being acknowledged by someone and not being so easily dismissed, or maybe it was just that she wanted to face more of her discomforts and fears after her late night talk with Daisy.

Whatever it was, whenever he was around, she felt like she was straining and stretching past the threshold of what was comfortable for her.

"You will have to allow me to make some recommendations to you for some proper classic literature, sometime, Juniper."

"Oh — ah, sure," she said. "When I'm feeling a little better, we can go to Hector's shop in the village. He usually has a good selection to choose from."

"Oh, we haven't been there in a good while," Mrs. Harlow enthused.

"Well, the reason for that may be that you're the one purchasing half of his wares," Mr. Harlow teased. "At the rate you buy books, dearest, you might want to open a competing shop."

"Oh, don't be so dramatic!" Mrs. Harlow retorted, eyeing her husband with glittering delight all the same. His mouth curled at the look, and the married pair stole a brief playful squeeze of hands. Theo observed their affectionate interaction with a vaguely offended blandness to his expression.

As Juniper listened to her parents tease each other, the room began to distort around her. She rubbed at her temple and closed her eyes in the hopes that she could stabilize her vision. She opened her eyes and looked at the guest she was meant to entertain, and he appeared on a tilted axis.

"Juniper, you would certainly love the libraries and the bookshops in Kingsborough," Theo said easily, his face now sporting an inviting, amicable smile. "You must allow me to take you sometime; perhaps you and your family can come visit in the spring to meet my mother and father."

"Ah, well — if spring wasn't the busiest of seasons—" she said.

Theo's countenance appeared bewildered.

She clarified, "It's the beginning of the planting season. Perhaps fall?"

Truth be told, Juniper didn't function well in places much larger than Faeridge. She would do what she could to avoid having to visit any place outside its borders when everyone was eager to travel after winter thaw.

"Surely you can take a season off from your little garden," he tutted, waving a dismissive hand.

Juniper's mouth pressed and she inhaled to speak when she heard the door open. Whatever she had planned to say died in her throat as her interest piqued. Despite her dizziness, she got to her feet to peer out of the sitting room toward the front door. She watched as Oleander came into the house and her face broke into a brilliant beam.

"Ollie, you're home!" she beamed.

"And you're out of bed," he scolded in a warm, almost indulgently admonishing tone, like she was a kitten who had strayed outside in the cold.

Theo watched the exchange as Oleander came to hover in the doorway of the sitting room with Juniper. The newly returned sorcerer propped a hand on his waist and lifted the other to feel Juniper's forehead.

"You look nice today, Juni," he said with quiet intimacy. "That being said, looks can be deceiving. How are you feeling?"

Theo felt a pang of hatred sent his way, despite neither of the boys' eyes meeting. Seeing the blatant display of familiarity apparently rubbed the unexpected guest wrong. Theo's mouth pressed and his eyes narrowed sharply.

Oleander looked from Juniper to Theo, feeling the weight of that haughty gaze. His brow knit and he gave a near imperceptible shake of his head, as if to warn Theo not to say what he was about to say, ready to give the man a rare advantage in order to protect Juniper from whatever clipped critique he was about to deliver. The tension was palpable, so much that the girl caught between it was rendered speechless.

The blond man ignored Oleander's silent warning.

Theo sputtered with quiet outrage. "Juniper. You have a guest—"

"*A fever,*" Ollie interrupted. "Juniper has a fever, Mr. Vervain."

Pale blue eyes bearing down on him, Oleander said firmly, "Thank you for coming to *check* on her, but I'm afraid she'll need to get back to bed if there is any hope of her recovering in a timely manner."

"Allow me to get you some tea, Mr. Vervain," Mrs. Harlow said pleasantly. "You don't have to waste the trip. I would love to talk to you about Kingsborough in the spring."

Theo opened his mouth to speak and then Juniper turned to look at him. His mouth closed upon seeing her face. She certainly had become pale since coming down. Even her lips looked too white, her eyelids too heavy.

She put a hand on Oleander's upper arm to stop a subtle wobble.

"Rest well, Juniper. We'll plan for the bookshop soon."

"That sounds nice," she lied.

"Let me help you back upstairs, Juni," Oleander insisted. "You look pale as death."

The fact that Juniper didn't refuse him told Oleander that he had arrived just in time to avoid a fainting spell.

Oleander followed her and herded her up the stairs. He heard her belabored breaths as she reached the top. The man's gaze held on her carefully, bracing to act on the slightest indication of distress. When she swayed after releasing the handrail, he gently stabilized her with a hand around her waist.

"Sorry," she said quietly as her weight leaned into him.

"Don't be," he answered. "Juni, why did you go downstairs if you were feeling so poorly?"

"I thought I'd be okay," she sighed. "I didn't want Theo to be cross with me."

He adjusted her weight in his hand before scooping her up into his arms as they finished the trip to her bedroom. Oleander got her situated on the edge of her bed and knelt on one knee to slide off her slippers.

"Juni, sometimes it's better to allow people like Theo Vervain to be cross with you when you can barely stand straight," he fussed.

Juniper hummed exhaustedly, looking with tired eyes down at her best friend. When he glanced up at her, he gave her a cheeky little smirk.

"And what is that smile for, Juni?" he teased.

"Am I smiling?"

"You are," he answered, as one hand reached up to steady another wobbling sway, her precarious balance threatening to spill her onto her side before he could get her properly ready for sleep.

"I suppose it's just that . . ." Juniper said as her mouth split further, "you taking my shoes off like that . . . it reminded me about the proposal scene in that one book."

"*The Cobbler's Wife?*" he asked, voice amused.

"Mhmn," she answered.

Oleander knew the one. He'd received it in one of her care packages when he was away at school. The hero of the story feigned a shoe fitting and subverted his beloved and the reader by drawing out an engagement ring once he was done.

The idea that Juniper was smiling at his resemblance to it was enough to make Oleander's heart quicken painfully in his chest. It gave him some hope that he was beginning to appear to her as the young man he is rather than the boy he was.

Then again, she was also delirious with exhaustion; it'd be foolish to take anything she said now as any indication of her feelings for him.

"Take off that apron, mn? I don't want you to get tangled up in it," he intoned.

"Do I look plain?" she asked, her words sort of blurring into each other.

The abruptness of the question was enough to make him gust out a chuckle.

"Plain? Never," Oleander affirmed with doting warmth. "Plain-as-day beautiful? Well, that's another question. Matter of fact, you're the most beautiful woman I've ever known, Juni."

Juniper's eyes closed and she smiled up at him as he rose back to his feet. He waited a few moments and, when it was clear that she wasn't going to remove the apron herself, he bent to reach around her, his hands gently undoing the knot.

Juniper seemed to think that he intended to embrace her, so she leaned into his shoulder and wrapped her arms around the back of his neck.

Oleander chuckled softly as he coaxed the apron away from her and set it aside. With her arms still about him, he carefully lifted her and laid her down comfortably in her bed.

"You're so strong now, Ollie," she sighed.

"Mhm, strong enough to take care of you," he answered with a tender voice.

Juniper gave him a cooing sound half hum, half giggle.

"Are you too warm, Juni?" he asked.

"No — I feel shivery, actually," she answered, resting the back of her arm over her head.

"Alright, alright, let's get you warmed up then, hm?" he said.

He covered her with blankets, tucking her tightly within. He even pulled a quilt from the chest at the foot of her bed and laid it over her. She exhaled in deep comfort, the weight and coolness of the sheets comfortable and soothing.

"Get some rest. No more gentleman callers until you're all better," he said, brushing some hair away from her face.

"Well, what about you?" she sighed. "You *live* here, after all."

The question made his heart thrum in his chest and his pulse thump in his ears as she looked up at him with sleepy eyes.

"That's right," he said a little breathlessly. "I live here, so technically I'm not a *caller*."

And Moon save him, Juniper actually frowned in response to that. Frowned when he pointed out that he wasn't in the running.

"Not a caller, but you are a gentleman," she cooed as her eyes closed. "Probably better than any of the others in town, I would say."

"How lucky for me that you think so," he said as he smoothed her hair away from her face. "But we can talk about your many suitors another time, Juni. For now? Get some sleep."

She let out a long, slow breath, her head turning to follow the tender path of his hand against the silken strands of her hair. He found himself wanting to spend the night watching her seek him out, to listen to her sleepy confessions. But the only thing he wanted more than that was for her to get the rest she so clearly needed.

"Good night," she whispered softly.

"Sleep well," he said.

And somehow, despite how much he hated it, despite the fact that he didn't know if he'd ever hear her speak with this candor and sweetness again, he left her room.

And let her sleep.

Adonshire

They couldn't be free from Theo Vervain for long. A day or two after his last visit, he made plans to come visit the Harlow household again. On the brighter side of things, he had, at the very least, given the courtesy of sending word ahead this time. Of course, that meant he likely would occupy most of Juniper's time that day. The idea of that was, for some reason, uncomfortable.

It wasn't the same kind of unease that she felt when it came to other social calls. She didn't feel the same impending doom as she did when they were preparing for Oleander's party. There was still the distinctive feeling of teetering on the edge of a blade as she got ready.

Juniper was sure to wear some of her nicer clothes, not wanting to risk the same lukewarm reception that she encountered days prior. She found herself feeling a little bit affronted by Theo's apparent distaste for her simpler garb, especially considering that when Oleander returned from working at the shop, he had seen perfectly fit to compliment her.

Theo had known that she was feeling under the weather, hadn't he? But perhaps he was right. Perhaps it wasn't polite to come down dressed so casually. Next time she would refuse the visit. Though, she had the feeling that would have been even more poorly received.

Juniper decided to wear something a bit more traditional. She opted for a charcoal dress constructed of durable silk. It was high-necked with eyelet lace lining the cuffs of the long sleeves, the collar of the dress, and the hem of the skirts. It had a few pleasant details here and there: the buttons were made of black pearls, and there was fine embroidery in the same muted color as the dress. She laced on some newer boots with a small, wide heel (anything else would be far too dangerous for her, clumsy as she could be).

It was pretty and practical.

She opted to arrange her hair up in braids to keep it from falling in her face as it was often wont to do.

On this day, she waited in the sitting room for their guest, sipping some bergamot black tea with a healthy amount of cream and honey in it. The warmth was a boon to her nerves, the cold of the winter seeming to wind her even tighter with tension than usual.

He finally arrived in the late morning, carrying with him a small parcel of books. They were bound together with some silk ribbon in a deep indigo. He joined Juniper on the sofa, his masculine body causing the cushions the slope somewhat.

"You're looking resplendent today, Juniper," he said with an easy warmth.

"You look very nice today as well, Mister Vervain," she returned, smiling.

It was true; he came to the house wearing a very nice blue jacket with golden embroidery of moons and stars and a serpent snaking up the length of each sleeve. It looked more like something that would be worn at Solstice than a casual visit with a friend.

"I brought you some books that I thought you might enjoy," he announced as he handed them over, stacked from smallest to largest and held together with a bow. "They aren't romances, but perhaps you will find yourself a bit more intellectually stimulated by the likes of these. They may even teach you something new."

Juniper smiled politely as she accepted them and looked the titles over. Each one was a book she had already read. She wondered about the proper way to navigate this situation. She supposed he would just want a 'thank you' and then she could give him the credit of introducing her to the works the next time they spoke. But something about that idea sat uncomfortably in her stomach.

"Thank you so much," she said, trying to hide her apprehension with the social maneuvering required.

"The small one is about the old war; it's written by a great general. That second one is a captivating read about the Goddess, both anecdotal stories and more empirical ones. Oh, this final one — one of my favorite epics — follows Oberon on his journey to becoming King of the Fae," he said.

"Ah yes, I've heard of them. Thank you again, Theo — I'm excited to read them," she lied.

Theo pressed his lips together and looked at Mrs. Harlow who approached him with a cup of fresh coffee from the kitchen. He said a quiet thank you and took a sip.

"Juniper, I thought we might go for an outing today, if you'd like. Get out of the village," he offered.

"Out of the village?" Juniper's fingers fiddled with the handle of her teacup. "Where were you thinking?"

"There is a small sister city to Kingsborough in development not far away; it's called Adonshire."

"Adonshire's a half day's train ride away, isn't it?" Juniper asked.

"Oh, we needn't take the train. The weather is fair; we ought to just fly out that way," he told her.

Juniper hedged a little, her legs crossing at her ankles as her mouth twisted. "I'm afraid I don't do well flying," she demurred softly. "I have a terrible fear of heights."

That seemed to surprise Theo, his expression shifting to one of consternation. A delicate line formed between his pale brows. "I see," he said.

"We could always try another day," she added quickly, trying to smooth the awkwardness over.

"I suppose we shall have to," he sighed, a hand raising to rub at the edge of his eyebrow.

He didn't say anything to betray it, but Juniper couldn't help but feel that he was irritated with her. The idea settled uneasily as she looked down at her tea and took a sip. There was a long moment of uncomfortable silence. Juniper thought of the night when she listened to Daisy and Oleander talk about Isla Estrella. She thought about how Daisy suggested that, perhaps with enough time and practice, she could learn to escape her fear of travel and of heights. Maybe this was the perfect opportunity to practice. Maybe this was the beginning of building her courage. Maybe this was the first step out of her comfort zone and closer to traveling the world with Oleander.

Juniper took a slow sip of her tea, letting the warmth of the liquid flow through her and calm her nerves. She set the cup down on its saucer, the porcelain clattering slightly as her hands trembled.

"I suppose we could go," she said. "It won't take that long to get there, right?"

The expression that bloomed on Theo's face was bright and full of approval. "It should only be about an hour, and you can hold onto me the entire time," he said.

It didn't take long to get ready, Theo clearly wanting to be on his way before Juniper had the opportunity to change her mind. They would take Theo's besom, a sturdy thing for lengthy travel. Instead of the thinner handles which were common for most besoms, this one was more akin to sitting astride a bicycle, offering more support for the rider to protect from fatigue.

After being afforded an opportunity to change into some more suitable garb for the ride (namely some besom trousers and more layers to protect from the cold), the two were set to be on their way. Theo stood waiting for her, freshly changed himself into some rather sporting besom clothes. A thick, quilted flying coat in princely white, and a pair of navy besom trousers and flying boots that, much to her surprise, looked as if they had seen their fair share of wear and tear from the elements. He held a pair of lady's flying goggles in his hand, his mount floating readily behind him.

When she approached, he handed her the goggles. They were fashioned of shiny brass in delicate curves of filigree. Blue-tinted glass lenses were meant to guard the eyes against the wind and the sun. The brass curved in what was almost a complete circle at the temple ends, a feature to reduce the chance of dropping them. Juniper noticed an inscription on the side, it was a protective sigil that would give her luck and good fortune should something go awry on the trip.

"Ready to go, Juniper?" he asked her.

Juniper heaved a shaky breath, stomach doing flips. "Ready as I'll ever be," she choked out.

Her hesitation seemed to bear no weight on the gentleman before her. He simply put out a gloved hand for her and assisted her onto the besom, climbing on in front once she was situated.

"Keep your arms about me, Juniper," Theo instructed. "I won't let anything happen to you."

Juniper's arms wound around him firmly, her hands clasping

each of his arms and not letting go. She held him close, her grip like a vice, as the broom began to rise off the ground.

The sensation was slow, but steady, and as the ground below faded away, Juniper's grip shifted, keeping her hands secure in their ascent. The wind blew around them, the cool air rushing past and ruffling her hair. She closed her eyes, feeling the warmth of the sun on her face, and the sensation of soaring through the air. It was a freedom she had never felt before, and it was exhilarating.

She kept her eyes mostly closed as they ascended further, not wanting to tempt fate by watching the tiny houses passing beneath them at such a terrifying pace. The wind was such that there could not be much conversation as they flew. Theo didn't move his gaze from the horizon in front of them, or at least didn't move enough when he did that Juniper could really tell at all.

Eventually, her eyes strained from the effort of being clenched shut, though, and she opened them to look up at Theo. She saw him in a slight profile, a different kind of smile on his face than she was used to seeing. It was brighter — truer.

The wind blew fiercely, sending his fine blond hair cascading back from his forehead, making him look more like a daring explorer than the composed aristocrat he normally appeared to be. He had a youthful radiance about him, a look of excitement and enthusiasm that seemed to be enhanced by the windswept hair that framed his face. His eyes sparkled with a newfound energy and his lips curled into a satisfied smirk as he embraced the moment of adventure. He was no longer the unruffled gentleman, instead, he was a fearless explorer, eager to venture into the unknown.

"You love it, don't you?" Juniper asked over the whip of the wind.

The voice seemed to spook Theo, his torso stiffened faintly

when she spoke. He turned his head to look down at her side-long, a glimpse only long enough to see her before going back to watching the skies.

"Love what, Juniper?" he asked, matching her volume.

"Flying. I've never seen you look so at ease," she said.

"Ease, you said? Nonsense. I'm always at ease," he clipped.

"Well, yes . . . I suppose you are, but you usually seem . . ." she trailed off as she looked for the words she would say next, "bored . . . I suppose," she finished.

Theo gave a sort of derisive half-laugh. He was quiet for a long moment after that, but his expression sobered slightly.

"I do," he finally said. "I do love to fly."

"You look the same way flying that I do when I look at my greenhouse. Like it's the easiest place in the world to be," she told him knowingly.

Theo looked back to her sidelong again, this time for longer.

That comported face he always seemed to wear fell, leaving something unreadable and enigmatic in its place. Juniper met his eyes behind his own emerald-tinted goggle lenses for a few long moments before he stared forward again.

"We're almost there," he said. "Hold on tight; we're going to start our descent."

Juniper's descent off the broom, however, was far from graceful. Luckily enough for her, Theo seemed more amused with her terror than irritated. He offered her a steadying hand on the small of her back as they stepped away from the besom, and with a final laugh, he suggested they take a break for a meal. Juniper gladly accepted, relieved to be on solid ground again.

The time allotted to eat gave her the chance to recover from expecting her own death to take place at any moment. Once given the chance to recover, however, she actually found herself enjoying Adonshire. It was still developing and so had some of the conveniences that might exist in Kingsborough along with the charm of a small town. It was certainly far busier than the village or even Faeridge was, but it was nice to get a controlled dose of that environment.

They had been to this shop and that, Juniper mostly watching Theo pick up odds and ends for comfort in his time away from the city, a gift for his Mumma, and other things. As the late afternoon sun began to dip in the sky, Theo smiled down at Juniper in a mischievous way.

"Well, we've killed enough time," he announced with sudden certainty. "I've been waiting to show you a surprise."

"A surprise?" she asked. "What kind of surprise?"

"You'll see," came his confident reply as he hailed a carriage for some more comfortable transportation.

The carriage took them through the busier streets of the developing city, out to the outskirts which gave way to some of the finest homes she had ever seen this far from Kingsborough. They first passed some small, tightly packed cottages with brick walkways and tidy gardens, and then, as they got further away, larger estates with sprawling acreages hemmed in by lines of trees. They finally pulled down one of the cobble-paved drives to a large home, about twice the size of the Harlow's back in Linseed Village.

It stood proud, like the manor royalty might live in. To either side of the drive stood great groves of pine trees, each standing at attention like a command of soldiers. Juniper idly wondered how they kept them so uniform and found herself a bit saddened by the magic that must have been used to keep the trees from pursuing the wild, powerful nature she often felt they possessed.

The windows were numerous, far more than Juniper could hope to count from her seat in the carriage. The house was almost blindingly white, reflecting the sunlight like it was the Moon herself. A large, black door framed by iridescent columns made of moonstone came into view. In the center hung a large golden knocker depicting the Vervain family crest; a sleeping lion framed by blooming sprigs of vervain, the flower for which the family was named.

As the carriage came to a stop at the front entrance Theo stepped out, rounding the back to open Juniper's door and offering her a hand. "Welcome to my family's country home, Juniper," he said with an air of satisfaction. "Moonstone Manor."

Juniper's mouth fell open with surprise as she slid down from her seat in the carriage. "This belongs to your family?" she balked.

Theo nodded and he led her by her hand up the white marble steps. "I'll have to ask you to forgive my staff; they aren't expecting me. Normally they would be here to greet you and welcome you to the house properly, but I assumed you wouldn't be too offended," he told her.

"Oh, no, of course not. We needn't be so formal," she said. "It's just me, Mister Vervain."

Theo gave a small chuckle.

"Speaking of which, why don't you start calling me Theo?" he asked. "I'd like to think that we're close enough now to drop the formalities between us, don't you think so?"

"Oh — I ah — just didn't want to presume," she stammered.

"I know, you're very sweet," Theo assured fondly. "Now come on, I want to show you the place."

"Okay," she agreed.

Moonstone was a sight to behold. The house was massive, with at least twenty bedrooms (less than half the size of the Vervain estate in Kingsborough, Theo informed her). Juniper, of course, had always heard of large houses like this but had never actually been in one herself. Houses like this usually came with parties of appropriate size, and she had no interest in embarrassing herself on such a large scale.

He showed her the library, the dining hall, the drawing room, and the music room. After that, he escorted her to the dining room window and showed her the many horses that peacefully grazed in the pasture and the spacious stables outside.

She met the butler and the matron of the house who kept the facilities running smoothly when the family was away for most of the year. The matron was a stout, full-bodied woman who appeared to be in her sixties or seventies. Her build, Juniper thought, resembled the pleasant curves and roundness of a tea pot and her wardrobe was similarly colored in pale blues, lilacs, and crisp, starched whites.

The butler was perhaps her opposite, standing near six and a half feet tall with the twiggy proportions of a scarecrow. Only, he had the poise of a prince and shapely calves — perhaps a rider?

"Allow me to introduce our butler, Mister Oakmoss and the matron of the house Missus Poirier," Theo said as he brought her over to where the two stood with surprised expressions. "Missus Poirier, Mister Oakmoss, this is the lovely Juniper Harlow. The daughter of father's old compatriot, Rowan Harlow."

Juniper blinked up at Theo. Theo's father and her father were friends? She'd never heard of such a thing. Before she had a chance to ask about it, however, the current of conversation swept her away.

"Master Theo!" the matron exclaimed as they approached. "I had no idea you were to pay a visit today. And with such a lovely young lady to boot! Don't tell me you're finally on the marriage market."

Juniper's stomach flipped at the mention of marriage, but she found herself distracted as she witnessed what she thought might be the faintest hint of a flush on the edge of Theo's cheek bones. He smiled, then. Perhaps the first true smile she had seen since meeting him as it actually reached his eyes.

"Missus Poirier has been invested in my marriage prospects since I was in swaddling," Theo explained. "Forgive her."

"And what else is there to be invested in since my own chicks have flown the coop?"

"Are you here for long, Master Theo?" Mister Oakmoss asked. "I can see to having your horses saddled; we can go for a ride."

"Before his retirement, Mister Oakmoss was a gifted horseback rider," Theo said as an aside to Juniper. "In fact, he used to race on the track in Kingsborough before they switched the sport to besom riding."

"The young master has an excellent seat. Unfortunate that he prefers his besom to his beasts," the butler said.

Juniper nodded, lost for words as she watched Mister Oakmoss muss Theo's hair only for him to fix it with a warm chuckle.

"You're going to make me regret introducing her to you two. She's going to think I orchestrated this to make me seem especially impressive."

"I'm sure she didn't need us to see that for herself, aye, Miss Harlow?" Missus Poirier asked. "Not hard to see what a dashing and capable young man Master Theo is."

"Truly a prize as a prospect," Mister Oakmoss said.

"And that is *quite* enough of that, thank you very much," Theo said quickly, his flush deepening. "I only wanted to introduce you, but you are intent on embarrassing me so we shall take our leave."

Juniper looked up at him to see, for once, that he actually *was* embarrassed.

Could it be that Theo was like her? That he simply felt the need to comport himself to such an extreme when in unfamiliar circumstances? That he simply felt more at ease when he was among people he knew and loved? Was this what he would be like if she got the chance to get to know him a little better? Warm and humble?

"Come, there's a great deal more to show you," Theo said, his hand on the small of her back.

"Nice to meet you Miss Harlow!" Missus Poirier called as they left the room.

"Must you be so loud?" Mister Oakmoss grumbled.

"How else are they going to hear me?" she retorted.

The sounds of bickering continued as they made their way out of the room. The sun was hanging low in the sky by the time they finished their tour.

Juniper had mentioned that perhaps it would be smart to start their return trip home when Theo put a hand up to quiet her. "There is just one more spot I'd like to show you before we head back. I saved it for last," he said.

Leading Juniper down long corridors covered in rows and rows of family portraits — all of them golden-haired dignitaries — they eventually arrived at a seemingly plain set of double doors.

"It's through here," he said, releasing Juniper's hand to grasp the handles of each door and open them wide.

Juniper smelled it first. The intoxicating song of thousands of blooms joining together in one of nature's finest perfumes. She thought for a moment that the room was filled with essences; that was until Theo stepped aside to let her walk in.

Past the door was an enormous solarium, nearly twice the size of her greenhouse in the village. The walls of the room were draped in an array of vibrant roses, with each petal carefully arranged in an intricate pattern. Deep reds, vivid yellows, and gentle pinks cascaded over the walls, the floor, and even the ceiling, creating a breathtaking display of color and life. Juniper stepped into the room and was immediately struck by warmth, as if summer had enveloped her. She couldn't help but gape at the vibrant colors that seemed to swirl around her, as if she had stepped into a fine painting.

Devoid of words, all she could do was step in and turn in place, taking it all in.

"What do you think?" Theo joined her at her side as he sought her opinion.

"It-it's amazing, Theo. I've never seen anything like this in my life." she sighed in awed reverence. "I've never smelled such fragrant roses."

"I'm glad that you like it," he said calmly as he stepped ahead of her and looked back at her. He looked perfect, framed by all the flowers behind him. "It's going to be yours."

Juniper's expression shifted from one of awe to one of confusion. *What could he possibly mean by that?*

His meaning became earth-shatteringly clear a moment later when he reached into his pocket and pulled out a small velvet box. All the color drained from her face as he opened it and revealed an expertly crafted golden ring. It was molded in the shape of a serpent with a glinting, rainbow opal wedged uncomfortably in its unhinged jaw.

That same old rope slinked around her ribcage and cinched so tightly that she couldn't take in a single breath, let alone *say* anything.

"My parents have given me this estate to use as a family home when I finally meet my future wife," he said, not flinching at her sudden tautness. "There is a portal in the magistrate building we visited earlier. I would be able to work in Kingsborough while my wife manages the household here."

Her heart squeezed painfully as she stared down at the ring.

"I think I've finally found the woman meant to fill that role," he said.

Had he even asked her parents? Did they allow her to come out with him to be blindsided by this unorthodox proposal? So far from home and so at his mercy. She needed to find a way to say no. How could she say no without angering him to the point where he just left her here to find her own way home? Was she even sure she wanted to say no? Thoughts raced through her. The edges of her vision began to darken, vignetting the ostentatious ring sitting in the small velvet box. She needed to get air in her lungs, she had to breathe.

She had to get out of there.

Juniper felt disconnected from her body as it twisted to turn away. She just needed to find a place to stop and sit. She needed a place to just . . . find five things.

But before she could get far, Theo's hand flashed out and grabbed the soft flesh of her upper arm, painfully. She winced and hissed a sharp breath in, the shock of being stopped setting her heart and lungs back in rhythm as she looked up at him.

When he met her gaze, his eyes were stony and hard. There was no sparkle in those indigo eyes — no stars — only endless night. She drowned in that glassy, bitter stare.

"Don't you dare," he warned with heavy authority. "Don't you dare embarrass me in my own home, Juni."

Juniper's swallow was loud and dry. His face became a blur.

"I will take responsibility for surprising you, but it's unacceptable for a young lady who is the daughter of a celebrated war hero to run off like some petulant child. It's just a marriage proposal. You needn't act like I'm a villain. And you should think about how your actions impact the reputation of your family," he scolded.

"W-what?" Juniper stammered.

"Don't you think it would be shameful for a woman of your age to turn down a smart match? Think of how it might look for the daughter of your father to turn down the most eligible bachelor in all of Kingsborough. How must he be raising you, to think so highly of yourself that you'd turn down the second most powerful family aside from the royal family itself?"

Juniper's chest heaved as the world shifted on a tilt.

Theo's eyes were focused on her, his gaze heavy and unrelenting. She couldn't look away from him. She couldn't escape.

His hand loosened and stroked from her upper arm down to her wrist where he lifted and turned her hand over. She watched numbly as he closed the velvet box and placed it in the center of her palm and then curled her fingers closed over the box.

"Think on it," Theo uttered. "Solstice is coming. I'll expect your answer by then."

Cold Water

Juniper had been a ghost since her day with Vervain. She could hardly find sleep after his proposal. That night, it was all she could do to turn over the entire scene repeatedly. She was utterly haunted by the choice laid out in front of her.

Never in her wildest dreams would she have thought that Theo had been doing all this to court her, but looking back over their interactions, she supposed she was being dense. After all, why else would a young man visit a young woman with such regularity and have such strong opinions about how she presented herself?

Her nerves were worn so thin that she had been up out of bed three times to be sick, losing even the small dinner that she had managed to eat.

Theo hadn't expanded on his meaning when it came to the reputation of her father. Would she really look arrogant if she turned him down? Would her father really face repercussions over something as trivial and silly as a marriage proposal? Why would what she did matter, anyway? She wanted to ask someone — her mother, her father? But doing so would give the situation away.

She knew that her parents would never force her to do something she didn't want to do, especially something so . . . permanent. But she had to think about more than her own happiness in this scenario. If her father's professional life was truly in peril by refusing Theo's proposal, it wouldn't only impact her mother and father, it would impact Ollie, too.

Oleander was just beginning his life as a trained sorcerer — if she stripped away the stability of his home life for something as trivial as a marriage proposal, it was quite possible that his career would be squandered. Juniper would have misled him for a second time; first by seducing him with the study of herbal remedies, then by ruining all his chances of success by destroying her own father's reputation.

Her head spun as she retched into the toilet yet again, sweat beading on her brow and drenching her nape. Her mouth was bitter with the taste of bile and guilt as she panted and reached up to pull the flusher. She sat back against the lavatory wall and wiped at the corners of her mouth as she tried to calm the churning of her empty stomach. Her eyes closed, but the room continued to spin, feeling more like she was on a boat in a stormy, turbulent sea.

She just wanted Oleander to come take care of her. She needed the comfort of hearing that everything would be okay, that she wasn't going to crush her family's success, and by extension, the wealth and wellness of so many others in the village that relied on their flow of money into the local economy. Her pulse pounded in her ears as her stomach began to lurch again, she tried to inhale slowly and calm herself, but it wasn't working.

She needed Oleander.

Her stomach decided to rear its ugly head again, and she was once more bent over the toilet, stomach fighting to empty itself more than it already had. In her exhausted haze, she thought she felt the brush of gentle hands in her hair. A ghostly touch gathered up her hair, removing the weight and burden of it from her sweat-drenched neck. Her head slumped against the toilet and as her head cleared, she realized that the sensation wasn't just a fever dream. A broad hand smoothed over her back in soothing circles, the light fabric of her shift clinging to her body, damp with sweat. Her eyes opened drowsily and found Oleander looking at her with open concern. Pale blue eyes flicked over her wordlessly as he silently fretted.

"*Ollie*," Juniper rasped.

"I heard the pipes," he said gently. "Are you alright, Juni?"

She didn't know how to answer that; she didn't want to lie — but she couldn't tell the truth either.

"Open the window?" she wheezed.

"Of course."

Oleander stood after a few more lingering strokes of his hand, going just behind her to open the bathroom window to the cool winter air waiting outside. The air gusted in insistently, rolling over her feverish body like a wave of fresh river water. Juniper heaved a soothed breath, eyes fluttering.

"Thank you," she coughed.

Oleander returned to her side and stroked over her back once again. Her heavily hooded eyes opened and rested on him. He was in his gray sleeping clothes; she couldn't remember the last time she had seen his pajamas. Was it the night Daisy stayed? Why did that feel like so long ago? So far away?

"I'm sorry for waking you," she said.

"I wish you'd done it sooner. How long have you been at it?"

"A few hours, I think."

"Moon above, Juni," he breathed with an emphatic pet of her hair, "you don't always have to handle things alone."

"It's not an ailment. I am having a horrible night with my

nerves. I know that there's no recourse, so it didn't seem wise to wake anyone to help me when there is nothing to be done."

"Pish, we can at least help you get through it; cold air, cool compresses, water," he said in light chiding.

"Water sounds lovely," she said.

"I'll be back with some in a moment."

His hand lingered on her back as he got to his feet and quietly padded away.

She slowly got herself back to rights and leaned against the wall of the lavatory again. The gentle breeze blowing in from the open window cooled her feverish body and made her shiver slightly. Already the churning in her stomach was beginning to quell. Knowing that Oleander would return soon and stay with her was proving to be the treatment she so desperately needed.

He returned with a tall glass of cold water from the tap — the water was kept from freezing by smart plumbing and simple charms, unlike the summer when there was need to cool it with magic — a light fog of condensation clung to the glass as he handed it to her.

"Small sips. Don't want to be making yourself sick again," he fussed in a quiet tone.

The sensation of the water running over her aching throat was heaven. She sighed, relieved as that coolness spread through her chest and stomach.

Oleander gave her a tender glance. "Are you chilly?"

"Yes, a bit."

He went back to her bedroom and grabbed a light blanket he knew she favored, returning to drape it over her before sitting next to her on the ground. He looked sidelong at her. "So, what do you find yourself worrying about?"

He didn't ask in a particularly worried or demanding way. It was asked the same way one might ask someone their preferred beverage, or their opinion on some far-removed controversy. That was the nice thing about Oleander, he didn't really pry. He simply opened the door and allowed someone to choose to step through or not. Part of her wanted to open the can of worms and spill out all of its contents. But she knew that if she did, Oleander would tell her not to worry about the consequences of refusing the betrothal offered to her. He would always put her own comfort above the comfort of anyone else, including himself.

"I'm just getting nervous about the Solstice celebrations. I haven't gone in the last couple of years," she lied.

"Ah, I see." He paused briefly. "What are you worried will happen?"

Juniper closed her eyes and pulled her blanket up to her chin. She heaved out a shuddering breath, a remnant of her earlier frantic tears that had given way to her fits of vomiting. "I suppose— I just don't want to impact the family's good standing by making a fool of myself," she said. "Mister Vervain seems fairly intent on spending most of the rite with me. He has such high expectations, and I'm constantly worried about meeting them."

She realized as she said it that those sentiments were honest. She really did feel as though she had to keep a sort of performance going with Theo. Even though she knew the steps to the dance, it was exhausting all the same to continue dancing.

Ollie's mouth tightened and his eyes narrowed. "Blast him, you needn't spend any time with him that you don't wish to," he retorted. "We could always play the game like old times."

The comment about old times brought a smile to her lips. Oleander and his protective nature. She adored it. "Another full dance card before the festivities even begin?" she teased.

"No other way to do it," he joked back. "I bet even Daisy would assist in the conspiracy."

Juniper gave a weak chuckle and tilted her tired head to look at him. Oleander really did have the uncanny ability to calm her worries. Talking so casually, so candidly, made her feel for a moment that her world wasn't constricting around her, threatening to crush her.

"I have the feeling that we won't be able to be so sneaky," she sighed.

Oleander's face fell as he looked down at her solemnly.

"Juniper," he muttered, the quiet sound drawing her focus back up to his eyes. "You know you have a say in these things. I know that you're as gentle as a summer breeze, but that doesn't mean that you must take whatever is handed to you."

"He hasn't done anything to warrant me rejecting his company or his invitations," Juniper replied.

"He doesn't have to *do* anything. You're your own person, hm? You could just dislike his pompous attitude and that would give you just cause to refuse his company!"

"That's not becoming of a young lady," she said, swatting at him weakly.

"Juniper, I mean it." Oleander sobered, his brows tensing slightly over those pale blue eyes. They were more fire than ice in his intensity. "The only requirement for not doing something is that you simply don't want to do it. If you don't want to talk to someone, if you don't want to go somewhere — that's a Moon-given right. Don't let anyone, not even Mr. and Mrs. Harlow, convince you otherwise."

Juniper's brow rose gently, and she bit her lower lip to keep it from trembling. She dipped her head lower and tried to soothe the ache in her chest. He made it sound so easy, so simple. It made her want to storm out in nothing but her shift and tromp up to the Hawthorne's hilltop home, bang on the door, and throw that blasted serpentine ring in Theo's face.

But she knew it couldn't be that simple. Not with so many people standing to be affected by that selfish choice.

"My sweet girl," Oleander cooed before lifting a hand to smooth down her sweat-dampened hair, "You believe me, don't you?"

"I do," she replied wetly. "I'll do what I can to spend as much of that night with you as possible, Ollie."

Tears stung her eyes as she finished that promise in her mind. It would likely be the last Solstice she would ever have with him.

Just Nerves

Oleander stayed with her until she managed to fall asleep against the wall. Luckily, she seemed to have calmed her nerves down, if only for now. She'd done no more retching after he'd gotten her through the last of it.

After getting her back in bed and closing the window in her lavatory, he returned to his own bedroom. He couldn't find sleep again, however; he was far too busy worrying about Juni. He had the itching feeling that there was something she wasn't telling him. He had seen her in many different states of distress, but none so bad as it seemed to be tonight. Never had Juni made herself ill from nerves before, not even for the rituals she dreaded most. What could be going on, and why would she be keeping it from him? That question kept him tossing and turning the rest of the night.

He continued fretting about it long after he rose for the morning, distracted by it as he prepared his tea. Perhaps . . . it was just that she was feeling too sick to explain the complicated bits about what she was feeling nervous about? He would just ask again when she was awake — ask her if there was something she hadn't divulged the night before.

Juniper finally came down around noon. She looked pallid but was at least well rested. Oleander joined her in the kitchen as she shuffled to fetch herself some tea. She didn't immediately notice his presence, though the energy coming off of her was so heavy. Something was definitely wrong.

He watched her do every task in preparing a cup of tea in slow motion. She got her cup. *Pause.* Prepared a sachet of tea. *Pause.* She seemed lost in a daze. Finally, when she seemed to forget that she needed to boil water in a kettle for three straight minutes, Oleander inhaled.

"Juni?" he intoned.

She stiffened slightly and turned to look at him. "Oh, good morning, Ollie," she mumbled.

His heart squeezed painfully. "You've been a ghost since you came home yesterday," he broached. "Won't you tell me what's going on?"

"It's the same as last night," she responded with a false smile. "Just nerves about Solstice."

"Is that really all it is? What's different this year than other years? Does it have to do with Vervain?"

Her mask fell at the mention of Theo, but Juniper shook her head.

"It's just Solstice. I promise."

Why was she lying? Why wasn't she telling him what was wrong? Juniper was always such an open book with him, so what had changed?

Maybe it was Vervain, but maybe not in the way he'd assumed. He knew about the day in Adonshire; that they had taken an outing there by themselves, though the particulars of how it went had not been shared. It would be just like Juniper to drive herself mad with guilt over something she decided she wanted.

The idea that she may have actually been charmed by Theo made him want to break things, but hadn't he decided that he would support Juniper in anything that would make her happy? Even if that very thing would break his heart?

He needed to focus. Juniper was his highest priority. If she didn't want to fess up just yet, he would simply need to be patient and dutiful until she wished to. You didn't wrench open a bud to make it flower.

So, he, as always, would have to wait.

Patience was something he'd needed to learn, studying herbalism. Its workings were often slow and subtle. But he had always admired that patience in Juniper and wished to emulate it in himself.

Unfortunately, no matter how much he tried to talk himself down over the course of the day with centering thoughts, nothing seemed to quite calm him. The tension was palpable and only seemed to grow by degrees in each passing second. He found himself often looking at Juniper, reflexively willing himself to somehow divine the answer she was keeping from him. At times, his mind devolved into miniature arguments with himself; those thoughts turned into a debate hall throwing around speculation and evidence.

And no matter how gently he approached her, or how often he shot concerned looks her way, all she seemed to do was avoid him. Conversation was thin and stilted. It almost sounded like how she spoke to *other* people, the ones that set her on edge. What had he done to make her afraid of his attention? They had been getting on so well. She even bid him to go home from the store by early afternoon. Juniper said it was because there was little left to do that day and he should go and enjoy his time elsewhere, but he had a horrible ache in his gut that she was pushing him away for a reason.

As much as he wanted to fight the issue, he merely contested that she should be the one to go home and rest, on account of how she had gotten the least sleep between the two of them last night. That remark seemed to rattle her slightly, but at least she accepted the terms and went home.

He was left alone at the shop, seeing as Daisy was at the Harlows' that day, sketching and painting in the greenhouse. The artist had attested that she needed to be immersed in inspiration to redo a tricky portion of the mural. She had said that it was a common occurrence, with a piece this large and involved, to find yourself realizing things that needed to change as you went along.

So, he was left with no one to talk to, no customers to service yet, and small chores to finish up. Nothing at all demanded *all of* his faculties, so the tedium left him to only worry away without anything productive to occupy his thoughts. After losing much of the night's sleep to the same intrusive thoughts, he felt the fatigue in his mind. It was worse than running on only a few hours of rest during the height of exam season, because at least then the labor was in *knowing* the answers.

He encountered Daisy on the trek back home, though he did not have the energy to do more than give brief greetings as they momentarily crossed paths. She cast him a worried look, but frankly, Oleander hadn't the patience to indulge her fussing or needling right now. She would just tell him to mind himself and be patient.

And Moon's mercy, he was trying.

Dinner felt excruciating, even though on the surface it was acceptably mundane. Mr. and Mrs. Harlow mostly carried the conversation, though they shared some subtle looks after reserved replies from Juniper, or Oleander, who was switching from glowering at his roast beef to tersely smiling and making an acceptably polite response.

After dinner, he announced that he would be going out for an evening flight, waving off Mrs. Harlow's concern for the late hour. He tried not to get hung up on how Juniper didn't seem to react in any way to his plans for good or ill, but it was difficult. She was normally so fussy about him — border line overbearing sometimes — especially with her fear of heights that she tended to project onto others.

He even hovered, repeating his goodbyes a few times.

Nothing. Not even a glance spared his way.

And the worst part of it? The worst part was that the late flight didn't do a single thing to calm his fears. Once arriving home, he still barely slept. Spending the night tossing and turning, too aware of every little creak and ache of the house, hoping Juniper would come knock on his door late in the night and confide in him.

She didn't though, and he was left only to suffer.

Velvet Box

Winter Solstice grew near, and each dwindling day filled Juniper with even more dread.

Oleander clearly sensed her anxiety; he seemed to know that something was wrong. It was everything she could do to simply comport herself and insist that she was fine, just recovering from the night of little sleep a few days prior. She could tell that Oleander knew that wasn't all that was wrong. It twisted her gut in a knot to see his worried gaze. It felt like betrayal to be in so much distress and keep it from him. The further betrayal, she realized as the hours ticked on, was that she would likely have to crush her dearest friend if she decided to accept Theo's proposal.

Her mind often drifted to the engagement ring that sat on top of her vanity, that golden serpent coiled its way around her heart and constricted so tight sometimes that she felt like it might stop altogether.

How could she go about telling Oleander what was going to happen? How could she go about telling him the impossible price that would be paid either way? She wasn't so full of herself that she believed she was worthy to marry Oleander, but she also didn't want to hurt him by accepting another man's proposal while he still claimed to be so in love with her. Regardless of whether she felt deserving of his affections, she had no interest in breaking the man's heart. But perhaps his feelings were changing, with how he had been acting lately. She had always told herself, and told him, that he would one day see that she was not worthy of the high praise and affection he always laid upon her.

Though, from the way her gut twisted and drew her towards despair, had she really been prepared for his mind to change? She felt a wretched hypocrite, not wanting the pressure of his high esteem but anguishing over the absence of his sweetness.

Due to her preoccupation, she had unconsciously pulled away from Oleander — from everyone, truly. Hour after hour passed, and often, by the time the sun had set, she hadn't even realized the whole day had passed her by. Unbeknownst to her, Oleander was watching her. Gauging her. In the greenhouse, at the dinner table, he continued to try to work out exactly what was bothering Juniper.

This had all started from a singular place, one buried seed of secret unhappiness, and he would either dig his way to it or dig his own grave if it meant she would be happy again. It was a maddening exercise that had been wearing him down for days; his mind desperately pacing over and over through every possible reason she was secretly nursing such misery and hiding it even from him.

He wanted to trust her when she told him it was merely a spell of fatigue after a bad night's sleep. But he had seen her fatigued and never had it manifested in such a manner. Something was horribly wrong; he felt it in his gut and in the intuitive tickle at the nape of his neck. It ate him alive to have her hide from him. It was a vicious cycle of denial, his patience becoming so thread-bare that each moment was a challenge of composure.

It was after dinner a couple of days before Solstice that he could no longer take the way things were. A horrible pit of dread settled heavily in his stomach; he was worried for her — worried for himself. This rift was summoning a side of him that he desperately wished to put to bed. All he needed was for Juniper to tell him the truth, and he could comfort her as he always did, and all would be well.

Oleander felt like a dog scratching at her door, but in his mind, she left him no choice in her insistence on shutting him out. He didn't want to bring the matter to anyone's attention at the dinner table, but once Juniper had fled back out to the greenhouse after not touching the food on her plate, he followed close on her heels.

She seemed to be unaware of him, even as he called after her.

He had to pick up his pace to catch up to her, and in his desperate effort to stop her, he reached out for her upper arm. He grabbed the fleshy part of her arm, perhaps a little too hard.

"Juni! Wait, wha—"

He didn't get the rest of his sentence out before Juniper spun to face him. Her eyes were wild and wide, and in the momentum from her spin, she brought her hand across his face in a vicious strike, offsetting the angle of his chin with the force of it.

The slap stung, but it wasn't something he couldn't take. More than anything, he was shocked at the uncharacteristic violence that came from a girl who was usually so gentle and kind. His head turned to look at her again, and he saw in her face that she was also shocked by what she had done.

He watched as she first looked at him in horror, her eyes frantic and fearful. That expression developed from fear to realization, her eyebrows dipping and curving, her lips falling into a saddened grimace. Finally, he watched as her eyes brimmed with tears and spilled them out.

His heart broke as he watched her slowly crumple apart in front of him. It was as if she had been incased in ice and the shock of the blow cracked it down its center and now she was bursting, leaking out at that fissure.

"Ollie — Ollie, I—" she stammered shakily.

She jerked against his grasp, and his hand tightened despite his worry it would worsen things, desperate to keep her from fleeing him again.

"Juniper, please!" he begged. "Please just tell me what's wrong."

She seemed to further fall apart in his hand, knees buckling. His other hand joined the first to support her sinking weight.

"I can't," she wept. "If I do, I won't be able to do it."

"Do *what*, Juni? Just tell me what's happening!"

"*I can't,*" she cried.

Something rose in him, some desperate emotion that made his hands tighten on her. "Juniper, don't do this to me. Don't shut me out," he growled giving her a firm jostle. "Not now, not ev—"

"Ollie—" she whimpered, "s-stop. I—"

There was a sound that jarred them both from their focus.

A loud *tack* sounded against the steppingstones, followed by another clacking sound and a skitter against the gravel by Oleander's feet.

Both of their gazes fell upon the object and Oleander's eyebrows knit together.

Juniper was frozen as he released her and knelt down to pick up a small, velvet box. She watched him stand and thumb open the box to reveal the ring she had carried and agonized over for days. His brow furrowed further, and his chest rose and fell as he glared down at the golden serpentine ring in its nest of blue silk.

"What is this, Juni?" he asked, even though his mind was already in the works of answering it.

"Oleander—"

"Did that — did he—" his voice built as a roiling anger boiled the blood in his veins. "Did that pompous, preening bastard propose to you?"

Juniper only trembled, either from the cold in the air or from her fearful response to his growing rage. The silence was answer enough.

Oleander's skin felt too tight over his muscles and bones. His jaw clenched painfully as he smashed the small box shut with a loud snap. He turned on his heel and stalked away from her, leaving the girl standing in the middle of the frozen night.

Violent Delights

Oleander didn't remember his flight to The Cradle. His mind was racing with a thousand thoughts. He didn't even know why he went to the lounge, something in his gut, he supposed. Intuition could be a funny thing.

His didn't fail him, he realized, as he entered. It took no time at all to scan the room and find an uncommon head of golden hair. His rage flared hotter seeing Vervain laugh easily with his friends, a billiard's stick in hand. He had half a mind to break the thing in half and beat him with it.

Oleander's hand's clenched into tightened fists as he strode with dark purpose toward the man. He was so narrowly focused on his objective that he didn't notice Dante approach him, his vision only widening to include him when his friend's hand grabbed his arm tightly.

Ollie only spared him the briefest glance.

"Whatever you're thinking of doing—" Dante started.

Dante couldn't finish his warning before Oleander jerked his arm away and continued his focused stalk over to Theo, who still laughed at some jest like he hadn't sent a poor girl's world tumbling down in a swirl of chaos. Like he hadn't directly tried to steal away the only thing that Oleander ever truly wanted.

Vervain noticed his approach too late. His face fell in surprise before Oleander ripped the billiard stick out of his hand and viciously backed him into the nearest wall. The art adorning the walls clattered with the force of Oleander's violence; the stick was up in his hands and baring down on the blond bastard. Oleander had much more brute strength than the willowy man did, and it was all he could do to hold the length of wood inches away from crushing onto his windpipe.

"Ambrose!" Dante shouted, trying to wrench him off of Theo.

"You fucking *bastard*," Oleander seethed. "How *dare* you treat her like a trinket to collect."

Theo laughed airily as his eyes narrowed on Oleander. "At least I don't chase after Juni like a desperate puppy," he wheezed.

"Don't you dare call her that. That name is for friends and family only. *Not* indelicate bastards like *you*."

"That's a bit rich coming from an Ambrose bastard," Theo said with a satisfied grin. "Calling me indelicate while you have me cornered like an animal. Talk about pots and kettles."

"You don't know anything about me," Oleander spat, face strained with anger.

"I know enough about your bloodline to venture a guess," Theo laughed.

"Mr. Vervain! Don't say anything more," Dante shouted over the scuffle.

"You're a madman," Oleander told him.

"Am I?" Theo said, sounding ever more unhinged in the adrenaline of the moment, his arms forcing the polished wood further away from his throat. "Madman I might be, but I am also the son of the Captain of the CAC. Maybe no one in this backwards town knows your name, but I do—"

"Theo—" Dante started, "Oleander — stop this, it's not worth—"

"Ambrose is an infamous name in the city, you know."

Oleander's force fumbled and stalled for a moment, the news starting to filter through the internal noise of his own rage.

Theo saw his chance to free himself. He used the lapse in Oleander's monstrous focus to push back against the billiard stick with all his strength catching Oleander off guard and forcing him back one step, gaining the higher ground.

"Oh — you don't know about that, still? Pity. I suppose that the Harlows decided to leave you in the dark."

Oleander's fury died in his stomach. Confusion took its place as the words started to fully sink in. *What was he talking about?*

"They didn't tell you? About that silly memory charm they put on you as a boy? I would have thought you would have spotted the threads of it by now," Theo said with far too much enjoyment. "Here, allow me to assist then—"

"Vervain, *don't you do it*," Dante shouted.

Theo ignored him, pushing hard again on the stick and sending Oleander down to one knee, his sharp white teeth gleamed with a sadistic grin. He was taking pleasure in twisting this knife. "You come from a legacy of violence, Ambrose!" Theo laughed. "A father who killed in the hundreds, and a mother who killed the man she loved to gain access to some sick, twisted cult in Kingsborough."

Some invisible cord snapped somewhere deep in Oleander's psyche. His arms went slack, falling to his sides as a dam of memories burst in his mind and unleashed horror after horror. It was like walking down a familiar corridor in your home and finding a horrible monster in every room.

· · ·

He remembered his father's face, strained with gentle worry as he asked after his mother. He remembered her shouting down the hall as his father lifted his hands to his ears to block the sound out for him.

He remembered the shattering of plates, the tearful pleading of his father to *please, calm down darling.*

He remembered the foreboding hover of his mother in the doorway of the family library, the eerie dullness to her black eyes that reflected nothing, not even the light.

He remembered . . . blood. Sticky and slick beneath his shoes. Chalk lines dissolving under copious amounts of it as his father stared unseeingly at him on the ground.

He'd heard her coming — heard the muttering and giggling. He'd thought to hide, but then he only ran.

Ran and ran until he couldn't even tell where he was. He'd hidden behind barrels and crates, slept under moldering stoops.

He'd vanished until he was found by some faceless man. And then there were trains and trees.

And then the Harlows.

Nothing was untouched. Nothing was unaffected. His entire life . . . everything he thought about himself felt . . . false. Felt like some humiliating farce. He was distantly aware of a force on his chest. He looked down and registered Vervain's fine snakeskin shoe just before it shoved him fully back on the ground.

"Is that the kind of violence Juniper deserves to be associated with? Does she deserve the name of a murderer?"

"That's enough, Vervain," Dante said with a finality so heavy that it made the entire room silent. Theo's eyes lifted from Oleander and he smoothed his hair back, the golden locks having been disheveled in the scuffle.

"Get out," Dante seethed.

"If you think—"

"Get out before I make you sorry that you ever came here," Dante demanded again.

Theo grew quiet, staring at Dante. Gauging him.

Dante's pupils were needle thin in his golden irises, his hands had grown horrible claws at the ends of his fingers — those fingers stained the deepest black, like he had soaked them in ink.

Theo scoffed with a shake of his head, throwing the billiard stick off to the side with no care for who or what it struck. It knocked a few glasses off the table, sending them shattering so loudly that it made Oleander flinch. The sound cut through his mind, as though some twisted mummer's cue for his own fracturing psyche.

Theo left the establishment; a horrible silence settled in his wake.

Dante got down to one knee and put a clawed hand on Oleander's back. He looked more like a frightened little boy than the day he'd arrived in the village.

Oleander's glassy, terrified eyes broke from their thousand-mile stare to look into Dante's.

"Ambrose—" Dante started with a soothing tone.

"You *knew*—" Oleander immediately accused, voice churning with fury and sorrow.

Dante's expression fell into one of deep regret.

"Oleander, it wasn't my information to share. I couldn't go against the decision of the ones providing for you," Dante soothed. "I would have been here the moment Mr. and Mrs. Harlow—"

"It wasn't their secret to keep," Oleander wept, tears spilling down his face. His entire world was shattering around him. The people he knew, the people he trusted most had lied to him his entire life. Nausea churned in his gut — his chest constricted painfully. He tore at his collar, popping two buttons off.

He needed to go.

Oleander stumbled to his feet, finger hooking and ripping at the ascot he wore around his neck. He gained momentum, running clumsily out of the door. His body came against some resistance, thudding into a person, he realized. He stumbled a few steps back to see Juniper looking up at him with reddened puffy eyes. All at once, the rage returned. It seared a path through his veins as he looked down at her.

Juniper, who he had always loved and done everything that he could ever fathom to support her. Juniper, who he had pined after and followed around like a guileless little duckling. Juniper, who had known this whole time what he was and rested in the comfort of his not knowing — willingly keeping him in the dark for her *own comfort.*

"Ollie — what's wrong? I saw Theo—"

The name of that golden-haired twit pushed him over the edge. He shoved her out of his way and stalked away.

"Oleander — wait," she begged.

"Don't ever talk to me again, Juniper," he said, turning on her with a palpable loathing in his eyes.

Juniper's own eyes filled with tears once more, mouth trembling.

Then he said words that broke her into a thousand tiny shards.

"I hate you."

Memory Charm

Juniper forgot how to breathe.

It was all she could do to just watch Oleander walk away, his steps heavy but unhurried, like he hadn't just taken the ground from beneath her feet, like he hadn't just ground her heart to paste beneath the sole of his shoe. She watched, detached from her body as he walked not toward home, but to another place — the train station.

She stood there so long that her body started to tremble from the cold, long after Ollie was out of sight. She felt the light sensation of an arm on her shoulders, gathering her with a light but firm grasp.

"Come on, love," Daisy said from somewhere far away. "Let's get you out of the cold."

She felt as if she were drifting in a vast emptiness for an eternity, the only sign of movement being the faint scent of a crackling fire and the addition of a man's deep voice to accompany Daisy's bell-like voice. The sensation of a heavy coat on her shoulders brought her back enough to look upon her surroundings. She took it all in — they were in The Cat's Cradle, it was empty save for Daisy, Dante, and herself.

With the world coming into focus around her, so did the sting of her pain.

Oleander's hateful glare was engraved on the back of her eyelids. Every time she closed her eyes she saw him there, looking spitefully down at her. What had she done? How did she come to earn his scorn?

It was Theo, wasn't it? Juniper's inability to refuse him, the impossible choice she had been left with. Oleander had finally had enough of her weakness. Is that what it was?

She supposed she was worthy of his scorn.

Daisy's hand drew soothing paths over her back as she sat at the empty bar with a steaming cup of tea in her hands. Chamomile and lavender, from the smell of it. A feeble attempt to calm her.

She didn't know how much time had passed, but eventually, her mother and father joined them. She heard Dante speak in hushed tones to her parents but couldn't quite make out what they spoke about. She did, however, catch her mother's gasp followed by a remorseful sob. Juniper looked over her shoulder, back at her parents. Her father was nodding solemnly at Dante while he gently consoled his wife. She was just about to spiral into guilt again when she finally made out something Dante was saying.

"It was only a matter of time before the memory charm broke, Mrs. Harlow. It's just a shame that it had to happen the way that it did."

Juniper's brow furrowed.

"What memory charm?" she asked.

"Why don't I go and try to find Oleander," her father suggested gently, "and you can stay here and explain what's happening to Juni?"

"He went towards the train station," Juniper replied numbly.

"I'll come along with you," Dante said.

Mr. Harlow hurried on assured feet into the chill of the winter night, Dante following suit.

Once the two men took their leave her mother sat next to her but remained quiet for some time. Juniper found that she didn't have the energy to grill her mother on whatever had happened. Her heart was still sore from Oleander's brazen hatred.

Daisy gently rubbed circles over Juniper's back as she idly tapped on her teacup, looking down into the floating bits of tea leaves that were suspended in the honey-colored liquid. Juniper's tea had cooled in her glass by the time her mother finally spoke.

"When your father and I heard that Oleander had been found after going missing for several months, it seemed like an obvious choice to bring him here," she said. "I don't know if you remember that time . . . we'd sent you to stay with a tutor in the Ash Forests." She twiddled her thumbs. "Oleander was wild, almost feral, when we arrived. He would fight and bite and run away. He was terrified of us, terrified of everything," she continued. "Naturally, we were at a loss for what to do. We knew we could care for him and help him heal, but it was near impossible to get close enough to do so. We worried that he would hurt himself, or worse, hurt you."

Juniper's mouth tightened hearing that. Both of those options sounding equally terrible. It would be no worse if she were hurt than if Ollie was.

"During the war, we used memory charms for the people who had seen the worst of the violence," Mrs. Harlow said. "We knew that Oleander had seen things — things that most grown adults would balk at. So, while it was questionably ethical, we decided to temporarily block those painful memories in his mind. We had only intended to do so until he was adjusted to the village and *to you*." Her voice became warmer. "But when he came, you gravitated to him so readily, and we saw you become stronger for him. We saw you be brave for the first time in your little life, and when he finally started to speak, we saw him rise to the occasion of protecting you. We didn't want to see either of you regress, not when you were doing so well together, and not when we saw confidence bloom." Mrs. Harlow sniffed and dabbed at her wet eyes with her black handkerchief.

Juniper's mind combed over old memories, not seeing them at the same vantage that her mother did. But she had been so young when he arrived, only barely learning how to process emotions at all. Perhaps that's why she didn't realize the difference. She only knew that she adored the connection to Oleander from the moment he arrived. They had become fast friends in that first year, even when he was selectively mute.

"He must have thought I knew," Juniper said in a near whisper.

"Why do you say that?"

"He told me to never talk to him again. He said he hated me." The words fell out of her mouth with unfeeling numbness.

Mrs. Harlow looked horrified, the guilt-stricken expression returning to her face.

"What did you . . . make him forget?" Juniper asked.

Her mother looked down at her hands where she fiddled with her handkerchief.

"We don't know exactly; we *can't* know everything he went through. But the reports from the CAC speculated that he may have been there when his mother . . . murdered his father. There was likely other abuse and atrocities leading up to that," she said.

Nausea rose into Juniper's throat at the thought of him being exposed to such cruelty as a little boy. And now, all those memories were spilling into his mind at the rate of a churning flood, and he was facing it all alone. She wished she had been a little more functional when he had told her he hated her. Maybe then, she could have stopped him. Now she might never have the opportunity to make it right. She may never be able to repay him for all the support that had given to her throughout the years.

Quiet settled between them. Daisy's hand still smoothed over Juniper's shoulders, and though she couldn't express appreciation, it did a lot to keep her grounded in reality. She didn't know how much time had passed before her father and Dante returned. Juniper spun around, her heart sinking when she only saw the two men. Her father inhaled breathlessly and confirmed her worst fears.

"He's gone," he said with numb finality. "He left a note at the ticket office."

Juniper's brows twitched faintly, her heart lighting up with hope — maybe he had calmed down enough to tell them where he would be going.

"What does it say?" she asked.

Her father approached her and handed her the small piece of parchment, an advertisement for the circus on the back of it.

"I am going to Kingsborough to learn the truth about myself. If any of you follow me, I will never forgive you."

Juniper's fingertips gently traced over the pen strokes, sensing the rage within them. The strokes were heavy — so heavy in some spots that they tore through the page.

She would have to find some way to be okay, she realized.

She would have to find some way to live a life without Oleander.

Kingsborough

Oleander seethed the entire way to the city.

It was a lot to process, both the information and the suppressed rage that filled him upon learning about his bruised and mottled history. The hours between the late night and the dawning of the new day were spent compartmentalizing his emotions. There were memories, yes. But it was as if they were all mixed in a giant cauldron and he was extracting each individual ingredient, one at a time.

He was so exhausted by the time the sun made itself visible, but there was no hope of sleep in sight. He simply sat slumped in his chosen seat on the train and watched the scenery pass by outside the window, trying not to wonder what Juniper would think of it — what questions she'd ask him.

Something painful twisted in his heart. He couldn't reconcile the idea of that gentle, kind girl with her deception. The shock and sadness on her face haunted him, but he shouldn't feel bad.

He couldn't.

They had all lied to him. His entire life with them was one

giant lie. Still, as he sifted through the wreckage of his psyche, he couldn't place the blame on Mr. and Mrs. Harlow for trying. There was so much that happened in his childhood that he had no understanding of. But now, as he processed it all again, he could make sense of that child's feelings with the maturity and intellect of a young man.

Theo's summary of events wasn't entirely right. That didn't come as a shock to Oleander. That fiend loved to twist narratives.

It was a steady decline into madness, for his mother. His father had tried to keep the darkness at bay for him, he now realized. He'd concealed worrying conversations beneath fond looks and gifts. Days that his mother would truly go beyond the limit of what was acceptable became days that he and his father would have an enjoyable day out at the circus or a trip to the besom races in the city. Perhaps his father had seen and committed atrocities during the war, but he had never shown that side to Oleander. With Oleander, he had been warm, and kind, and supportive.

All this time Oleander thought that his understanding of Juniper's unique flavor of mental anguish was just something he innately came upon. He realized as he combed through his past that it was something he learned from his father.

His father, despite his wife's sadistic side, loved Oleander's mother dearly. When she would descend into a frothing rage — rage Oleander now recognized in the way he wanted to hurt Theo only hours ago — his father was the only one who could calm her. The man had been able to soothe that rage in her to quiet, flickering candlelight. It would just be a touch or a calm uttering of her name, and of the rage would drain out of her like compressed steam in a teapot.

It felt bizarre to finally have context for who he was — to remember more than just names or faces. Perhaps some of the blame was on him. Sure, he didn't ask for a memory charm, but he hadn't gone looking for his past either. He had been plenty happy to continue living with the family he'd found in the Harlows. But they could have at least told him about what they had done. They could have at least given him the choice to know or not know. This was his history, after all. This was *his life*. How could a boy become a man with only half of the facts about himself?

He wondered if that was why Juniper's reception of his long-time feelings had been stand-offish at best. Maybe knowing the cruelty he'd come from soured the idea of him as a potential husband.

He wondered now if he had misinterpreted the tears in the garden. Maybe she really wanted to marry that golden-haired buffoon.

Oleander rubbed at his temple, a headache growing there. He needed to stop thinking so hard about this. There was no way he was going to be able to sort this out on a single train ride. He did his best to keep his mind on the landscapes zooming by for the rest of the ride.

When he reached Kingsborough, the sun had already dipped below the horizon and the city glowed with an uncomfortable incandescence from the use of electric lights instead of witch's-fire lamps like the ones they used in the village. Oleander rose on stiff legs and stretched his arms above him before rolling his shoulders. He'd not moved the entire train ride, and he was feeling the effects of that decision. He rigidly trudged off the train into the bustle of Kingsborough. Even at this late hour, the city was alive with noise and chaos. There were so many *people*. It was far more crowded than he remembered, even with Oleander's memories restored.

In his exhaustion it was all a bit overstimulating, the noise, the shouting, the smells. He looked about until he found a ticket office and strode over to it.

"Hello, have you a map of the city?" he asked gruffly.

"Aye," the ticket seller said. "It's going to be fifteen shards, sir."

Oleander reached into his pocket, grabbed his purse, and paid the required funds, sliding the money to the clerk. Oleander was still looking in his purse when the thick folded parchment was given to him. He didn't even think about money. He needed to find a bank. If the Harlows hadn't just cut him off completely, that is. The thought of that made his tongue taste bitter, but he swallowed it down and looked at the clerk.

"Could you tell me where the nearest bank is, sir?"

"Ah, up the avenue and near the city hall. Best hurry though," the clerk answered as he drew a pocket watch from his waist-coat pocket. "They'll be closing soon."

"Thank you," he said, and he was on his way.

He only narrowly made it to the bank in time; in fact, he was nearly turned away at the door when they realized he would be making a withdrawal from a non-local account. But Oleander mustered the energy to use some of that innate charm of his and flashed an imploring smile at the young lady getting ready to bar the door.

"I know, and I'm terribly sorry for putting you out," he said. "But I've only got two stags and a handful of shards, and I need to secure lodging for the night. Believe me that I'd never do this if it weren't for the bind that I'm in, Miss."

The young woman pushed up her glasses and her mouth worked. She looked over her shoulder as if to see if a supervisor was nearby and then looked back at Oleander.

"Come on, then," she said with a bit of haste.

The banking system relied primarily on the energy of ley lines to quickly communicate with one another. The distance between cities and countries could easily be bridged by hitching a ride on the energetic connection between two locations of spiritual significance. He didn't know the details but had found an interest in it while at Conservatory.

"Where will we be withdrawing from, Mister . . ."

Oleander's teeth clenched a bit, but he mastered himself.

"Ambrose. Oleander Ambrose. My branch is in Linseed Village," he said.

The flash of recognition across the girl's face was enough to make him want to throw something, even though she comported herself quickly.

"Just a moment. Let me go make the connection, it won't be long."

The woman stepped away to a table strewn with massive maps of stars and landmarks. He watched as she placed a copper nugget here, a shard of citrine there, and then put her own hands on a copper plate and closed her eyes. Behind her, a quill set to furiously writing figures on a piece of parchment which snaked down from a massive roll affixed to the wall. She relinquished the bond with the ley lines, and she went to the paper and tore off the information required for Oleander's withdrawal.

"So, I found the account, but I'm afraid for you to pull out the money, there is a condition that must be met," she said.

"And what is that condition?" He tried and failed to master his ire.

"Oh, it just requires that you read and acknowledge a message from the primary account holder — a Mister Heywood Harlow?"

Oleander shook his head and put out a hand for the missive, fully prepared to not even skim the message before signing it.

She handed it over and he looked down to sign, only for his eye to get caught on one particular sentence — really, a particular name.

"Spare Juniper your anger. She knew as much about the memory charm as you did."

Curiosity piqued, he decided to read the rest of it.

Ollie,

Mrs. Harlow and I fully intend to support you in your quest to discover more about yourself. We will not seek you out, but please know that we are worried for you all the same.

Your account will remain in your name, and you're welcome to access it to fill any needs that arise while you're in Kingsborough.

Mrs. Harlow and I just ask that you spare Juniper your anger. She knew as much about the memory charm as you did. We didn't want her to accidentally undo it by mentioning something about your history. I regret leaving you both in the dark for so long. I hope that I will one day have the opportunity to apologize properly.

With Love,

Mr. Harlow

The missive did not bring him comfort. If anything, as he signed the bottom of the parchment to prove that he acknowledged the message, fresh anger roiled in him once again. "Here you are," he said somewhat curtly. "I need to withdraw two hundred and fifty stags, please." It was an exorbitant amount, but he wasn't interested in a repeat of this little loophole Mr. Harlow had learned to exploit.

The woman remained silent as she started to thumb out the bills for him. She seemed to have sensed his irritation and had no interest in catching the sharpened edge of it. She stacked the bills and bound them in a bespelled black ribbon, which knotted itself into a meticulous little bow.

"Here you are, Mister Ambrose," she said.

Oleander accepted the stack of money, tucking it neatly into the pocket of his coat, and tipped the brim of his pointed hat as a gesture of gratitude.

"Enjoy your day, ma'am," he said.

"Happy Solstice!"

The holiday greeting made his stomach tighten as he went for the door to exit.

It was supposed to be a happy Solstice. Now it wouldn't be.

Deference

*D*espite the shortened daylight of winter, the time that followed Oleander's departure was long and painful. It was all Juniper could do most days to get out of bed, drink her bespelled tea and climb back into bed. She hadn't returned to her work; it felt as it belonged as much to Oleander as it did to her. Daisy would send word about the progress of the mural and the gallery space in the loft, but Juniper couldn't find the nerve to go see it herself.

The novel she had been reading lay open, its face tented down on her nightstand. She had tried to go back to reading her romance stories, but the idea of love had grown bitter and sorrowful ever since Oleander had left. She couldn't understand why.

A couple of days after Oleander's escape from the village, Theo came to darken their doorstep once more. Juniper was tempted to turn him away when her mother came to fetch her, but the threats to her father's livelihood convinced her otherwise. She got ready as quickly and thoroughly as she could and came to join him for a walk to the bookstore.

Morosely distracted, Juniper didn't notice when Theo asked her a question. She only clued in when he gave her a little bump and jostle of her arm which limply hooked with his.

She looked up at him and blinked.

"What do you think, Juni?" Theo prodded quietly.

"Hm? About what?"

"I asked you a question," he tutted with chastising impatience as they walked past the tailor in town. Seeing the building had brought up thoughts of Oleander walking her there to be fitted for the dress for his party — the dress Ollie said she looked beautiful in.

She looked up to Theo, her hand tightening where it rested on the crook of his arm.

"Oh — of course, I'm sorry. Could you please repeat what you asked?" Juniper requested, with the appropriate amount of chagrin.

"I was asking you what you thought about wearing white to the Solstice rite? We should coordinate," he said.

Ah, that's right. He had been talking to her about attending Solstice together. Another invitation she couldn't refuse despite desperately wanting to.

"It's customary to wear darker colors, isn't it? For the longest night of the year? Usually, you wear whites and yellows and such for the Summer Solstice."

Theo shrugged. "I hardly think it matters. Besides, wearing what everyone else is wearing is droll. If you want to appear posh, it is better to subvert expectations."

She didn't want to wear white for the Winter Solstice. It was the most formal occasion of the year and wearing white would feel far too much like donning a wedding dress. The idea made her feel queasy.

"How about lavender instead?" she asked.

"Eugh, I despise that color," Theo said.

Juniper looked down at her cloak for the day; a thick woolen lavender one with salt and pepper fur trim. She grimaced internally and made a note to take all the lavender out of her wardrobe.

"We'll wear white," he said with a sort of unbudging finality.

"Mm . . . all right," she said, too tired to fight him on it further.

Juniper realized that if they were to get married, this is probably how it would go. They would discuss this or that, and Theo would disagree with her on something, yet she'd yield to him when he insisted. It seemed that she was too meek to assert herself, or maybe she was just too exhausted and defeated to try. It certainly didn't seem to bother Theo, though. No, he seemed quite comfortable in his position as her superior and accepted her deference with absolute pleasure. He would certainly fall into his father's position with a natural command. He fell into it quite easily with her, she thought.

Moon above, she missed Oleander. Being with him was as simple as breathing. She had taken him so much for granted. But he made his feelings very clear. He would never forgive her if she tried to come find him. She knew that she couldn't live in a world where Oleander hated her. She just couldn't do it. Besides, she couldn't navigate Kingsborough on her own. She was too much of a coward for that.

She only had a few more days to give Theo her answer to his proposal; she doubted he would take very kindly to being left behind as she fled to his hometown where she adamantly told him she wouldn't be able to handle the crowds. For her own sake, the sake of her father, and for Oleander, she would need to remain in the village.

"So, have you thought on my offer?" Theo suddenly said.

"I've been thinking on it, yes," she said.

"You can give your answer early, you know. I know some women are sentimental about Solstice, but I'm not," he said.

Her mouth pressed into a forced smile. "I'm afraid I am one of those women," she said.

"Ah," Theo said before looking down at her with that same dangerous charm she had once found exciting. "Keeping me on my toes, are you?" he asked.

Her eyes dipped to her shoes, and she huffed half-heartedly.

Theo patted her hand in a slightly encouraging way as they made their way up the stairs to the bookstore. "You'll come to enjoy it, Juni, being my wife. Down the line, you'll look back at this time, and you'll laugh at the discomfort you put yourself through."

The idea of that seemed unlikely, to say the least.

First things first, the library.

It was where he found so many answers in his school days, after all. He spent much of the morning hours toiling through reference cards and newspaper archives to find every spare scrap he could regarding his family.

What he found was harrowing.

Obviously, the news clippings were relatively sanitized, for the sensibilities of the reader. But he knew the sort of gory truths that lurked behind words that already offended and horrified any sensible soul. He was sorely tempted to destroy one article that featured a photograph of his mother, to keep her from looking at him with hollow, inked eyes. He knew every detail of that face that the printing lacked. The memory of her haunted him every time he closed his eyes.

That article was the first one he put back.

After, he took refuge in a fine café, where he alternated between being a nervous wreck and indulging in what felt like some form of twisted astral projection, a desperate attempt to flee from his troubled mind. Despite not actually finding any respite, he was unable to retire from his investigations for the day. That meant doing more of the same at some other scenic locale, or in his rented bed, waiting for the nightmarish memories to haunt him in his rest.

By the time evening neared, he took to roosting in one of the drinking establishments near his housing. Although he was desperately exhausted, the urgency to confirm the truth gave him the energy to charmingly ingratiate himself into sporadic groups of gentlemen as the night went on. Specifically targeted, of course. They had to be old enough to have recollected the events that transpired in the city when he was a mere boy and of accommodating nature that he could coax them into humoring such grim discussion. He was, of course, just Oliver Winslow, a young man from the far countryside who had heard about those nightmarish times from a neighbor and was just morbidly curious if the old man spoke true.

Some of those conversations were *extremely* difficult to keep character as they spoke in horrified or judicious tones of the misdeeds they had heard of and seen. The closest he had come to truly cracking was when one old veteran spoke with glassy eyes about how he'd seen the now-dead Ambrose husband once, on the battlefield, and the brutality he'd left in his wake.

Oleander had braced to hear every sort of wickedness about his mother. But all he remembered of his father was the kindness of a good man. And it was after that conversation, deep into the night, that he found himself wandering to the bar for a seat of solitude. He was intent on just nursing something to sober up, maybe a bite to eat too, although his stomach was so knotted that he could scarcely bear anything at all other than the beer he'd been drinking alongside his sources.

He was halfway through a cup of cold coffee, blacker than

death and just as bitter, when something so very small went so very wrong. There was something about the tone of the breath of the man slumped on the bar beside him, a sort of heady wheeze—

When a man died like that, he didn't scream. There were no moans or groans or honorable final words. When a man died like that, his lungs caught, his throat locked, and the wind passed through him like a half-broken instrument. There was no dignity or grace or honor in it. That had been how his father had died, staring him in the eyes; perhaps willing his gaze to speak what his dying breath could not.

The ambiance of the bar had turned into a deafening roar. There was a vague awareness that he was sitting but not quite breathing, as though a rope had constricted about him, sapping the life out of his body while his mind was too preoccupied to notice. He wanted to crawl out of his skin, he wanted to scream, he wanted to do literally anything but sit there and stew in this — whatever this was.

But he couldn't move. He couldn't breathe. He *was* breathing, even though he felt like he wasn't. Too much and too little at once, but despite the inhalations into his lungs at such an erratic pace it felt as though he was suffocating. He—

Couldn't breathe.

In the village, perhaps his state of despondency may have been noticed by an amicable neighbor or friend, which could have led them extending their compassion and rousing him from his dolor. But this was Kingsborough, and the courtesy of strangers was often only paid as was expected by politeness. And men losing their minds drinking at a bar was far from an unusual sight; he was just scenery to the other patrons milling and laughing around him.

He needed to breathe.

It was what he always told Juniper, when her body betrayed

her like this. This was exactly the same as her episodes, he realized then.

Just breathe. Deep breaths. In and out. Slow and steady.

His lips twitched in a silent babble. A cold sweat beaded on his pallid face and beneath his collar. He focused on anything. The grains in the wood, the bitterness of the coffee on his tongue as he took a shaking sip.

When that wave of relief finally broke, it was swift as it was sudden. Gone was the tide of panic, leaving in its wake a deep, bone-aching exhaustion that seemed impossible to be the work of such a short period of time. It was as though his body had been held in a state of imminent phantom death for an age, a prison of eternity transpiring over mere moments to those outside of it.

His legs slipped from the stool of their own accord and made for the door, as if they had sensed his need for air that didn't smell of smoke and liquor. He stumbled towards the door, wanting to escape the stifling atmosphere. Once by the lamplit streets, Oleander cast his gaze upwards. He couldn't see the stars very well in Kingsborough. Too many lights. Not like home, where they sprawled out forever.

Mrs. Harlow once told him that the phenomenon was a lesson in its own right. The stars were beacons of brilliance; their vast magnificence incomprehensible, yet appearing so small because of their immense distance. A candle or a streetlight here and there muted them easily but only because they were right there before you. It was easy to miss their radiance when too preoccupied, losing them to the black of the sky.

He missed home. The wide horizons not claimed by mortar; the pure air, the rolling countryside so pleasant to the eye.

He missed Dante, that smug tomcat. His best mate.

He missed Mr. and Mrs. Harlow. The ineffable kindness they had shown him . . . instilled in him.

He missed *Juniper.*

He'd spent two years missing all of it, all of them, and he'd run off when he'd finally earned his return home. It broke his heart, and he felt he'd never deserved any of it. They had been too good for him, always. The blackened bitterness he felt now was the charred remains of a Beltane fire, no more than charcoal.

He had been a burden on those who should have never been touched by someone bearing the weight of such darkness, even by proxy. Though they had betrayed him in their silence, he had never been worthy of their charity. They should have left him here to rot, that way, he would never have hurt Juniper as he had. She would have been better off without him. Lonelier, yes, but he would have never entered her life under false pretenses only to ruin her tenderness forever.

But that was a lie. He knew it was. Though his heart longed to succumb to the depths of despair, he was aware it was simply his own cowardice. Merely the wailing of a mind struggling to join the pieces of himself together and wanting to just choose the easiest option: Out.

But while he was miserable, lonely, and perhaps a bit drunker than he had anticipated being, he couldn't go and find some overlooked cranny in the urban sprawl to huddle in as though a stray animal again. He wasn't going to surrender into lunacy just to avoid facing them again. That was a boorish and idiotic notion he refused to humor, despite the temptation to erase himself from the lives of the people he, truthfully, couldn't bring himself to hate.

What if he got them to reinstate the charm? Would that be possible? Difficult, likely. But he could go back to being little Ollie, go back—

There was no going back, though. It would make him a coward to pretend he was still the Oleander that had only existed with the Harlows. He wasn't either of those boys; not the one before the charm, nor the one after. Going back to how things were was moot, he would only end up here once again and probably have far more to lose by then.

He had no idea who he was. He needed answers — context. Not just hearsay and news clippings.

What he needed was to pay a visit to the source.

He needed to go to the Chaos and Crime Department.

White Dress

A little over a week passed at a breakneck pace before Solstice arrived.

The mood in the house was still as morose as it had been since Oleander left. Juniper supposed everyone had been looking forward to a Solstice with Oleander after two years of him being absent for the holiday.

Everyone tried to make the best of it that they could, though. They needed to trust that Oleander would get what he needed and hopefully come home. All the same, everyone had the same agitated edge to them, making even typical stressors seem bigger than before. The atmosphere was tense and the gaping void that Oleander had left behind was palpable.

The proposal that hung before her was as appealing as a hangman's noose. She supposed that her decision was already quite made for her, wasn't it? Oleander already hated her; he had said as much. She could say yes without the guilt of hurting him or making him hate her more for dashing his hopes and dreams.

So why did it still feel like approaching her own death?

Theo was handsome enough; he was charming when he wasn't extorting her. Maybe he was right, maybe she would come to enjoy the marriage after the ceremony was done.

Only time would tell.

Juniper's mother was helping her get dressed in the absurdly opulent gown Theo had sent her. It was a gift for Solstice, he explained, ordered special from the city.

It really did look like a wedding dress: A high-collared bodice, bespelled to keep its wearer warm in the freezing cold of Solstice night, was crafted from delicate lace; the skirts were heavy and cumbersome, with four layers of fabric in the outer layer; and a long, voluminous train that lifted and floated as the wearer moved, preventing it from becoming muddied.

As her mother worked on pinning her copious hair into a stylish updo, they met eyes in her vanity mirror. Both exchanged smiles that didn't meet their eyes as Mrs. Harlow pinned white crocuses into the folds of her bun.

"Are you excited to attend the rite with Mr. Vervain?" she asked.

Juniper heaved a heavy breath in response. "I suppose," she muttered. She really should have tried to sound more enthused, but Moon above, she was so tired. It was all she could do to just make it through this day.

Mrs. Harlow's brow tensed faintly as she looked down at her daughter's demoralized eyes, staring at the enchanted hairbrush sitting on her vanity.

"Juni," Mrs. Harlow said quietly. "If you don't want to go today—"

"I can't very well refuse this late," Juniper interrupted. "He would be put out."

Her mother finished pinning the final flower and set a hand on each of her shoulders, the weight in them comforting — steadying.

"Darling," she said. "It's easy to get caught up in the expectations of the people around you but remember, at the end of the day, it's you who must live with the choice. Remember that your happiness is no more or less important than someone else's."

Tears stung her eyes, and she fanned at herself lightly with her hand, not wanting to smudge the kohl used to accentuate her eyelashes.

"I thought you wanted me to attend more social events," she said.

"Not if doing so will render you so upset, my dear," Mrs. Harlow said, brows lifting in gentle concern. "Juni, my hopes for you going to more social events were only because I want you to have a full and happy life with wonderful friends to keep you company."

Juniper sniffed and met her eyes in the mirror again. "I thought it was because you didn't want me to be a spinster," she admitted.

"Of course, I would like you to have your own family — not just because I would make a *fabulous* grandmother." She chuckled. "but because when your father and I are gone, an empty home can be terribly sad." It looked as though tears were beginning to accumulate in her mother's eyes, as well. "Juni, your father and I . . . we just want you to be happy, so if you don't want to go today . . ."

The door chime rang then. Theo coming to fetch her, no doubt. Juniper's heart sank gently. This conversation was too late to matter. No matter her mother's wishes, Juniper had stumbled into a predicament that would not be solved with sentimentality. The success of her entire family hinged on the way she answered Theo Vervain's proposal.

Juniper sighed and stood, looking in every way the part of a bride-to-be. She rounded her vanity seat and started to make her way out of the bedroom.

"Wait, Juni—"

Her mother's call for her made her pause and look back.

Mrs. Harlow fiddled with her fingers in the same nervous way that Juniper always did.

"I know that my fussing — I know that I've made you feel as if you have been doing something wrong. That something was wrong with you—"

Juniper looked at her mother and saw herself mirrored there. Nervous. Hedging. Small.

The doorbell chimed again, and Juniper heaved an impatient breath.

"We have to leave," Juniper said. "Let's go have a happy Solstice."

Solstice

Winter Solstice was by far the biggest event of the year in Linseed Village. The entire main street was converted into a large, outdoor festival. It was always formal, like what Juniper imagined it would be like to visit the ballet in a larger city. Everyone wore their finest attire and came together in the spirit of the generosity of the Moon Goddess.

In the center of the festivities was made a grand altar of offerings. Each offering was wrapped in pretty parchment and labeled with the name of the person who had gifted it. At the conclusion of the festivities, the items on the altar would be claimed by the attendees, commencing with the poorest in the village and working up to the wealthiest. This was an attempt to even the odds of the year and provide those with the most need, the opportunity to possess something finely crafted or handy for work.

It was in this way that the Harlows often engaged in charity without outright gifting or embarrassing the person in question. The correct gift always seemed to reach the correct person one way or another.

It was usually Juniper's favorite holiday of the year, not for its revelry but for the tradition of giving gifts. Even when Juniper wasn't attending the rite, she still prepared at least four or five gifts to place on the altar to the Goddess and to those who were the most needy. She took heart in the fact that if nothing else was enjoyable that night, at least the gifting portion of the evening would be.

Theo Vervain arrived at the family cottage in an immaculate white carriage, pulled by white horses. The carriage interior was lined with golden satin upholstery and the windows, made of stained glass in shades of citrine and amethyst, veiled the winter landscape outside. It was luxurious to be sure, but Juniper felt almost embarrassed riding in it for the mere mile and a half between the cottage and the village square.

Theo sat beside her, looking every part the crown prince and her, his little princess. He wore a fine silk suit in white with golden embroidery of serpents on his lapels. If he had intended on talking to her about the proposal, it seemed he wouldn't do so yet. It was a relief to Juniper, especially considering that the engagement ring had been missing since Oleander ran off with it in hand.

The carriage pulled up to the edge of the party where a shimmering mesh of energy locked the bitter mid-winter cold out of the fire-warmed square. Theo stepped out of the coach and rounded the back, opening the door and holding out an austere, gloved hand for hers.

She put her hand in his and stepped down, heeled slippers crunching in the snow. He smiled easily down at her, and she struggled to return the expression.

He turned, placing her hand in the crook of his arm and patted it as her parents came out of the carriage behind them.

"Smile, Juniper," he said under his breath. "All eyes will be on you tonight."

The warning made her dizzy, near to the point of swooning. Was that supposed to be encouragement? Didn't he realize that the entire reason she didn't come to these social events was because of that very fear? She did her best to inhale as much as she could before that invisible rope snaked around her ribcage, the way it always did. She didn't respond, she just passed on a half-hearted attempt of a smile as they stepped through the energetic mesh into the warmth and bustle of the party.

There were three colossal brick hearths strategically placed throughout the area, radiating warmth to fend off the chill and provide refreshments to festival goers. A variety of meats, produced from the nearby Beckton family's hunting endeavors, were expertly arranged on the spits, while Dante, with courtesy of The Cat's Cradle, and with the generous subsidy of the Harlows, supplied the venue with hot drinks. There was already dancing and music.

Truthfully, they had arrived quite fashionably late, which Juniper was beginning to learn was a nightmare.

Theo hadn't exaggerated; every eye truly was on her. But she couldn't blame them. After all, she was there, dressed in white during the longest night of the year, when everyone else was wearing the customary grays, and violets, and blacks. Juniper had to resist the urge to hide her face behind her hand.

She looked up at Theo, hoping he would have perhaps realized the faux pas of arriving dressed like this. Unfortunately, he looked all too happy to have everyone's notice. The angle of her glance must have tipped him off because he looked down at her.

He smiled affectionately as he led her to the table with the dance cards laid out for the ladies in attendance. He leaned down next to her ear and whispered, "Smile, Juni."

There was no kindness or warmth in his command, despite the care in his face. He drew back, still smiling as he reached for one of the cards on the table and parted from her. He brought it up and gently bound it around her wrist with those elegant hands she once admired.

Now she wanted them nowhere near her.

He took up the attached pencil and wrote his name in elegant script — on every single line of the card. There was a bitter irony in looking at it. It was something Oleander had done since she was old enough to dance at these gatherings. But it just felt wrong like this.

Theo smiled at her and offered a hand.

She didn't smile as she took it.

Theo led her to the dance floor as one song started to meld into another. He waited for the beat and started to lead her in a waltz. He must have felt the music gave him enough cover to speak more frankly without being overheard, because he was a little louder this time, a little more irate when he repeated for a third time, "*Smile.*"

The repeated demands were wearing on her nerves, but not in a way she was used to. She didn't feel afraid; it was an entirely different emotion boiling in her tightened belly. It was hot and uncomfortable and made her clothes feel too tight. Her teeth ground in her mouth as she stared at a golden button on his jacket, seeing her ridiculous over-done face and hair reflected back, warped and odd as she felt inside from this farce.

"Juniper—"

"I heard you, Theo," she finally snapped. "I am not feeling the cheer of the season, I'm afraid." Theo didn't miss a beat in their dance despite looking miffed by her outburst.

"If you think that you can talk to me as my wife—"

"We. Are not. Married."

Theo paled, pressing his lips and looking around as if checking to see if someone was eavesdropping. He lowered his voice, sounding almost frantic as he said, "Does that mean you intend to refuse me and leave your family to ruin then?" he asked.

Juniper shook her head, feeling impossibly trapped by this infuriating man. She looked away. Anywhere she could, making sure that people weren't staring or whispering. When she did, she was surprised by what she discovered.

Not a single person on that dance floor was looking at them. No, they were all involved in their own dancing, their own conversations.

Despite what Theo had told her, despite what she lived in constant fear of, no one seemed to care about either of them. At least not today. She instead saw blissful young couples giddily twirling around, making eyes at each other in their finest clothes of the year. She spotted fathers gracefully waltzing with daughters who were still too short to dance with without hitching them on their father's hips. She saw Daisy and Dante sharing a private laugh.

And she saw her parents.

She saw them looking at each other with so much love, even despite the way things were falling apart around their family. Despite all the worries.

She remembered her father talking to her once about how her mother had healed him from his wounds when he was pulled out of the war. He had called her his sanctuary and salvation. She had only just now realized what that meant. It was easy to take in those words and hear only platitudes, but as she looked at her parents, she realized they were no such thing. They really did find refuge in one another. Not only were they each other's shield from the outside world, but more importantly, they were each other's dearest friend. Just like she once was with Ollie.

Just like she was with Ollie.

The realization of that rang in her ears like a bell, clear and bright. She looked up to the man dancing with her. His starless night eyes looked down at her, wreathed with taut irritation, with the paranoia of a man who only cared about status and appearances. Devoid of anything but expectation and requirement. There was no love there. Only ownership.

Her mother's words only an hour ago floated to the forefront of her consciousness.

Remember that — at the end of the day — it's you who must live with the choice.

All at once, Juniper knew that she couldn't live with this choice. She couldn't live with Theo as his wife while she was in love with another man. She couldn't marry Theo when she loved Oleander more than anything else in this world.

Her feet stopped in place, causing Theo to clumsily step into her, almost bowling her over.

"If you decide to ruin the reputation of my family because you're a spoiled fool that can't accept rejection, then Moon have mercy on you, Mr. Vervain," Juniper said as she helped stabilize him, hands on his upper arms holding him out at arm's length. "I've been such an idiot."

She released the man and turned herself about, looking for her destination.

Theo grabbed her wrist, hand constricting hard enough that it hurt. Her head whipped to look at him and found him red and strained with anger and disgust.

"After all the ways I have doted on you, all the money I've spent — *you will not leave me here.*"

Juniper scoffed and looked at him incredulously before tearing her hand out of his with enough of a struggle that other dancers were beginning to lose focus on their own steps.

"If your money is so precious to you, send my family a bill," she spat. Then she turned herself in the direction of the train station.

And she ran.

Nightmares

Oleander awoke with a start, springing to a sitting position, panting and drenched in sweat. His pulse hammered painfully in his neck as his hand clutched his chest over his heart. He caught a glimpse of himself in the mirror on the wardrobe, dressed only in his underthings — an undershirt and shorts — and yet he was still completely drenched in the winter chill of the tenement he had rented.

The nightmares were relentless. They had been since that damned charm broke.

He was struggling; he couldn't delude himself into thinking he wasn't. He had told himself that being away was what he needed, but in the absence of what he knew to be family, he felt a hard spiral down into the darkness of his life was imminent.

Oleander slid out of bed and raked his hands through his sodden hair. He strode to the small breakfast table in his tiny room and poured himself some water from a tin pitcher set there. He gulped it down, savoring the chill that spread through his adrenaline-warmed chest. He worked to steady his breath as he focused on that soothing sensation. He repeated the same words he had always said to Juniper during her episodes: *Breathe, count, exhale.*

After sorting through his feelings for a day or two, the anger he had felt toward Juniper faded into bitter regret. At first, he didn't believe Mr. Harlow's note. Years of suppressed anger wouldn't allow him to think the world was anything other than dark, violent, and ugly. But the image of Juniper's stricken face and the gentle care and love she seemed to always exude made it impossible to reconcile with the thought that she was some kind of calculating harpy.

It was a bittersweet truth he had arrived at, one that cast him as a villain at a time when Juniper desperately needed someone. He had left her in the clutches of Theo Vervain, but what else could he have done? He couldn't very well put this burden on Juniper, nor could he very well trust himself to act gentlemanly around Vervain. Seeing the engagement ring had made him so angry that he was ready to murder the fellow.

No, he knew he needed to sort this out on his own before returning home to Juniper. He wanted his apology to be true and genuine. He didn't want to bring this darkness home to the woman he loved. Oleander would have to trust her to take all the encouragement he and others in her life had given her, and advocate for herself.

He knew that she could do it if she tried.

His past was much darker than he had ever imagined, and trying to reconcile his first eight years with the ten he had spent with the Harlows was proving difficult. It felt like two people dwelled within him: the feral boy who had been neglected and forgotten, and the young gentleman he was today.

He took one more drink from the water and placed the half-emptied glass on the breakfast table. A few steps took him to the wardrobe, where he pulled out a clean washcloth. He then walked over to the basin in his room, which had already been prepared with water, and set to work cleaning the sweat off himself.

His blood seemed to be cooling, causing goosebumps to prickle across his arms and legs as he washed in the cold water. He stripped off his makeshift night clothes and changed into a new pair of shorts and another undershirt. The soiled ones were placed in the hamper the old woman who owned the tenement had told him to use (she was an old laundress and included the service as a part of the lease). Once he was satisfactorily clean, he stripped the bed of its sweat-soaked linens and remade the bed with fresh sheets; the landlady had by then learned that he needed more than the average tenant.

After doing all that, Oleander didn't find himself particularly tired. Once the sun was high in the sky, he put on the plain clothing he had purchased from a nearby clothier. They were nothing like the finery he had at home, but they still had their own appeal. He wore a pair of navy workman's trousers, a plain, thick cotton shirt, and worn brown suspenders. His shoes were the same fine ones he'd arrived with, the only hint of his recently divorced affluence.

Something felt good about being a common man. He'd never felt particularly embarrassed by the Harlow's wealth or his privileged upbringing, but there was a certain grit to the city when he looked like any old fool.

He sat at the desk in his room, a small one squeezed awkwardly between the door and the wardrobe — neither could be open while the desk was in use — and took his fountain pen and a piece of parchment from the desk to write a letter home.

Oleander took his time drafting a two-page missive before folding it with care and sealing it with wax. He scrawled the address on the back of the folded paper before standing and slipping into a tweed jacket and a matching tweed pointed hat. The letter went into his inside pocket, and he made his way out.

His intention for the day was to go to the Chaos and Crime

Department to see if he could gain access to the public records about his mother and father's case. He hoped, perhaps foolishly, that knowing the details of his father's murder would allow him to heal from the tangle of emotions and memories within him. Of course, there was always the chance that he would just uncover more nightmarish truths, but living in the dark was no way to live at all.

If he timed things right, he could make it by the time they opened. He'd go to the post box, stop at the bakery on the corner — they had delicious breakfast muffins — and then take the trolley to the CAC.

His morning went as planned, save for a moment when he was distracted by a shop with beautiful glass teapots that he thought Juniper would like. He felt embarrassed and ashamed when he realized he wished she was there with him, knowing he had ruined any chance of that with his outburst. Regardless, he knew she would have loved this shop if she'd had a chance to adjust, perhaps a few days of watching it from a window before she ventured out to experience it herself.

Kingsborough was a city worthy of its royal inhabitants with huge old structures and a massive clocktower of greenish glass; though there were some unsightly elements, such as crime and the slums, these were unavoidable in any city larger than Linseed Village. Even the CAC building had its own majesty to it. Austerely carved columns, marble steps, and golden gargoyles protecting the building from spells of deceit and the baneful magic of those slighted by the justice system.

Standing at the base of those copious, shallow steps, Oleander fiddled with his hands, clenching and unclenching. The unease in his stomach had him regretting eating breakfast that morning. "Now or never," he told himself once, before heading up the stairs.

Once inside, it took Oleander a few moments to get his wits about him. Witches and sorcerers seemed to do nothing by half-measures; the inside of the building was actually far bigger than the outside let on, some kind of glamour, probably. After approaching three desks and bearing his trauma at each one, Oleander was finally directed to the Ledgers and Records department. He was exhausted by then — and a little bit angry after spending two hours dealing with the frustrations of bureaucracy — but he approached the plain wooden counter that separated the lobby from shelves and shelves of tomes behind it. There was a little glass bell sitting on the counter with a sign that said, 'ring for service.'

He stood up on his toes and looked around to make sure no one was just about to return from fetching something or a trip to the lavatory before he picked up the bell and gave it a little shake. The sound of the small bell seemed to echo throughout the endless corridors of files and books, never growing louder, almost as if there were bells evenly spaced throughout the shelves, passing on the message to the next one in line. After the ringing ceased, he heard a voice, very small and far away.

"I'll be there shortly!"

"O-oh! All right!" Oleander called back.

It was a few more minutes before a person came walking on quick, short legs from the very end of the visible part of the room. They had pale white hair and reddish-pink eyes and stood at just below Oleander's chest when they finally reached the counter and greeted him with an adorable gap-toothed smile.

"Welcome to Record and Ledgers . . . er Ledgers and Records?" They stopped for a moment to hedge on the order before shaking their head. "You get it."

Oleander laughed softly for perhaps the first time since he left the village.

"Yes, I do, thank you."

"How can we help today?" they asked him.

"Ah, I'm here to get records on my family, here is my identification," he said as he pulled out his pocketbook and handed it over to them.

The person snapped their fingers, and a pair of half-moon glasses appeared in their hand. They hastily sat them on the bridge of their nose and tilted their head slightly up to peer down through the lenses and read the details on the papers. The small person's expression fell gently before they pushed their glasses up and closed the pocketbook, handing it to him. "I'm very sorry, Mr. Ambrose. I'm afraid you'll have to speak directly to the big man upstairs to gain access to the files. The Crown's worried about copycats an'all that," they said.

Damn this bureaucratic nonsense, thought Oleander.

"Would you like me to call up to the top an'see if Captain Vervain has the time?"

Oleander grimaced at the name. He really had no interest in any more dealings with the Vervains, but it wasn't as if he had the luxury of choosing.

"I'd very much appreciate that, thank you," he relented.

"Won't be but a moment!" they said, before scurrying to some unknown location again.

Captain Vervain

Oleander's knees bounced at such a rate that the bench he was seated on was beginning to squeak.

When the clerk said they would have to call up to Vervain's office, he was fully prepared for the answer to that inquiry to be a resounding 'no.' However, on this day, the stars aligned in such a way that Captain Vervain was indeed available.

He didn't know what was worse: the fact that he was moments away from learning the depths of his own family's scandal, or the fact that he was likely to learn it from someone as pompous and arrogant as a Vervain. He found himself wishing he had worn his statelier attire — he wasn't looking forward to the once-over he was likely to receive in his matching tweed hat and jacket.

Upon arriving at the office at the top of the building, Oleander had been informed that he would likely have to wait a quarter hour. Each moment was painful and drawn out. A clock as wide as a dinner table hung above Captain Vervain's door, and each tick of the minute hand made him flinch.

"You get used to it," the secretary said through a mouth full of chewing gum.

"I can't imagine how," he responded.

It was twenty-two long minutes before the door to the office opened and Captain Vervain's last meeting exited the room. Slightly obscured by the taller man he said goodbye to, he heard the standard departing pleasantries and watched them shake hands. The strangers departed, leaving Vervain the senior behind, who finally set his eyes on Oleander. Familiar indigo eyes rested on him, though they were much less shrewd than the ones he was accustomed to. They curved pleasantly with a hint of sadness, accompanied by a small smile as the man approached him.

Oleander stood from where he sat somewhat stiffly. "Er—m-my name—"

"I know, Oleander Ambrose, no?"

Oleander deflated with relief; thank the Moon he wouldn't have to explain it all again.

"You're the spitting image of your father," the Captain said. He stood aside and gestured for Oleander to join him. "Let's talk in my office."

Oleander found himself . . . surprised. Though Theo Vervain looked as if he could have been a carbon copy of his father as a young man, the elder Vervain was immediately disarming, even despite his high station and the pressures that plagued his professional life. Perhaps that bastard of a man had learned his conniving from his mother?

They entered the office and Captain Vervain shut the door behind them. He led Oleander to a huge mahogany desk, polished to a mirror-like shine. Curiously, he sat not across from Oleander, but in the chair next to his.

"Your son is nothing like you," Oleander blurted.

The captain seemed taken aback by the comment, his pale eyebrows furrowing a bit. Then, as if needing the moment to process what Oleander had said, he gave a warm laugh. "That's right, you're living in Linseed Village, I forgot—" he said. "I take it Theo has found some way to overwork himself, even though we sent him there to *relax*."

"Overwork is — you know what, it doesn't matter," Oleander said shaking his head and rubbing the edge of his dark brow. Now wasn't the time for that conversation.

"I'm sure I'll hear all about it from his side in the next few days," he said. "Let's focus on what you're here for, hm?"

The captain waved a hand and a book about three inches thick floated its way to the table from the shelf and settled quietly down in front of the two gentlemen. Captain Vervain crossed one ankle over his knee and leaned in towards him, his elbow propped up on the armrest of the chair.

"Now, Mr. Ambrose," he said, his mirth sobering to a concerned intensity, "it is up to you to decide the level of detail you'd like to explore on the subject of your parents. The case of your father's murder was one of my first as a Captain in the CAC and also one of the most harrowing."

"You said I looked like him," Oleander said. "Does that mean you knew him?"

"Myself, your father, and Mr. Harlow were all in the same unit during the Sorcerer's War," he said.

"I see," Oleander said.

"Now, I can give you that book and you can read it cover to cover, if you like. I'm a man who believes in allowing opportunities for discovering the full truth of something," he said. "But after years in this position, after almost losing my own life many times, and after seeing the atrocities that people are willing to commit against each other, I am also a believer in the idea that you don't always have to dive headfirst into the abyss of human cruelty."

Oleander looked at the book warily.

"There's . . ." Oleander started, sounding again like a boy

instead of a man. "I remember so much darkness but they're the memories of a child. I just want to contextualize it."

"That book," he said, pointing a gloved finger, "is a cut-and-dry account of everything we have learned about your mother and her crimes. No detail omitted; no stone left unturned. I can hand that book to you right now, and you can learn every atrocity your mother has committed.

Nausea rose in his stomach again and he swallowed down the taste of bile at the back of his throat.

"Or—" Captain Vervain continued, "or you can simply leave that book shut until such a time when you can no longer stomach the not knowing, and we can have a nice lunch where I can tell you all the things I know about your father."

"I want to know about what Mother did — why she did it—"

"Mr. Ambrose, there is no sense in cruelty. There is no rationalizing or understanding it, not when it is to this degree," he said.

Oleander looked at Captain Vervain. For a long moment, they stared at each other. The words the captain said echoed through his head as he processed them. They settled and became real, and Oleander realized what he was really after by coming out here. He wasn't looking for himself — he wasn't unearthing some hidden facet of himself — Oleander knew the man he was today. He knew himself already.

What he had been after was a way to understand why his mother would take the person he had loved most in the world away from him. He wanted to know why the Goddess, in all her kindness and nurturing, would allow such a bright and selfless man to be taken away by the worst betrayal: to be killed by the person they had loved most in the world.

He felt a seismic crack in his heart and a different dam entirely broke in him. Swelling past the bitterness and anger he'd felt for days was a debilitating sadness. Grief of the worst kind flooded every sense of him and welled up in his eyes, spilling over onto his face in huge tears.

Captain Vervain inhaled a shaky breath of his own and put a hand on Oleander's shoulder. "He was a good man, Oleander."

"How could she take him away?" Oleander let out a weak sob and gasped in a needy breath.

Captain Vervain didn't answer. He just held quiet vigil and allowed a grieving boy his chance to weep.

After being allowed his catharsis, the Captain cleared his day, and over lunch *and* dinner he fielded every question that Oleander had, from his father's favorite meals to the circumstances of his own guardianship after being orphaned.

The captain was forthright in answering everything, though there was some measured reservation about his father's time in service. Oleander had wished to find corroboration of his father's alleged violence in the war. Those particular remarks were carefully measured, with the soft justifications a man might hold in loyalty for a comrade valiantly doing his duty. Oleander felt some guilt for pushing the man who had clearly not left his own duties unscathed, and so he turned his inquiry to less challenging topics. He had every question answered that had popped into his head since the memory charm broke, but he found himself at a loss afterwards. He had grown quiet as he pushed around the remnants of some beef stew he'd eaten.

Captain Vervain looked at him as he finished a bite of his own food, and then, as he went to scoop up another spoonful of the rustic dish, quietly asked, "Shard for your thoughts?"

Oleander looked up at him and then back down to his food. "I have felt so jumbled up this last week, not knowing if I carried the legacy of my father or my mother. I thought I would feel like I knew my identity better after learning all of this, but I still don't feel any different than when I left the village."

"Why would you feel different?" Captain Vervain said.

Oleander balked at him slightly.

"Well, I just learned about my origins—"

"It's not our origins that define us, Oleander," he said with a cheeky smile. "If it was, my dear son wouldn't be half as neurotic as he tends to be."

Oleander pressed his mouth shut to avoid cackling at the expense of Theo.

"Oleander, we choose every day what kind of man to be. Every day we wake up and we choose to be kind or cruel, to love or to hate. We choose the clothes we wear and the dream in our heart. If ever you wake up and you're not pleased with the man you see in the mirror, simply choose to be a different one. Your father once told me something similar, after the war, about how he was choosing to be a better man for those he loved. I have learned that lesson in my own life."

"You make it sound easy," Oleander grumbled.

"It's not easy, but it is that simple," he said. "You make a choice, and you take actions consistent with that choice. Don't let your mother, who hasn't been in your life for the last ten years, define who you are today. Don't even let the Harlows define that. Only you can choose who you want to be."

The poignant words soothed the ache in his heart like the comfort of a warm blanket.

"You really think it doesn't matter? The scandal around my name?"

"I know it doesn't, Oleander. I know it for a fact."

Oleander inhaled a deep breath, filling his lungs with all the fear and distress of the last week, and then exhaled, releasing it all out of his system.

"Thank you, Captain Vervain. For everything."

There was a levity to Oleander as he took his leave from the building, the sky already dark and that strange incandescence returning to the city which never seemed to sleep. He had a lot of decisions to make that night — mostly about whether he would return to the village or not.

With the knowledge that Theo would soon be returning to Kingsborough, he knew that Juniper would not be in immediate danger of having to deal with that bloated puffer fish of a man. However, Oleander would be more likely to follow in his mother's footsteps if he risked running into the Captain's son. Regardless, he was kind of enjoying the city. There was a vitality to it that wasn't present in the village. There was so much he wanted to do and see. Maybe he would take a month to just live here and experience things; take the time to process his feelings and then go back to Linseed.

That seemed like the most viable plan.

He made his way to the trolley stop and easily hopped aboard a moving one, slipping a few coins into the collection tin at the back. He hung on the back railing, letting the biting winter air brush over his face and invigorate him. He watched the city pass him by at the loping pace of the trolley as he removed his hat. When it finally arrived at the street he was staying on, he hopped off and considered going back to the bakery to pick up some more breakfast muffins, and perhaps an entire cake to eat that night for comfort, but something caught his attention on the way.

There was some kind of drama happening about half a block down. A few people cooed at someone as they hemmed her in like a frightened animal. He only heard weeping and pleading, and he started to wander towards the disturbance out of morbid curiosity. Perhaps it was an arranged marriage gone awry.

It must have been with such a ridiculous white gown as that.

Tweed Jacket

Juniper, once on the train, was left to contend with all the daft choices she had made.

It wasn't regret — no — that wasn't what she would call it. She was proud of herself for being brave enough to tell Theo off. But now she was on a train to Kingsborough, alone, without money, and without any clue as to where Oleander could possibly be within the city.

Moon above, what was she thinking? Well, the answer to that was obvious enough: She wasn't.

She had been so caught up in the revelation of her feelings that she had simply acted. She had used the last of the money she carried to get on the train, and now she only had hours to herself to think. What must her parents think? What if Theo really did squander her family's name to ruin? What would the people in town think? What would she do if Oleander refused to see her? What would she do if she couldn't find him at all?

She ran through each of these questions in a cyclical fashion until she had worn herself so thin that she slipped into a fitful sleep, which lasted from dawn until late morning. When she woke, as the train began to fill with other people, she found herself particularly self-conscious as she sat in her ridiculously ostentatious dress. After a while, she decided to use the lavatory on the train to dress down what she could.

She drew out the pins and wilting flowers from her hair, letting it fall to its full length around her waist. She removed the bespelled train and wrapped it about herself like a shawl. It didn't do much to make her look any more casual, but at least she could feel the comfort of being slightly obscured by the gossamer fabric from the view of rubbernecking strangers.

Regardless, she still felt prying, curious stares. She even fielded a few questions from well-meaning but nosy strangers. Thankfully, most of them seemed to pick up on her aversion to communicating, or at least found her awful stammering awkward enough to not want to continue their conversations with her.

As the hours passed, her energy began to sap away. Each new passenger and the loud screeching of the train coming to a stop at another platform wore through her delicate nerves like moths chewing through a forgotten pair of woolen tights. By the time the train pulled into Kingsborough Station, it was all she could do not to bolt off the train and into the city.

She just needed to focus on finding Oleander. If she could find him, everything would be okay. Everything would be okay.

But Juniper had never been to Kingsborough; she had never even been to a city at all. So, as she hurried through the train station to make her way out into the city street, all the color drained from her face.

Kingsborough was a monstrosity.

It was like a forest of brick and mortar. She turned this way and that, searching for signs of Oleander's whereabouts. She tried to still her mind, to think with logic, but the more she tried, the more it felt like the buildings were closing in on her.

A trolley bell clanged loudly behind her, making her jump out of her skin and scaring her so horribly that she immediately broke into a frightened sprint in the opposite direction. She didn't stop, she didn't look anywhere, she just needed to be somewhere that wasn't so loud and new. She needed the quiet of a garden or the smell of old books in a library.

When her lungs were burning, she stopped at the corner of two major streets, her ribcage fighting against her corset.

Too tight — it was too tight.

She might die if she didn't get her corset loosened. She reached fruitlessly behind her and tried to fumble with the buttons of her high-necked dress. When she failed to do so, she felt desperate for air and simply tore at the delicate lace, the pearl buttons popping off and scattering on the street below. She tore the bodice of the dress down, revealing a shift and her corset beneath, and she started to fumble with the lacing of her corset.

"Child! What *are* you *doing?*" a shocked and offended voice said behind her.

Juniper turned to see the wrinkled face of an elderly woman glaring down at her in disgust. Remembering herself, Juniper realized she was stripping in public. Her feet clumsily set off into a run again but caught the ball bearings of the pearl buttons below her, causing her to tumble to the ground, splashing into a freezing puddle of grime and half-melted slush. She scrambled back to her feet and broke into a sprint, her bodice streaming in a clumsy tangle behind her. She ran down an alleyway, hoping to find privacy, but she only found more people. Curious gazes fell on her as she gave a desperate, guttural scream of frustration.

Immediately, people approached, fearing that the girl had met some unseemly character in the alleyway she had just emerged from, as she was half-dressed.

A woman and her husband approached. "Hold on dear,

you're alright," she said with hands raised as she looked to her husband. "Go see if you can find him dear." The man disappeared into the alleyway, running to find some assailant that didn't exist.

A small collection of others approached in short order, leaving Juniper with no choice but to back up against the cold, gray brick of some unidentified building as she sobbed.

"Can't breathe — I can't breathe," she gasped.

"Does anyone have a calming potion on them? This girl needs help!" a woman cried as she tried to approach Juniper.

"No, no, no, no—" she wept as she sunk down to the ground.

She knew, somewhere in her racing mind, that these people meant to help her, but she felt caged in by them. All she needed was a room to disrobe in, just a breath of air to breathe.

The husband returned from his pursuit, panting and wiping his face with a handkerchief. "I couldn't find him," he said.

Juniper wept as she uselessly tried to reach for her corset laces.

"Can't breathe, can't breathe," she whimpered.

"Excuse me."

The sound of the calm voice excusing itself pierced through the cacophony of the chaos going on around her.

"Do you know this girl?" a stranger asked, sounding more angry at him than anything.

A coat, heavy and rough, was placed on her shoulders; the body heat captured in the fabric permeated her frantic haze.

"I was supposed to meet her at the train station, she's never been to the city. Unfortunately, my trolley was delayed," Oleander said with all the calm that seemed to naturally cultivate within him. "She's my fiancée," he said.

"Well, she gave us all quite a fright; she ran out of the alley half-naked."

"I do apologize that we worried you all, I'm going to take her home right away," Oleander said. "Thank you so much for helping her, you gave me a chance to catch up to her."

Her body left the cold, stony ground, and the warmth of a strong body cradled her tightly. She smelled honey and mint and sage. It was her Ollie.

Oleander continued walking with her and the crowd parted.

Once the chaos quieted and the warmth melted through Juniper's frozen nerves, she managed to look up at her savior, her friend, the love of her life. She was flooded with relief at the sight of him. He even deigned to smile that beautiful smile down at her.

"O-Ollie—" she hiccuped.

"Shhh—" he said. "You're alright. I can't believe you took a train all the way out here by yourself, Juni." The smile he gifted her with was a marvel, tinged with a little bit of wetness even. "I'm so damned proud of you."

The praise was so much a boon to her that she found herself sobbing.

"Will you forgive me for coming to find you?"

"Shh — there's nothing to forgive," he said.

"But your letter," she sobbed.

"Don't worry about that." He became more sober then, looking down at her with brows dipped gently. "I jumped to conclusions when I was upset. I've learned the truth of things now. I was a fool, and I'm sorry Juniper. And I will spend the rest of my days making up for my ill-treatment of you lately."

She sniffed softly and heaved out a shaky breath. "I'm sorry too, for not knowing. For shutting you out," she said.

Oleander inhaled tightly, his chest warm. Even when she was upset, she was such a precious thing. He hefted her up a couple more inches and kissed her on her temple. "It's alright. You were only a child when I came to live with you, how could you have even guessed? And I . . . can hardly blame you for feeling as though you couldn't confide in me. I've been a powder keg waiting to blow as far as that man was concerned, and you could probably tell. You had every right to strike me when I grabbed you like that. And you could do it again, if you'd like," he said, voice turning soft as he teased and even presented his cheek.

A tearful laugh bubbled up from her, shaking her head. "I'm also sorry for that. I hardly know what's gotten into me."

The stare he gave her then was heart-breaking.

"You have every right to defend yourself from me, Juniper. I promise you that. If I ever make you feel unsafe, you run for the hills and do whatever you need to protect yourself. Do you understand?"

The pained sobriety in his voice, saying such words, would have been confusing to her before she had learned the truth herself. But she wished nothing more than to reciprocate the support he had given her all these years. So, Juniper merely leaned into his chest, relishing his presence. They had only been separated for a little while, but it felt like ages — it felt even longer than the two years he had been away.

In the month or so he had been home, she had come to depend on his presence, not only for moral support, but also for his physical presence. She craved the feeling of being held by him, carried by him, dwarfed by him. Juniper never wanted to be separated from him again if she could help it. She willed herself to calm down as he walked with her in his arms, cradling her with care.

"Where are we going?" she finally asked after her breathing steadied.

"I'm renting a room in a boarding house. It's just up the street here," he said. "We're going to get you in a nice warm bath, and I'm going to see if the landlady has another dress for you to wear." He looked down at her filthy skirt with a raised eyebrow. "White on Solstice, eh?"

Juniper grimaced.

"Vervain's idea," she grunted.

Oleander scoffed and shook his head. "Of course it was."

Silence fell between them as he neared the boarding house.

Juniper looked up at him, hesitating for a moment before delivering the confession she'd come here to give. But when he looked down at her, she lost her nerve.

"I said no," she blurted.

"No?" he asked. "To what?"

"The proposal. He had only given me until Solstice to decide, and I said no," she said.

A piece of his soul left his body when he realized how his own impulsiveness almost took away the one thing that he'd wanted in life.

And then he realized — he still wanted that.

After the dust settled with the chaos of the last week, in his heart of hearts, he still wanted to marry Juniper. That clarity gave him some comfort. He looked down at her and grinned.

"That must have been scary, Juni—" he said.

"It might have been a mistake. We might wind up being the first to pick gifts at next year's Solstice because of it," she said. "But I couldn't go through with it."

She looked up at him as he reached the door to the building. *Ask me why* she tried to implore with her eyes, *ask me why I said no.*

But he only smiled down at her as he set her to her feet.

"Let's get you washed up," he said.

A Solstice Present

The landlady in the boarding house had almost fainted when Oleander had carried her in. She'd started muttering about overnight visitors and propriety, and Oleander once again fed the line about Juniper being his frazzled betrothed whom he had failed to meet at the train station in time. Oleander spun a tale of someone stealing Juniper's baggage and asked about a change of clothes. The landlady didn't have anything herself but insisted on going to purchase them on Oleander's behalf. He couldn't very well be seen buying a young lady's underthings, she had chided. Oleander gave the lady a generous budget to do so, and then set Juniper up with a bath.

Juniper blew bubbles in the hot water of the bath, trying not to feel stymied and flustered. She had consulted her vast catalogue of romance novel confessions but had struggled to find one to use. She sunk into the water and closed her eyes. It wasn't that she was worried about Oleander not returning her feelings; she was almost certain that he did. But after all the years she had not taken him at his word about those sentiments, or laughed them off, she wanted to make sure that the moment was something he could treasure as a memory for a very long time — like her parents did.

She resurfaced from the water and stood up in the now-cooling bath. She smoothed her hands back over her hair and brought it to the side to wring out. She stepped out of the tub and dried off with a fresh set of linens set out by Oleander. She then slipped into the ruffly night shift that the landlady had given her to wear until she could return with some more appropriate clothes. It looked kind of silly, and she couldn't imagine being comfortable sleeping in something that was practically its own cushion, but it would keep her decent for now.

She stepped out of the communal washroom and walked down the corridor to Oleander's room, knocking on the door.

Oleander called from within. "It's unlocked, Juni."

She stepped in and shut the door behind her. He was lounging on his bed when she entered, but he sat up on the edge when she walked in.

"Feel better?" he asked.

"Much."

Their relationship was such that neither blushed at the fact that she was wearing only night clothes. They had grown up together, running through the house in their nightclothes, and Oleander had cared for her when she was ill and couldn't muster the energy to dress fully.

"Have you a hairbrush?" she asked. Oleander indicated his wardrobe, where a simple boar-bristle brush sat. She grabbed the brush and started to comb through her soaking hair.

"Are you tired? I thought I could give you use of this room and wait for the landlady to return with your clothes and prepare another room," he said.

"I'm not that tired," she said. "The bath woke me up. Besides, I want to talk to you about everything that's happened since you've been gone."

"Maybe we'll go out to dinner then," he said.

"Good places out here?"

"Yeah, there are a few," he said.

She set down the hairbrush on his desk, an awkward silence fell between them; the first they had ever experienced in all the years that they had known each other. Juniper could hear her heart thumping in her ears, and she wondered if he could hear it too. The confession tingled on the tip of her tongue; so tangible she could taste it. But it wouldn't do to just blurt the words out like an idiot. She stared at him for a long moment, considering.

Seemingly feeling her gaze, he looked over at her.

"Shard for your thoughts, Juni?" he asked.

Her mind went back to that day he walked her to the tailor in the village. The fateful day that the Goddess put Theo in her path to show her the truth of her own feelings. She remembered his gentle stroke of her face and the angling of her chin to meet the angle of his. She remembered how emotion choked her then, and how it was choking her now. How it had been doing so since he returned from Conservatory and perhaps even before then.

She had truly loved him for so long.

"I have a Solstice gift for you," Juniper said.

Oleander's head tilted in that way that she loved, like a confused puppy.

"But you only came with the clothes on your back," he said.

"Close your eyes," she told him.

He huffed a laugh and shook his head, but he obeyed.

Juniper approached him on quiet feet and, when he sensed her near, he opened his hands and turned them upward, waiting for his gift. She was gentle when she moved his hands out of the way, watching as his brow furrowed in confusion. She stepped up close enough to feel his breath gust against her décolletage. His head angled up slightly, searching. She stood between his knees and lifted her small hands to cup either side of his face.

His eyes opened, piercing her heart with their striking blue. She lost her nerve for a moment, staring down at him, beautiful in every way.

"Juni—" he whispered, half question, half hymn.

"How do you do it?" she asked, suddenly overcome with emotion.

His brows arched softly.

"Do what?" he asked.

"How do you . . . put up with it all? With my fragility, with my nerves? How could you possibly want me even when there's so much about me that I can't fix," she said.

The air was dense with the question. The inquiry was simple, but it was also much larger than either of them. Her own deficiencies had become such an obstacle in their trajectory to each other, requiring so many detours and even a bit of backtracking, but at the end of the day, it really was as simple as not understanding how a boy as wonderful as Oleander could find it in his heart to love her. It felt like a trick sometimes; like a dream that would dissolve as soon as she grasped it.

He placed his hands on the curve of her waist and her skin tingled beneath the stuffy fabric of her shift. "With love, Juniper," he said. "There is nothing about you that needs to be fixed. I don't love you in spite of your struggles. I love every bit of you, including your struggles." he said. "Watching you try every day to be more than you were the day before is my inspiration — Juni, you are my muse."

Juniper's eyes welled and two tears fell onto Oleander's face.

He lifted his hand and swiped another tear off her soft, flushing cheek. Before he could lift his other hand to repeat the gesture, Juniper closed the small distance between them and pressed her lips to his. His free hand froze in a shocked hover, unsure of where to go.

The kiss started chastely, two inexperienced mouths meeting. Tentatively, like the first cautious steps into the brine of the ocean. But it soon developed into something more. Oleander's eyes closed, and he shakily inhaled through his nose. His frozen hand found its place on her, resting where her waist met her hips. He scooped his other hand back into her wet hair and tangled it there. Both hands pulling her into him with brazen need, holding her tighter. The sensation of it made Juniper gasp, and Oleander used the opportunity to seize her lower lip between his own, needing to taste her.

She shuddered, the breath drawing on her vocal cords like a bow over the strings of a violin. His hand coursed from her hip to her lower back, and he pulled her down to sit on his lap, using the new angle to deepen the kiss further. His mouth sought to claim hers, and she was happy to yield as their lips parted and their cloying breaths mingled. Juniper's fingers slid into Oleander's hair and curled at the roots in a needy tangle. The touch drew a growl from him, the sound reverberating through her teeth — her chest.

She chanced the barest stroke of her tongue against the edge of his lower lip. He answered with a sweet, overwhelming undulation of his own. She tasted the remnants of a butterscotch candy he must have snacked on while she was in the bath. She whimpered, weakly this time, and he immediately pulled away from the kiss to look down at her with fearful concern.

"Juni? I'm sorry— Are you—"

Juniper gave a single happy breath and looked at him. Her hands smoothed back to hold his face in her hands once again and she laughed.

"I love you, Oleander," she finally said.

Oleander's lungs emptied all at once, his heart ached in his chest with how full to the brim it was.

"Marry me, Juni," he gusted.

She huffed a brilliant smile and nuzzled her nose against his, stealing another kiss.

"I will," she said.

All's Well

Oleander and Juniper spent a few more days in Kingsborough after sending word of their safety to the Harlows. They spent most of their waking hours together, only parting when neither could keep their eyes open for another moment and only because the landlady would likely keel over if she found them sharing a room when she brought up tea in the morning.

Despite being glued at the hip, Oleander somehow found time to sneak away long enough to buy Juniper an engagement ring. He presented it to her on the train ride back to Linseed Village — a simple silver band with a raw amethyst set in the center. It was the first time Juniper's focus didn't stray to the passing scenery during a train ride; she was far too busy smiling down at her ring finger the entire way back home.

Theo Vervain was gone by the time they returned, which was a relief to all involved. Juniper didn't care to know how he'd responded after her rejection. The threat of her family's reputation being shot was still a concern for her, but Oleander assured her that it was something they didn't need to fret about. After meeting Captain Vervain, Oleander knew the man wouldn't allow his son to do something so petty and ridiculous — not to a brother-in-arms.

He had also personally inquired as to whatever fallout his Juni had left in her wake. From what Oleander could glean, the man had been quite frazzled after the young lady was seen streaking off into the night. While Juniper thought the villagers would find her behavior to be reprehensible, there was more skepticism as to why she would have fled so blatantly from the dance floor.

Theo had also been seen trying to take umbrage with the Harlows at the edge of the festivities and made the mistake of ordering them to curtail her behavior. Mrs. Harlow verbally boxed his ears so thoroughly that he looked properly chastised. Mr. Harlow only served as a sufficient masculine set-dressing to ensure the boy could not dismiss it as mere 'hysterics.'

Theo's intentions came to fruition. The sheer audacity of him to presume forcing their daughter's hand had caused much gossip in their absence. So much so, that when Oleander and Juniper returned, they were met with a congratulatory welcome in the village.

The Harlows were, of course, entirely ready to offer every consolation and assurance on their daughter's return, expecting her to be disconsolate and uncomfortable for what had happened. But she seemed to be in such fine spirits upon her return that the point seemed moot. Frankly, seeing Juniper so unfazed had been such a relief. It was all a bit of unfortunate silliness, so if their daughter saw fit to put it behind her, they certainly were not going to make a fuss of dredging it up.

Mr. Harlow was just relieved to have some measure of peace in his household again — though his wife would certainly see fit to keep it busy with all the planning that came with a betrothal.

After some time enjoying the bliss of new love and recovering from the drama over the winter, Juniper and Oleander dove back into their work together. They completed preparations and opened their store, Ambrose Nursery, shortly after the new year. Juniper had come up with the name, inspired by everything Oleander had gone through during the time they had been apart. At first he had reservations about it, but seeing as they would soon share the same surname, it made the most sense. Besides, you can't change the connotation of a name without using it. At least that was what Juniper had said to convince him to agree. He wasn't sure if his family name would ever divest itself of its blood-drenched legacy, but if anyone could help that endeavor along, it was his intended.

In addition to opening the shop, the new couple worked on their winter-thriving seeds. It was a series of triumphs and frustrations but fulfilling all the same. Their failed attempts provided enough stock to keep the store attractively full, even if they didn't reach their goal immediately. The quality of the products was still higher than their competitors'.

Daisy's paintings, and Juniper and Oleander's products began to draw more tourists to the area. Juniper, still prone to becoming overwhelmed, found some solace and pleasure in the social elements of running her shop. It was much easier to converse with people when there was a shared enthusiasm — now Juniper got to discuss plants every day — and people seemed to appreciate what she had to say.

The wedding took place in the spring.

It was a small affair with only their dearest friends in attendance.

They had it in Faeridge amidst the sea of wildflowers. Oleander had insisted upon it when Juniper confessed that she had wished for him to kiss her when he took her there on her birthday. Hallowed ground, he had called it.

Mr. Harlow officiated the union, Dante was Oleander's best man, and Daisy was Juniper's maid of honor. Mrs. Harlow wept as she watched her husband perform the handfasting ceremony with pale blue and charcoal cords, the colors of the bride and groom's eyes.

Their kiss was quick and chaste. Juniper didn't want to make their friends and family uncomfortable, whereas Oleander didn't much care. But he had already sated his appetite for her kisses many times over; stealing them while hidden behind monstera leaves in the greenhouse, cornering her against the countertops in the kitchen, and stealing moments lying in her bed while her parents slept in the wee hours of the night. Sure, it wasn't exactly proper, but neither party could seem to keep their hands to themselves, and if nothing else was certain, their future together was. A few stolen moments of intimacy wouldn't change that.

Their first night as a legitimate married couple was full of blissful love and connection. Both parties nervous — embarrassed — but also, so happy.

Summer arrived as Juniper and Oleander took their honeymoon in Kingsborough to see all the bright, electric city had to offer. For once, Juniper was excited about the prospect of traveling to an unfamiliar place. Truly, she was excited to see the world with Oleander, but for now, Kingsborough was a great start.

Oleander hefted their trunks onto the cart, while Juniper worked at hitching their horse to it. She was patting the horse's neck as Oleander came around to the front, his sleeves rolled up to his elbows. "You sure you packed enough, my love?" he asked as he dabbed his forehead with a handkerchief. "Your trunk was hardly half the weight of my own."

Juniper shot him a look and a smile played on her lips. "That's because you're a dandy and you have more clothes than makes sense," she teased.

"I am *not* a dandy," he grumbled with a playful nip at the shell of her ear. "You're just infuriatingly practical."

Juniper leaned into him, turning away from the horse to dote on her husband instead. She stood on her toes to peck him chastely on the lips as his arms wrapped around her. "I left room for souvenirs," she said. "I want to make sure we thank Dante and Daisy adequately for their help while we're away."

"How thankful do you intend on being?" Oleander asked with raised brows.

Juniper swatted him lightly on his chest.

"I've never been on a real trip before, I have to make up for lost time," she retorted.

They had spent the last few weeks preparing for their departure. They would be there for a fair amount of time and Juniper wasn't one to leave all her friends in the greenhouse to just anyone. She had spent no less than a month training Daisy and Dante on the intricacies of taking care of them, even going so far as teaching them some herbal magic to use in dire circumstances. They both endured the lessons with amusement and endearment, even though all parties knew that the appeal of a greenhouse was that it already catered to most of the needs of the plants just by virtue of how it was constructed. They were happy to provide Juniper with the ability to enjoy her honeymoon to the fullest, unbothered by the thought of her garden suffering at home.

"Always making up for lost time," he said with a kiss to her temple. "I hope you feel that way about all the affection I'm going to give you on our honeymoon. I have a season's worth of love to give you after you spent all of spring refusing me in the name of your parents' comfort."

"I'm sorry, but you don't have to deal with Mother's conspiratorial chit chat at the breakfast table, Mr. Ambrose!"

"As if I don't brag about you every chance I get, Mrs. Ambrose," he crooned. "Would it kill you to return the favor?"

Her heart fluttered every time he called her that — every time she got to sign her name with his attached to it. She wondered if that feeling would ever go away, or if she would revel in it forever. She sighed and smiled dreamily up at him.

"You had better go get your jacket and hat if we're to make it to the train station on time," she told him. "Kingsborough awaits."

"I would never *dream* of missing our train, my love. I'll be back soon with Father."

She smiled as she watched him go back into the house, climbing up into the carriage to sit amongst their things. She was no longer the reclusive herbalist in the cottage on the outskirts of town. She had grown in her ability to face uncertainty, to confront the prospect of someone not liking or understanding her. Juniper had finally begun to learn which opinions mattered to her and which ones had no impact on who she was as a person.

Yes, she still had many of the odd fears and behaviors she always had. It was still nerve-racking to place orders at restaurants or buy tickets at the train station, there was still the rare customer who would force an uncomfortable smile when she extolled the virtues of the nutrients found in cow manure, or caught her speaking to her seedlings when they wandered into her store, but that was alright; she knew she wasn't meant to appeal to everyone.

She found the comfort in being an acquired taste, a delicacy for a special chosen few, so long as Oleander was counted among them. She wasn't entirely sure that it would always be easy, wasn't sure she would always feel so brave, but she knew that she had the support of the ones she loved to make it through the times that were truly frightening. She had done it once before, and she could do it again.

Oleander returned only a few moments later with her father and climbed into the carriage, sitting beside her. He adjusted his hat and smiled down at her.

"Are you ready, Juni?" he asked her.

The question was asked with real curiosity for the answer, as it always was. Even now, he was checking in on her to make sure he wasn't pushing her too far, too quickly.

"I'm more than ready," she said without even a hint of hesitation.

"Then away we go," her father said as he took up the reins and clicked his tongue, setting their horse in motion.

Juniper watched as the cottage — her home — grew smaller in the distance. She watched as she left the place that had served her so well, protecting her and swaddling her. It was time to fly the nest and find a new perch or two. To learn what other places in the world could hold her the same way that this one had for so long.

The idea of something new — something unfamiliar — no longer filled her with dread. Now, it filled her with curious hope. The same way the first few pages of a new love story did.

Only now, the story was her own.

And she couldn't wait to see how it unfolded.

Epilogue: Bested

Theo Vervain never failed.

Not until he'd met Juniper Harlow and Oleander Ambrose.

There was a persistent, nagging ache that lingered in his chest. It'd started the night of the rite and only seemed to get worse. He rubbed over the lapel of his coat, as if he could quell the ache lingering there. Hawthorne, before Theo's departure, kept asking him if he was feeling ill. It was only natural with how Theo's appetites had diminished; both for food and for diversion. Truth be told, he'd had a hard time finding the motivation to leave bed since hearing about Juniper and Oleander's engagement through the rumor mill. And now, all he had to do was ride his besom to Adonshire and reflect on his broken heart.

He supposed that's what it was — a broken heart. An ailment he always scoffed at, but now that he was experiencing it first-hand; he was the one who felt like a fool. The worst part was that he'd brought it upon himself.

He didn't have to read Juniper's silly romances to know that a marriage proposal served with a side of extortion didn't work. Yet . . . yet he'd seen the terror on her face when he showed her the ring and felt his own nausea churn so hard in his gut that it just . . . fell out of his mouth. And he'd said it with such conviction.

And then there was his abhorrent behavior at the rite. He felt even worse than he did when he'd shouted at his mother. He was the worst kind of wretch. He had so long thought of love as some schoolgirl's idle fixation that when the Moon dropped it on his lap he had no idea what to do with it. He'd had no idea what to do with it and he crushed it in his own hands like an oaf. And what was worse? He'd used his father's position like some spoiled child. He had *disappointed* his father, potentially spoiling the relationship between his father and an old friend of his from the military.

He had only tried to help — to try and encourage Juniper to act like the lady she was. If she could have just acted with propriety and poise, she could have run circles around the women in the city. She could have been the perfect wife, and he could have been the perfect husband to her.

He should have never left Kingsborough. He should have just stayed there and worked. Then he would have never been haunted by dreams of Juniper's beauty. He would have never made an idiot of himself. He would have never fallen in love with a woman that had her heart won since she was twelve. He would just be the same over-achieving, poorly sleeping man he was before. And at least a few months further along in his career, following in his father's footsteps like any good son ought to. His thoughts cycled on failure after failure all the way to the magistrate in Adonshire. He thought of how it would be to admit his failure to Mr. Oakmoss and Mrs. Poerier and felt sick all over again.

When he made it to the front desk he showed the clerk behind the counter his arm band, the one he wore as a novice detective. "I'd like to take the portal to Kingsborough, please," he said.

The woman narrowed her eyes at him. "Portals are meant for official business only. If your matter isn't pressing or you're not on duty, I'm afraid you're going to need to book passage on a train."

"I have an emergency meeting with Captain Vervain," Theo said.

"The son of the Captain has a *meeting* with the Captain?" she asked. "Or are you just trying to take advantage of magistrate resources?"

"Would you like to find out? You could always prevent me from making that meeting. If I were you, though, I wouldn't risk the reprimand or my coveted position at the Adonshire branch. But that's just me."

The clerk's eyes widened slightly before she pressed her lips and gestured toward a flight of stairs about ten feet away. "The Kingsborough portal is through the doorway marked eleven."

"Thank you," Theo said and wasted no more time in leaving the front desk. He walked up the stairs and found himself in a corridor lined with doors. Far too many doors than what would seem possible, in fact. Each one a different color or finish and each one only about six inches away from the one before it.

All of them were portals.

He found the door labeled with two gilded numbers; this particular door had the ivory and golden coloring of the building in Kingsborough he was going to. Theo held onto his besom tightly and opened the door. There was nothing but a void on the other side. Inky darkness as far as the eye could see. He always hated this part, but he couldn't abide a train ride. It would take too long.

He closed his eyes and drew in a deep breath, holding it. There was no air in the portal, and losing consciousness within was ill-advised. He stepped into the void and shut the door behind him. There was a sickening feeling of falling sideways, then down, then up. When he opened his eyes again there was another door before him, pale light coming through slatted windows above it, gobbled up by the incessant dark of the portal. He opened the door and stepped through, finding himself in a similar corridor to the one he'd just left behind. He wobbled slightly on his feet as he exhaled in a gust and then drew in a deep breath. He walked out of the corridor, down the hall and finally, into the foyer of his father's office.

"Ah, Novice Detective Vervain! I thought you were still out of town," the secretary said. "Here to speak to your fa— I mean . . . Captain Vervain?"

Theo cringed internally, remembering with perhaps too much clarity that he had once barked at her for referring to his father as such while they were working together. Why was it that every failure of composure suddenly felt like a brand on his conscience?

"Is he in there?" Theo asked.

"Yes, he's been going over some files for a recent string of crime in the city. I'm sure he'd be happy to see you, though. He could probably use a break."

Theo nodded once. "Thank you," he said, walking past her desk and into the office. He closed the door behind him and looked at his father sitting behind his desk, looking exhausted as he flipped through a massive tome. He recognized it — the Ambrose files — the ones about Oleander's family.

Captain Vervain lifted his eyes from his work and closed the book.

"You made it home quickly," his father said.

Theo swallowed tightly, nodding once. "It felt negligent to

engage in further diversion," he lied. "There's work to do, after all."

Captain Vervain heaved a sigh, standing up from his desk and coming around it. He walked toward Theo until he was only a few steps away.

"I've had a letter from Rowan Harlow," he said.

"Ah," Theo said, not knowing what more would be welcome.

He dropped his eyes and waited for the lecture he was due. He knew he had made a royal mess of things. He just wanted it to be over and done with so that he could start making amends and earn back his father's love and trust. But the lecture didn't come. Instead, Captain Vervain simply opened his arms to his son.

Theo looked up at him, his eyes wide with surprise. "You should be reprimanding me," Theo said.

"My very responsible, very by-the-books son just made unauthorized use of portal to hurry home to his father after going through his very first experience with a broken heart," his father said. "I don't think a reprimand is what is needed right now. I think my son needs a little care and comfort from his father."

There was a pause.

"Of course, if you would prefer a reprimand . . ." his father teased.

Before Captain Vervain could finish, though, Theo dropped his besom on the ground and stepped into his father's embrace. He felt the comforting weight and strength of his father's arms envelope him, and squeeze him close. He felt the press of a quick kiss to the top of his head.

"My poor boy," his father said, patting his back. "Love is rarely what we expect, and it can hurt more than we hope. I'm so sorry your first experience with it ended like it did, but don't worry. Love will find you again, and next time, you'll know how to treat it."

Theo didn't know if he believed it. He didn't know if he ever wanted to love again after how poorly he handled it the first time. He couldn't think about any of that right now, if he was honest. He could only wrap his arms around his father.

Bury his face in his father's coat.

And cry.

Acknowledgements

Forgive me an indulgent list of people to thank, this is going to read like an over-long academy award speech, but there are so many people whose hands touched this book, without whom, *With Love, Juniper* never would have come to fruition.

Thank you to my best friend, Eden Carroll, without you, these characters would have never existed. Thank you for allowing me to expand on a little role play idea we came up with together and create this narrative that healed so much of my inner sixteen year old.

Forever in debt to Rachelle Raeta, Candice Winzen, Eden Carroll, and Shea Peters for your careful, caring beta reads when this story was in its infancy. With your excitement and editorial tweaks, I had the confidence to bring this story to the world and shout about it on social media, which is one of the hardest things to do for a silly little nerd who struggles with talking about herself.

Oliver Carter, thank you for your first copy edit on this

book, much of which has become some of my subsequent editors' and readers' favorite lines. I will always be indebted to you for "Plain-as-day beautiful!" and the word "unpinkify." Thank you for honoring my voice and loving this story as much as I do.

Thank you to Lauren Devila, who saw a pitch of this book and decided to take a chance on it when starting your journey with Inked in Gray. I can't wait to get lunch again soon.

Vanessa Redmon, your copy edits took a good story and made it shine. I will never not appreciate the sting of an excellent edit. Thank you for polishing this narrative.

Dakota Rayne, thank you for never being irritated with my constant sliding into your DM's with questions about everything from book covers, to launch parties, to marketing ideas. I have loved working with Inked in Gray and hope I can do so in the future.

Vis, Wolf Layman, Alex Gann, Christopher Anderson, and Todd "Typhon" Muse: Thanks for your continued support and cheerleading. Thanks for being half of who showed up with regularity to all of my digital bookish events. Thank you for giving me feedback on the cover of my book cover as I stumbled through illustrating it. Thanks for being eager to buy my book. And thank you for being my little pocket of weird where I can always be myself.

Wolf Layman, Adrienne Lothy, Jon Paul Hart, Aaron Broom, Zoë Partyka and Magpie for joining my silly little Kitchen Table MFA and giving me regular feedback on the parts of this book I was workshopping.

Thank you to the Top Three Author writing sprint group, especially AJ Harper and Laura Stone. You guys are an endless font of information and knowledge that I'm so glad to know. The open-door community you've created is a smooth stone in the pocket of my mind that I regularly thumb for comfort when things are scary.

And finally, thank you to my family and my husband, who always had an excited word when new publishing news came through.

About the Author

Amanda Cessor is a queer, neurodivergent author living with their husband and pets in beautiful Crestline, California. She has short stories published in Full Mood Mag and Merciless Mermaids: Tails of the Deep. When she's not writing books, she's either doing hair or playing TTRPG's.

To keep up to date with their upcoming projects, follow them on instagram at @amandacanwrite, substack at amandacanwrite.substack.com or on tumblr at amandacanwrite.tumblr.com.

instagram.com/amandacanwrite

Also by Inked in Gray

If you enjoyed *With Love, Juniper*, please consider also reading *As We Convene: An Anthology of Time and Place*, or any of the other Inked in Gray novels and anthologies. Support our small business by buying direct at InkedinGray.com

We also appreciate any and all reviews! You may leave a review on Goodreads, Amazon, or on our site at Inkedingray.com